# The Imaginist

## Elizabeth Glanville

Dear Louisa,

Thank you for coming to my launch, & congratulations on becoming a mummy!!

Lots of love,

Cousin ~~Rose~~

BETH x

*Long-listed for the 2010 Sony Reader Award for Unpublished Writers, in collaboration with The Dylan Thomas Prize*

Copyright © by Elizabeth Glanville, 2012

Cover design by Tanya Back, 2012

Published by Lulu.com

ISBN 978-1-291-24767-1

4

## About the Author

Elizabeth Glanville is from Cardiff and lives in London. She graduated from Cambridge University in 2005 and is a writer, journalist, teacher & novelist, and has been a newspaper editor.

*The Imaginist* is Elizabeth's first novel. It was long-listed for the 2010 Sony Reader Award for Unpublished Writers, in collaboration with The Dylan Thomas Prize, as were her unpublished novels *Oceans Apart* and *Learning to Fly*. Her short story 'Mistaken Identity' - based on *The Imaginist* - was short-listed in the 2013 ReadWave Anthology Competition.

Elizabeth has had short stories, poetry and travel writing published, and has written for a number of newspapers. She is part of a writers' collective, 'Authors for Charity', and has contributed to their children's book, *Tales of an Old Wizard*.

Elizabeth is also studying for an MA in Psychotherapy and Counselling and has written for the online magazine, *Contemporary Psychotherapy*. Her non-fiction book, *The Quarterlife Crisis: Tips to Beat the Trials of the Twenties,* is available to buy at lulu.com, and to download at amazon.co.uk.

In 2010 Elizabeth came 1st in the RW Poetry and Flash Fiction Competitions, and two of her short stories came in the top ten in a competition run by Little Acorn Press. Her poem, 'Great Expectations', was long listed in a contest by poethood.com and she came 2nd in The Bradt/Independent People's Choice Writing Competition. In 2012 her travel writing was published by Kasini House, in the book *This Is What's There.*

# www.elizabethglanville.com

Find out more at www.elizabethglanville.com, on Twitter @bethglanville, or on Facebook at Elizabeth Glanville, writer.

# The Imaginist

*For my family and friends*

www.elizabethglanville.com/the-imaginist

*"Isn't it funny how day by day nothing changes, but when you look back, everything is different?"*

*C.S. Lewis*

# The Imaginist

"Noooo...my baby! Stop, get off me! I just need my baby! Skye...!" Christine's tears mutated into muffled sobs as she collapsed into her husband's arms, rivulets of soil-stained tears chasing one another down her cheeks. "My baby...my Skye...she can't leave us like this, she can't go...she had her life...she had..."

"Sshhhh..." Chris was vaguely aware of her husband's breath against her ear. "Sshhh...I know, it's ok..."

"It's *not* ok!" Chris struggled to break out of Mike's grasp as she continued to sob. Then, as she felt her husband's grip weakening, she curled herself up in a ball at his feet, her black coat encasing her dwarfed self until she resembled a lone rock perched up high on the Brecon Beacons.

The last of the mourners slipped away as Chris felt Mike's arms wrap around her shoulders. This time she allowed herself to fall into them, smelling the muted whispers of brandy on his breath as she willed herself to evaporate into the atmosphere, and vanish forever with her daughter.

"But she's my baby. How did it happen? Why our Skye? Why? How could we let this happen?"

"Sshhhh now, shhhhh...I've got you..." As Mike rocked her from side-to-side Chris became aware of the sound of an infant's cry. Its delicate screams and innocent demands seemed mocking, reminding her of what she had lost. Her tears began to gather once more, but this time they fell silently.

"Louise..." Chris whispered. "Louise...Skye...my baby, my poor baby...my baby..."

11

# The Descent

# Chapter 1

"Now are you sure you've got your tickets? And did you get that cheese sandwich from the kitchen? You didn't forget that top drying in the airing cupboard, did you?"

"Yes, Mum! Here's my ticket, and here is the sandwich, and yes, I did get the top. Would you like to see that, too?" Louise made a show of going to open her suitcase but the older woman batted her hand away with a shriek.

"Don't you dare open that thing again, your dad nearly pegged out trying to fasten it! Hey," Louise noticed her mother's eyes suddenly sparkle, "did you see his face when those red pants fell out?"

Louise held Chris's gaze for a second, before they both burst into giggles. "Oh Mum, that was hilarious! He just about managed to keep his cool through the detangling lotions and party shoes and belts, but it seems that lacy thong was just too much! Well, that and Flumpy." Louise chuckled at the memory of her father wrinkling his nose as he extracted a faded, one-eyed bunny from between the teeth of the zip. She'd shoved Flumpy back into the case, smothering Mike's protestations that she was too old to be taking away her childhood sweetheart with reproaches over his lack of sentiment although, on second thoughts, she had indeed popped Flumpy back on her shelf. Though she still made sure she did it when Mike's back was turned.

"I kept telling him to sit on it, but he just wouldn't listen! I don't know. But those pants! I can't stop chuckling about it!" Chris dissolved once again and Louise smiled as she thought of how her father's face had flushed before turning pale, as he'd caught sight of that thong trying to escape from its prison. He'd proceeded to resume his task with vigour until the most essential elements of Louise's life were squashed into the dark, polyester lined cavern, safely ensconced in a sealed and padlocked plastic shell from which they which they couldn't possibly escape.

"Anyway, have you got a book for the journey?" Louise came back to the present as fingers snapped in her face. Her nostrils filled with a whiff of her mother's ever-present lavender hand cream, tainted with the fumes of stationary taxis.

"Yes, Mum. But I'm only going to London you know, I'm not going on a boat to Australia!"

"I know love, but I just, you know. I worry about you."

"I know, Mum. But I spent three years at university, and you weren't around then to make sure I had my book and my sandwich!" Louise flicked her hair out of her face, but her humour suddenly turned wry as two hands of icy fingers wrapped themselves around her stomach.

"Don't you roll your eyes at me, young lady! Anyway, I know. But that was before..." Louise watched her mother wring her hands, then smooth imaginary creases out of her skirt. "Louise," her voice dropped. "Are you sure you're doing the right thing? It's not too soon...?"

"Christine, she's going to be fine. Now let's go up to the platform and see her off, there's a match about to start, you know." Mike winked at Louise and she grinned back at her father, squashing the prickly wave that washed through her stomach far back down into her abdomen.

16

"Ooh, ooh! It's only nine minutes until the train goes! Quick, get up there you two!"

Louise took a deep breath and turned back to her mother. "Mum! It doesn't take nine minutes to walk up to the platform! It's only about thirty yards away!"

"Well, you never know. It might be late!"

Louise smothered a smile and glanced over at her father who shook his head, rolling his eyes skywards before following his wife. Chris was all but running up the steps to the platform, oblivious to the suitcases she knocked into and the angry glares that followed.

"Right, you've got seven minutes and thirty seconds to decide where to stand. Where do you think would be best? Where do you think the doors will open?"

"I don't know, Mum! Here will be fine!"

"Now, make sure you don't end up on one of those seats where you travel backwards, you know how prone you are to travel sickness."

"Mum! I've told you a million times, I haven't been travel sick since I was three! Will you just calm down? A few minutes ago you were worrying and now you've gone mad!" Louise bit her tongue as her mother's features recoiled into a frown, and uttered silent thanks for the passing cargo train that drowned out Chris's response with the roar of engines, the clanking of carriages and the screech of metal against metal as wheels scraped over rails. She placed a reassuring hand on the scratchy woollen wrap her mother refused to replace, giving a gentle squeeze before allowing the moment to pass.

"Six minutes, Louise! It's nearly here!" Christine soon bounced back, squealing the words above the sounds of the fading freight and draping her arm over her daughter's shoulder, as Louise turned her gaze on her father. He finally made it to the top of the stairs, his scarlet forehead glistening, and promptly dropped her suitcase onto the platform while exhaling theatrically, much to the surprise of the elderly lady in front of him. As Chris and Louise stood in that awkward embrace, and Mike hopped from foot to foot in case they missed kick off, Louise fiddled with the heart shaped charm on her necklace, every so often jerking her fingers away from her mouth whenever she realised she was nibbling at her cuticles yet again.

"Here it comes, Lou!"

Bang on time the rumbling purple beast rolled up to the platform, and Louise sucked the scent of oil and grease deep into her lungs as carriage doors were flung open, and groups of day trippers spilled out from their temporary cells.

"Get in, get in!"

"Mum! Stop it!" Louise moved out of the way of alighting passengers - as well as out of her mother's poking range - before turning back to her parents. "Well, I guess I'll see you soon."

"Oh, you'll have a great time love. Look after yourself, and make sure you eat properly! Good luck with the job search and finding a place to live, let us know when you're all settled in!"

"Will do, Mum! Bye, Dad!"

"Take care of yourself, Lou." Mike spoke gruffly as he enfolded his daughter in a hug, and Louise took a moment to relax into his arms. She inhaled the familiar scent of coffee mingled with wood smoke, and let his weight support her like she had done as a child. As they broke apart she saw that his eyes were damp. "You are up to this, aren't you? I know what I said to your mother but, you know, I just want to make sure." He spoke in an undertone, his copper tinted eyes boring into her matching pair.

Louise nodded brusquely and squeezed her back teeth

together. "Mm-hmm."

"Ok." Mike relaxed his grip. "Well, give us a ring soon. And anytime."

"I will." Louise sniffed and blinked a few times, then the train conductor blew his whistle and doors started banging down the platform. She spun around to face the entrance opposite and threw her case up the step before following after it, just as a man in navy slammed the door behind her. Once her case was secure Louise pulled down the window and leaned out on top of the frame.

"Send our love to Amy, won't you? You'll be with her for a fortnight, right? Before she goes off around the globe?"

"Yeah, well about ten days. I'll pass on your message, Mum!" Louise grinned as the train started to pull out of the station, feeling much more confident now she was finally on board.

"Bye!" She yelled, picking strands of hair out of her lip gloss as the warming breeze snaked through her curls. Mike's mouth moved but Louise couldn't make out the words so just waved back in acknowledgment, but as the train began to gather momentum she heard the unmistakable Celtic lilt of her mother's voice following along in the wind: "make sure you don't end up travelling backwards!" Louise smiled, then withdrew into the carriage.

*     *     *

Ryan woke up when the sun finally managed to pierce the crack in his Bournville velvet curtains. As he came back to consciousness he became aware of the muffled voices drifting in from the living room; no doubt Ash and his mate were slobbed out on the couch, the papers spread out between them and the TV chattering on with some kind of nonsense from across the pond. He couldn't face that right now.

Closing his eyes and willing sleep to return he tried not to think about the day stretching out ahead of him, void of structure and anything that could help pass the time, before returning to his abysmal temping job on Monday. Ryan spent Monday to Friday counting down the hours until the weekend, then his time off awaiting the return of the week, just so that he would have something to pass the time and fill his day. The irony of it all stuck in his throat, like a burr to woollen trousers.

In that sweet time between sleep and wakefulness, when Ryan could still pretend that everything was ok, his thoughts drifted back to Zoe. If he focused on switching off his waking brain and remaining in the safety of the inbetween he could just about manage to convince himself that she was still there, sleeping next to him in her old cock-soc t-shirt and nothing else, her cinnamon coloured hair splaying out across the pillow and her rounded hipbone peeping out beneath the hem of her shirt. Ryan rolled over and reached out across the wrinkled sheets, which had been yanked out of place by his tossing and turning underneath a fifteen tog duvet during what was turning out to be one of the hottest weeks of the year. But Zoe wasn't there.

\*       \*       \*

"I feel alive, I feel alive, I feel alive and I'm feeling good, waow! Oops sorry, hang on, I've got it here…somewhere…just bear with me…"

"Miss, can you move to the side please?"

"Yeah sure, sorry about this…I put my ticket in a safe place and now I can't find it. I always do this!" Louise glanced up to meet the ticket inspector head on, hoping that a mild flirtation would encourage him to let her slip through the gate un-ticketed, but all she got back was an icy glare. "Man, where *is* it?" As Louise allowed her head to fall back in frustration she noticed the sweeping, stained arches above her, and couldn't stop her mind from wandering to times gone by.

"Miss, do you *have* a ticket?"

"Sorry, sorry, I do…maybe it *was* in here…receipt, seat reservation, here's one from Cardiff, aha! I've got it!" Louise waved the card triumphantly in the ticket controller's face, but he just indicated the slot in the gate. She meekly inserted the ticket, snatching back her fingers as the machine guzzled it up.

Out on the concourse Louise paused to take in the rush hour city-ites hurrying past in suits and boots. She tugged awkwardly at her well-worn joggers and combed her fingers through curls which were quickly mutating into frizz, due to the ring of sweat surrounding her hairline. She glanced around for signs to the Circle and District lines then marched off, swinging her handbag on her shoulder, her stride slightly wider than usual.

"Excuse me! Sorry, do you mind if I just, ooh! I'm sorry! I…" Louise broke off as she looked up and caught the stony glare of a man in a suit, reclining against the edge of the tube train, whose foot was trapped underneath her case. With a gulp of warm, sweat-fragranced air Louise yanked up her luggage and dropped it on the other side, narrowly avoiding knocking over a pram. Even the baby seemed to be glowering at Louise with a 'what the hell do you think you're doing?' expression on her face, while a few rude mutterings about tourists surfaced, uttered quietly enough so that the speakers couldn't be identified yet loud enough for the words to reach her ears undistorted. But Louise held her head high, straddled her case and ignored the commuters, then satisfied herself at Notting Hill by giving the fingers to one particularly rude man before she got swept away with the crowd. They ascended en masse from the overheated, musty underbelly of the tube network, past a busker playing a rather deflating version of the Beatles' 'Here Comes the Sun' on his piano accordion, and out onto the heaving pavements.

"Ow!" Louise scowled as yet another shopper walked into her suitcase. "Where are the fucking directions? Why can't I get *organised*?" She fiddled around in her bag then exhaled, pulling her hair up into a ponytail and enjoying the feel of the sun beating down on the back of her neck, before letting her waves tumble down to cover her shoulders once more. With a deep breath she plunged her hand back into her bag, continuing to obstruct the paths of commuters and tourists pushing to get into the station like children fighting to reach a new toy, then heard someone bellowing her name.

"Loueeeeeeeese! Loueeeeeeeese!" She paused in her rummaging and looked up, scanning the crowd to locate the source. She broke into a grin when she clocked the young woman bouncing up and down on the other side of the road, waving her arms wildly while her bright blonde ponytail flicked narked passersby in the face.

"What are you doing here?" Louise yelled as she flew across the road to the angry honking of the 452 bus. "I thought I was meant to come to your house!" She nearly choked on an invisible cloud of Ralph as she arrived on the other side of the road, and swept Amy up in a hug.

"I knew you'd get in about now, so thought I'd head down and see if I could surprise you! Which I did! God, you're going to love it here, Lou! I'm so glad you managed to move up before I go, it's going to be like uni all over again! Though, of course we are a good few more years older and wiser..."

Louise caught Amy's eye and the pair burst into giggles.

"In theory, Ames! Anyway, it's so good to see you, it's

been far too long! Come on, let's go back to yours and dump this beast, smarten up and then head out and get some drinks. We've got so much to talk about! What do you say?"

"I say speak for yourself, you're the one who looks like you haven't seen the inside of Oasis since graduation. I think I'm plenty smart enough!" Amy leant over and yanked down the collar of her friend's polo shirt as Louise pulled out of her grip with a laugh.

"Ok, I was travelling! I have better clothes in here!" Louise kicked her suitcase, but she got more satisfaction from the sharp pain that spread through her big toe than from the clout the case made as it toppled over.

"Excellent, I'll give my mates a ring." Amy hauled up the suitcase. "Let's go!"

"Ooh, look at you, all city-ed up with your mojito! You slot right in now, Lou. But you need to calm that excitement, just be cool, have a casual slurp, look like you belong…fuck that's strong!" Amy coughed as Louise cuffed her on the arm.

"Don't be a dick, Amy. It's just that there's such a buzz here! It's so exciting, I can just smell the glamour!"

Now it was Amy's turn to reprimand her friend with an ice cube between the eyes. "Alright, now who's being a dick? Listen to yourself, since when did you take up poetry?!"

"I'm just excited, leave me alone! Ooh, that mojito's refreshing. Anyway, do you know of any flats going around here? You said the grapevine was the best way to find somewhere, right? And you are my best grapevine!"

Amy shook her head and put down her mojito, picking a stray bit of mint out of the tiny gap between her two front teeth. "I don't actually, at the moment. Which is unusual. It's a shame, though, that I didn't realise you were moving a bit sooner, before my room got taken on. It's not bad either at six fifty; it's a big room and a great location."

"Six fifty?! Is that, um, a standard amount to pay here?"

"Well, yeah. What were you expecting? Didn't you look it up before you came?"

"Um, well yes, I did look online. A bit. But I get distracted, you know what it's like!"

Amy arched her right eyebrow as Louise rushed on.

"And everyone wanted people to move in so quickly, then they all wanted me to view a place before they would even consider me and I couldn't come up just for viewings, so I figured I'd just wait until I got here..." Louise paused, thinking back to those hours spent tracking Jed's latest moves, the thrill of the occasional messages and the nights indulged in fantasy...but she reprimanded herself as she called to mind the sudden appearance of his profile picture with his new girlfriend, looking hauntingly happy and sickeningly smug. She shook her head sharply. "But I thought I saw places going for less than that. I mean, I just don't know how I'd afford that at the moment. Shit, maybe I should have thought this through a bit more..."

Amy rattled the ice cubes in her glass. "Well, like I said, it's not too bad. For here."

"Seriously?" A shiver fluttered down Louise's spine as she took another minty sip of rum and soda.

"Uh-huh. But there are cheaper options out there, if you're happy to have a single room or live a little further out. Try the outskirts of zone two, or just into zone three."

Louise drained her mojito, buying herself a few seconds by letting the ice cubes linger against her lips. She sighed as she replaced the glass on the table.

"I don't want to think about rents and money and things now, Ames. Let's just have a good time. You know, I'm so glad I made this move. I mean, I love Swansea, and I will miss

24

it. It's a great place, but it's no London, is it?"

Amy shook her head, smiling. "No, it's not. I've had an amazing few years here and I'm sad to go, but you know. London will always be here. I want to travel but I do want to come back."

"And what about Kat? I know it's not been the most, um, consistent relationship," Louise grinned at Amy's snickering. "But hasn't that been going on for, like, a year now?"

"Well, you know...if she's here when I get back then she's here, if she's not then she's not. She's nice enough but she's not the one. And I'm expecting to meet plenty of ones on my travels so I don't want to be tied down!" Amy elbowed Louise in the ribs and winked as the girls burst into giggles. "Ooh, look! There's Jen and the others! Come and meet everyone!"

*      *      *

On the other side of town Ryan saw off another bottle of Stella, simultaneously wrestling to get his wallet out of his jeans' pocket. It seemed to be getting harder to coordinate the two. Eventually he managed to free his Mastercard, and waved it around the circle of his new found drinking buddies.

"Another round, all?" He shouted above the mixing of the DJ, revelling in the appreciative cheers and slaps on the back. He turned to the barman and gave his order, then added a round of tequilas with a couple of extra shots for the wait. As his mind fuzzed over he relished in that safe, familiar sense of drifting away from himself. It started in his legs as his muscles began to soften, then moved up through his body as his trunk filled up with nothingness and he lost himself to the music and booze. He knew he would pay the price for it come morning, but at least the pain of the hangover would numb the pain of life and give him something to focus on.

## Chapter 2

"So, where do you want to go today? Here, take this you slob."

Louise took the proffered mug, cupped her hands around it and took a slug of milky coffee. "Mmm...I know it's summer but there's still nothing like a nice cup of coffee first thing, is there? Last year I tried to get into those iced frappuccino things, but they're just wrong. Coffee is meant to be hot."

"Lou? Where do you want to go?"

"Oh, sorry. Umm, how about Covent Garden? We used to go to the market there on school trips. I like the cobbles! And all those funky little shops and restaurants, it's like going back in time!"

"Louise! My God you're such a history geek! There are more exciting things in London than cobbles, you know. And it's so full of tourists."

"But I like it!"

"Alright! You're the guest. And then I'll take you to one of my favourite places for lunch. Deal?"

"Deal."

"Right, then finish your coffee and get ready. Let's go!"

"London life hasn't half turned you bossy," Louise grumbled, as she buried back down under the covers.

"Get UP!" Amy hoiked the duvet off Louise in one

swift movement then ran back to her bedroom with it, giggling like an overexcited hyena. Louise accepted defeat, took another slug of caffeine and forced her mind to focus on the present.

"Ah, this is so lush! It's magical, isn't it?" When Amy didn't reply Louise looked across at her friend, who was staring back at her with a repulsed grimace.

"Magical?! I wouldn't exactly...for fuck's *sake*." Amy turned to glare at a couple arguing in German while gesticulating wildly at their Eyewitness guide, oblivious to their flapping elbows which were alternately poking Amy's back and handbag. Appearing not to have not heard Amy's berate they carried on jabbering over each other, as Amy huffed and puffed and made a big show of moving out of their space.

"Ow!"

Louise suppressed a giggle as her friend caught her heel in a cobble, only avoiding toppling over by grabbing onto a toddler who was wobbling along beside his buggy.

"Omigod, I'm so sorry!" Amy flushed and turned pleading eyes on the boy's mother, who grabbed her bemused son by the hand, glared at Amy and marched off towards the market hall. "See? I told you this was a bad idea." Amy folded her arms and tossed her head.

"Oh Ames, just think of the history. Ooh, I'm so sorry!"

"S'alright," drawled the Aussie surfer dude she had careered into, smiling with one side of his mouth and peering at Louise over his sunglasses. He winked at her then sauntered off in his Havainas. She glanced over her shoulder, but he didn't look back.

"Can we get a coffee?" Amy whined, flapping her hands around her armpits. "But *not* here?"

Louise sighed. "Ok, come on moany. I've spent enough

money as it is, you should never have taken me to that jewellery stall. And David and Goliath. Or Lush."

"I didn't force you to spend your money! Come on, let's head down to Leicester Square, I guess you'll want to see *that* too. We can get a coffee on the way. Then, when you've bought your souvenir tea towels and coasters and t-shirts and crap, I'm taking you over to Brick Lane for a Turkish lunch with apple tea. Then we'll finish up at Oxford Street before we go home, if you think you can control yourself in that massive Topshop…"

"Shouldn't have thought so!" Louise pulled out her brand new Oyster card. "Let's go!"

"You can put that away, we're walking."

*     *     *

"Morning you…or afternoon, even…" Ryan stirred in his sleep as a spider ran across his nose. Reaching up to brush it off he started when his fingers met with another, and his eyelids shot open as the memories of the night before started to surface.

"Um, hey. You." Ryan's stomach lurched. "Please get the fuck out of Zoe's side of my bed, and don't even think about leaving your number." Although that was only in his head. "Er…how are you?"

"Good," Sam replied. "Very good, in fact. And I know something that would make me even better…" With that she whipped off his Carlsberg t-shirt and rolled over on top of him, brushing her chocolate-drop nipples against his lips before straightening up like a phoenix rising. His stomach churned, but that didn't stop him from reaching up to take a nipple in his mouth while running his palm over her curvaceous buttocks.

See, that was the thing with one-nighters. It was so easy. Whereas with Zoe it was intense, and scary. He had felt

29

out of control of his feelings and hadn't known how to deal with them. He was sure it was love, though he had nothing to compare it to. In many ways it was what he'd always dreamed of, but he'd never expected it to be so frightening and to leave him feeling so open and vulnerable, and dependent. When they were together he felt consumed by her, and when they were apart he felt he might burst with his need to be near her. And that was before everything that had happened. So, as it approached that time where Zoe insisted they 'talk it out', and 'consider their future together', he ended it.

*　　　*　　　*

"Man, I'd forgotten how amazing London is. It's been ages since I really spent some time here!"

"Oh, here we go again." Amy muttered, before smiling as sweetly as Emma Bunton with a cup cake.

"There's just so much happening and so much to see! Even just the buses called after Monopoly places, and the black cabs, and the underground!" Louise flopped back on Amy's sofa.

"Are you done?"

"With what?"

"With your tirade of wonderfulness! You've been at it all day!"

Louise felt her face begin to heat up. "Yes. Sorry Ames, I just get so carried away! But yes, I'm done now. God, I'm knackered!" She let her head fall back onto the top of the sofa.

"Good. Well you need to wake up now because we need to make dinner plans! Come on, open those eyes. What do you fancy?"

"Where do you get your energy from, Ames?" Louise struggled into a more upright position. "Oh I don't know, is there a good pub around here?"

"A pub?! Come on, we can do better than that! We can get Chinese, Japanese, Thai, Indian, Mexican, Italian, Tapas, or try something a bit different like Lebanese or Brazilian? *Que piensas*?"

"Umm, Thai? I usually go for Chinese but perhaps I should try something a bit different?"

"Excellent! I know just the place! Get changed into something nice - you never know who you might meet - and we'll go!"

Twenty minutes later they were back out on the streets of Notting Hill, Louise tottering along in borrowed heels behind Amy, who confidently led the way in her needle-thin stilettos.

"Where are we going? Are we going on the tube?"

"No, just local. You're going to love it! Come on, keep up!"

"I can't! I haven't worn heels in years, my feet are already starting to hurt."

"Well you'd better get used to it now you're in the Smoke! You want to look the part, don't you?"

"Yes." Louise told her brain to ignore the burning sensation in the balls of her feet, and marched ahead to attempt to catch up with Amy. "I really, really do."

"What was that, Lou?"

"Oh! Er, nothing. It's ok."

"Cool. You know, I do like shopping around High Street Ken. You sure you're alright back there, Lou? I mean, don't get me wrong I love Westfield and all that, but it's just so massive, and always heaving. It's much more manageable here, everything's smaller and less crowded. Anyway, here we are. Ta-da!" Amy stopped abruptly outside a traditional looking pub, presenting it with a flourish of her arm.

31

"Here?" Louise spun around on the spot, panting slightly. "I thought you didn't want to go to a pub? I thought we were going for Thai?"

"Ah, but we are. But first, just look. Isn't it beautiful?"

The building was covered in hanging baskets of flowers in all shades of yellow, red and violet, while further beds outlined the name of the pub, bursting with the bright colours of more peonies and pansies. Barely a speck of bare wall remained.

"It's my favourite spot in London, this. Aside from my bed, maybe. You know, when there's someone in it. Like..."

"Amy!"

Amy giggled. "Nah, seriously. I love this place. It's just so beautiful, it's like a little haven in the middle of the city. Don't you think?"

"It is gorgeous," Louise pulled her phone out of her handbag. "And they do Thai, do they? I'm going to set this as my background!"

"Yeah. It's yum! And the restaurant inside is even better than this." With that Amy pulled open the door and ushered Louise through.

The interior of the pub was disappointingly normal - the lounge had that familiar smell of beer mixed with damp carpets and cooking and the decor consisted of old pictures of the city, dated beer mats and historic marketing memorabilia of little-known ales. Most of the tables had been taken so people were propped up at the bar or leaning back against pillars, while nursing pints or glasses of wine. It was nice enough but didn't seem too different from the pub Louise had worked in back in Aberystwyth, although the clientele seemed a bit better off. And she wouldn't mind betting that drinks were about three times the price. She turned to look at Amy, who pre-empted her question by grabbing her hand and leading her deeper into the tavern.

Louise followed obligingly, although somewhat distracted by the high prevalence of men in shirts and ties. But her attention was soon diverted from the bachelors (she had managed to glimpse enough ring fingers to allow the use of that term for the collective) as Amy led her into the conservatory towards the back of the pub.

"Oh my God, look at all the flowers! They're everywhere! This is gorgeous, I feel like I'm outside!" Louise closed her eyes and turned her head towards the early evening sunshine streaming in through the glass roof.

"And look at the butterflies!" Amy grabbed Louise's hand and brought her back.

Louise let her gaze wander over plastic butterflies balanced on the flowers, light fittings and table tops. More were stuck to the walls and around the window frames. She inhaled deeply, savouring the sweet scent of flowers mixed with the delicate chimes of oriental cooking.

"Go to the toilet!"

"What? I don't want to go the toilet."

"Just go!"

"Well, I'll go in a bit, when I need to. Amy, you're grinning like a maniac!"

"Oh, just *go*!"

"Why?!"

"Get in there and you'll see!"

Louise frowned once again, but turned towards the bathrooms while Amy wandered off with a waitress.

She pushed open the door to the ladies then stopped, her smile spreading until she laughed out loud. Again the toilets were covered with plants and flowers; hanging over the sinks, balanced on the windowsill and in flowerboxes on top of the loos. The bathroom was also decorated in butterfly stickers, all over the walls, in the corners of the mirrors and even on the toilets themselves. As she took in the interior design she made use of the free Molten Brown White Mulberry hand cream, then studied herself in the mirror.

"Why are you stressing all the time?" Her reflection responded with a giggle. "It's all going to be fine; you're going to get a job, and find a flat, and get a boyfriend, and make some friends. There's no need to worry anymore, you're here now and it's all going to work out."

The face in the mirror suddenly became a lot more serious. "Remember this moment, Louise." It said. "This is what it feels like to be happy. And soon, before too long, you're going to feel like this every single day." Louise knew, deep down, that either way that would be true.

"Pad Thai?" Louise nodded, dropping the menu back down on the table. "Chicken? Pork? Prawn?"

"Umm, chicken, I think." Amy signalled to the waitress and ordered the food, then Louise jumped in with a request for a bottle of sparkling white.

"To celebrate!" She explained as the bottle arrived, before decanting the effervescent liquid into the accompanying glasses.

"To your new life in London!" Amy toasted. "Ooh, that's really fizzy! So, are you ready for it all then? It's not always as glamorous as it seems, you know. London is busy and fast paced and exhausting, and it can be a pretty unfriendly place at times."

"Mm-hmm, I could do with my life picking up pace a bit. I'm excited!" Louise paused. "Did you find it unfriendly?"

"Well, it was a bit different for me because I went into a grad scheme, so work provided quite a social life in itself. But it wouldn't have been so easy if I hadn't had that." Amy took a swig of wine. "And I guess I've been lucky with my flat. Rachel and I don't spend much time together but she's still around, you know? And we do sit down together sometimes and have a glass of wine after work, and that. I've met people through her and she's met some of my friends, and like I say it's just nice having that to come home to. Know what I mean? But there's just so much to do here. It's nothing like Basingstoke." Amy pouted. "Ooh, here's our food, let me just make some space."

"You're making me a bit nervous now, Ames." Louise pushed the menus out of the way. "I figured everything would just all fall into place. But maybe I'm wrong. I mean, I don't even have anywhere to live yet. Let alone a job to go to. Thanks, this looks lovely!"

"Look," Amy speared a prawn and pointed it at her friend. "Firstly, you've got a decent degree behind you and some gap year experience." She hesitated. "What exactly is it you've been up to these past few years, anyway? I mean, I know you were planning to go to Australia and that you've done some work at home, but it's been hard to keep up…" Amy trailed off and popped her prawn into her mouth, flushing pink and wrinkling her nose.

Louise shook her head and laughed lightly as an invisible cloak of chainmail draped itself around her shoulders. "Don't worry, it's fine. I have been a bit all over the place. Even I'm struggling to keep up." She giggled again then grabbed at her glass, flicking her eyes around the room as she took a few gulps. "This is good wine, Ames! And the food is beautiful."

"Yeah, I love it here." Amy let her gaze drift across the room. "Anyway where were we? Ah yeah, what exactly is it you're looking for on the job front?" Louise exhaled and let her shoulders fall as she turned her attention back to her friend.

"Um, well I guess PR or sales or something. Maybe recruitment. That's what other graduates seem to do, and there seems to be a lot of opportunities. Oh Amy, have I done the wrong thing? I have a bit of money saved up but not loads, I guess I got so excited I didn't really think properly about what I was going to do once I got here. And I don't really know anyone, except you. It's just that people seem to come to London after uni and travelling and that, so it seemed...I don't know...right?"

"It is, don't worry. It'll work out, it just might not be quite as linear as you were expecting. And you do know people, right? Your mates from uni are here? Those other humanities geeks?"

"Amy!"

"Well, you know. Anyway, once you're in a job you'll meet loads of other people and things will take off. You're nice! You're friendly, outgoing and approachable and interesting. Sometimes. When you're not banging on about tube trains and cobbles and things." Amy grinned slyly as her friend kicked her under the table.

"Remind me why I'm staying with you again?"

"Because," Amy spoke as if she was talking to a toddler, while waving a piece of pepper at Louise's nose, "your humanities friends are all geeks." Amy dissolved into giggles as Louise brushed her friend's fork out of her face.

"Bugger off, you." But she smiled as she tucked into her Pad Thai, enjoying the feel of red chillies biting at her tongue and the fragrant taste of coriander that permeated the dish.

"Thanks, that was delicious! Can we get the bill please?" Amy wiped her napkin over her mouth and delved around in her white suede handbag. "Where's my bloody purse? It's on me,

Lou."

"No! You don't have to do that! At least let me get mine." Louise reached for her own synthetic clutch but Amy waved her words away.

"Seriously, I want to. It's your welcome to London present!" At that moment the waitress returned and Amy handed over her card. "Too late now, anyway. She's gone to get the machine."

"Thanks, Ames." Louise leaned across the table and squeezed her friend's hand.

"No worries. Wine at the bar?"

"Oh, yes!"

Amy tapped in her PIN then led the way back into the main bar, while Louise marvelled at the heads she turned as she strutted past tables of diners. Amy seemed completely oblivious.

"White wine? I'll get them!"

"No! You just bought dinner! Let me get them." Louise's protests were met with a vicious shake of the head and a wave of the hand, but before she could try and persuade Amy otherwise a deeper voice cut in.

"Ladies, allow me…" the owner of the smooth yet commanding tones leaned over and requested two glasses of Pinot Grigio from the bar maid, smoothly slipping a crisp twenty into her outstretched hand. "Keep the change." He winked, and she blushed as he turned his attention back to Amy and Louise.

"Jake. Pleasure to meet you." He proffered his hand and smiled at the girls, who returned the grin and introduced themselves, suddenly becoming rather more subdued and stuck for words than they had been all night.

"And this is Andy." A second guy who had been hovering in the background stepped in and the introductions were repeated, before Jake turned back to the bar and ordered a couple of pints.

"So, what are you girls up to tonight?"

Louise noticed that Amy's eyes were studiously locked on Andy's jaw so decided to leave her friend to answer that one, wondering how Andy would react when he realised just how futile his advances were; Amy did enjoy looking at men but she never, ever touched. He glanced up when Jake handed him his pint then refocused his attention on Amy, while his comrade moved around to stand beside Louise.

"Are you from London?"

Louise glanced back over at Amy, who was chatting away to Andy while still managing to keep an eye on the other pair. As she caught her eye Amy grinned in an encouraging manner, and Louise turned back to Jake.

In a different age he may well have been described as dashing, with his slightly stocky build, dark hair, distinguished air and quiet confidence. He had a twinkle in his eye and his smile made him look as if he was guarding a special secret. He smelled of expensive aftershave and, if she dared to even think such a cheesy line, success. She took a deep breath before answering his question.

"Just moved up, from Swansea."

"Cool! I have an auntie in Llandudno." Jake paused.

"Oh, right. Well I've never actually been to Llandudno, but, um, I hear it's nice."

"Ahem...so when did you move here?" Jake flushed slightly and slipped a hand into his pocket, before withdrawing it and resting it on the bar. Louise smiled and relaxed against the counter.

"Just yesterday, so it's all pretty new at the moment."

"Yesterday, eh? And what do you do? Are you living around here?"

"I'm staying here with Amy for a week or so, but I start flat hunting tomorrow. And job hunting."

"What are you looking for?"

Louise shrugged. "I'm quite easy, really. Not like that!" She tapped his cotton-covered arm at his raised eyebrows, hesitating for a second to appreciate the firm muscle hiding underneath, before yanking her arm away and flushing at the out of character confidence the wine had induced in her. "Something along the lines of PR or recruitment. Something that will bring in money and make use of my degree, that's pretty much my request!"

Jake bobbed his head. "Well, you should find something easily enough around here. But don't forget to get on the nightlife too. Where are you heading later? Maybe we could show you girls some places...?" He held her gaze for just a second longer than necessary, before hiding behind a prolonged swig of Guinness.

"Sorry, Louise, you've just got a smudge of lipstick..." Jake leaned over and ran his finger down Louise's cheek, despite the fact that she hadn't worn anything other than clear gloss since a bad experience at a school disco when she was twelve. But the moment was spoiled somewhat as Amy appeared out of nowhere and seized Louise's arm, digging her nails into the soft flesh by her armpit.

"Come to the toilet with me!"

"Ow! I don't *need* the toilet." Louise eyed her mate pointedly, experiencing a not-so-mysterious sense of deja vu.

"Come *with* me." As Amy tightened her grip Louise realised that she wasn't going to win, so grinned apologetically at Jake and allowed herself to be dragged off back to the butterfly haven.

"Ok, I'm just going to check my make up while you go

then. Have you got an eyeliner? What are you doing?!" Louise toppled into the rim of the sink as Amy grabbed her by the shoulder and spun her round.

"They're engaged."

"Who's engaged?" Louise tentatively bent over and poked a scarily life-like looking Red Admiral.

"Jake and Andy!"

"Nooo!" Amy gained Louise's full attention as she revealed her news, almost proudly. "They're gay? Wow, I'd never have guessed."

"Who's gay?"

"Jake and Andy!"

"They're not gay!" Amy clouted Louise over the head with her friend's own pearly clutch, catching Louise rather neatly on the temple with the oversized diamante clasp. "They're not engaged to each other! They have girls waiting for them at home!"

"Oh." Louise rubbed her skull and snatched her bag back from Amy. "No, they can't be! How do you know, anyway?"

"The shithead told me! We were just talking and he said something about his fiancee! He even said 'fiancee'. And when I questioned him he was just like 'well, yeah I'm engaged, do you have a problem with that?' And then he started stroking my arm! Can you believe it?! And," Amy lowered her voice, "Jake's fiancee is expecting."

"Expecting what?"

"A baby! For God's sake Louise, how much have you had to drink?!"

"Oh! Quite a bit, actually, Jake was rather plying me with them…"

"Wanker."

Louise was about to jump to his defence when she

realised it was true. But that didn't stop her chest from slumping as his potential went out the window. She took a deep breath. "Yeah! What a knob head!"

"And Andy. I mean, he's certainly not my type. But you know!" The two girls stood in silence for a moment, shaking their heads and tutting. "Well, fuck them." Amy swept her hair off her face and picked up her bag. "I'm outta here."

Louise stared after Amy, hesitating for a few seconds before sneaking another blob of white mulberry, then hurrying along behind.

"Ladies?" Jake pulled out his wallet as the girls approached. "Another drink?"

Louise's heart fluttered as she caught his eye, and despite her brain trying to direct her otherwise she opened her mouth to accept. But she didn't get the words out in time.

"Fuck you." Amy raised her fingers at Andy.

Louise glanced at Amy, then back at Jake, then imitated her friend's action before picking up her wine glass to take a final swig.

"We're off."

Louise emphasised Amy's statement by banging the glass back down on the table, before swinging around and stalking off after her friend.

"Score." Amy offered Louise her palm and the girls high-fived, but suddenly even just slapping hands seemed like an effort. Louise tried to tell herself she was just tired, but for the briefest second she felt that dreadful sinking feeling inside her tummy again, that one that made her feel as if something inside her had just died. She couldn't help but glance back over her shoulder as she stumbled along the pavement, but the street was as quiet as morgue.

"Tea?" Amy offered as they entered into the flat. "Let me just dash to the loo!"

"No, thanks. I just need to get back to my sofa. You've bloody worn me out!"

"What are you going to do tomorrow?" Amy called through from the bathroom. "I'll be gone by seven."

"I'm going to lie in and drink lattes! And then I guess I'd better try and find a flat. And a job. Hey, can I have your laptop password?"

"Sure, it's Aberames, capital A. Have you got somewhere to start?"

Louise waited until the sound of running water eased. "Well, there's a few graduate schemes out there, and some sales and marketing things that I did look at in third year." She paused as the tap went on again. "Then I'll check out some PR places. And I guess I'd better give my CV a once over, as well."

"Wouldn't be a bad idea," Amy asserted, although it was a bit muffled through a towel. "What about flats?"

"Yeah, I'll have a look at some of those sites too. I'll worry about that in the morning, though. Good night, Ames!"

"I was going to come and have a cuppa! No worries though, you must be knackered and I'm just rabbiting on!"

"Oh! No, come have a cuppa! I thought you were going to bed."

"No, it's ok, I'll leave you to it. I shouldn't be too late anyway. Sleep well, Lou!"

Louise lay back, closed her eyes and smiled with relief. As much as she enjoyed Amy's company she wanted to be left alone now, to re-create that feeling of well-being she had briefly experience in the toilets of the pub. Just for five minutes. Honestly. Not a second more.

In her mind Louise was walking into a classy bar on Carnaby Street, that was packed to the rafters with Jakes and

Andys. But these ones weren't engaged sleaze balls. She was dressed in a designer suit with spiky high heels, her Givenchy make up impeccable and her hair straightened and gleaming. As she approached the bar to order a glass of sparkling wine a man who could quite easily be a model for Calvin Klein swooped in and paid for her order.

"So what do you do for a living, then?" The man asked, leaning over so Louise could smell his musky aftershave and see herself reflected in the glimmer of his dark eyes.

She chuckled. "I'm in PR, been in the field for a few years but expanding now, going to set up my own business. I've just been checking out offices and premises actually, and I'm going to start looking for staff soon."

The man nodded, then reached in and put his hand on her waist. "You know, I could tell when you walked in that door that you were someone special. I knew you wouldn't just have a run of the mill job, knew there was more to you than that. I can see it in your eyes, in the way you dress, in the way you hold yourself. Shall we get dinner?"

As Louise had only popped in for a quick post-work drink and had no further plans she nodded in agreement, reddening slightly as his hand slid down to rest on her hips.

"Allow me." He picked up her coat and slipped it around her shoulders, before offering his arm and leading her out into the magical land of the city at night, where anything is possible and dreams are not only formed but realised.

Louise smiled to herself and wrapped her arms around her waist, imagining, for a brief second, that they belonged to her mystery admirer.

"Night Lou! Glad you're here!"

Louise jumped, cracking her elbow on the frame of the couch as she remembered where she really was. "Night Ames, me too!"

"And don't forget that you're cooking tomorrow night!"

But Louise had already drifted off to a place far, far away.

## Chapter 3

*Dear Ryan,*

*Thank you for your recent enquiry regarding writing reviews for Music Mania. We have considered your samples and would be happy to print your work in the 'unknown bands' section, as and when possible. Do feel free to send through any more pieces and we will notify you upon publication.*

*Yours,*

*Lara Scanlan*
*Assistant Editor, Music Mania Magazine*

Ryan re-read the e-mail as his face cracked into a massive grin. And then he read it again, just to make sure. Ok, so it was a long way off having his own page, and it was all voluntary, but he had to start somewhere.

"Right, drink time." He clapped his hands together. "Who's about? Where's my phone? Hmmm...work people? No. Ash has that thing, uni people? Nah, I'll have to do all that bloody small talk. What about that girl, whatsername? Janie? Jamie? Janine?" He went to 'J' and scrolled through his contact list. "Jaylene! Aha. That's the one."

"Hi! You've reached Jaylene's phone. Leave a message and I'll get back to you. Bye!"

"Um, hey, Jaylene. It's Ryan here. We were, um, chatting in that bar in Hoxton the other night. Anyway, I wondered if you fancied getting a few drinks later? I'm celebrating. Gimme a call!"

Ryan hung up and flopped back on his mattress, feeling flattened. He fiddled with his phone for a few seconds before his fingers found the contact list, and he watched as they scrolled down to 'z'. He hesitated when he reached Zoe's name. She'd always been so supportive of his passion for music and his need to write, and would have been delighted to have heard about this. But things had changed and he had lost the right to text her at whim and just pop up in her life. He raised his eyes to gaze out of the window, up at the tiny segment of blue that peeped out between the surrounding flats and offices. It looked like a light viewed from the bottom of a 500 foot mine shaft. With a sigh he pulled his attention back, and then he hit delete.

"And send!" Ryan grinned as he saw off his first official contribution to Music Mania. He'd written a piece about a band he'd seen at a pub in Hackney the other week, called Grass Shoots. They seemed pretty fresh, although there stuff was somewhat predictable. But they had potential and a bit of publicity could give them more confidence to work on their originality. He forwarded the e-mail to Chaz, the lead guitarist, then opened up another blank document. This seemed like the perfect time to get started on that novel that had been brewing at the back of his mind.

But as his fingers hovered over the keyboard his mind went blank; he could almost hear the monotonous beep coming from his neurones as they refused to rise to the challenge. He gazed distractedly round the room, at the plethora of unwashed coffee mugs, the piles of CDs - starting to double as coasters as they were being made redundant to his Mac - and the scattered bits and pieces of clothing. The sheets on his bed were wrinkled and the duvet was draped half across the floor and half on the bed itself, with one pillow at each end of the mattress. Bed making had always been the one thing that he and Zoe couldn't agree on - she insisted on smoothing the sheets and spreading the duvet out every morning, and in her own flat would strategically place a few scatter cushions around the head. He'd remarked that the term 'scatter cushion' was misleading and 'putting cushion' would be more accurate, but she had just called him a philistine, and said that she wasn't going to waste her breath talking about the subject with someone who seemed to think that rolling up the duvet into a ball and dumping it in the middle of the mattress equated to 'making the bed'. But he'd only made that much effort to please her, as she'd get cross when she found the duvet straggling onto the floor. Now he could just leave it where it fell, the way that nature intended.

The door slammed as Ash came home and, as usual, flicked on the kettle. He had recently started in some finance firm in the city so was rarely around during the week, and now seemed to exist solely on a diet of caffeine and beer.

"Mate?" Ryan called out, wandering towards the kitchen.

"Alright, mate?" Ash stuck his head out of the door, looking rather tired and drained but nonetheless the typical Cityboy in his pinstripes and brogues. Ryan wasn't sure where he had learned that word, and it unnerved him somewhat to be able to recognise the style of his flatmate's shoes.

"You're home early, eh?"

"Yeah, for once. What you up to?"

47

Ryan watched Ash meticulously spoon one and two-thirds of a teaspoon of coffee into a mug.

"Not a lot." He shrugged as he thought about his laptop sitting on his desk, patiently awaiting his return. That sudden flash of creativity seemed to have seeped out of his system to leave him feeling more drained than ever. "I was going to get on with some writing, but I'm not really feeling it now. Think I'll just get on it in the morning. Fancy going for a few beers?"

"Well…" Ash paused as he topped up his black coffee with cold water, then knocked back half of it in one gulp. "Fuck it, why not? Just let me have a quick shower then I'll be right with you. Horse?"

"Yep, cool." Ryan opened the fridge and pulled out a can of Stella. "I'll get going on this, just give me a shout when you're ready."

Meanwhile, the empty paper on Ryan's computer screen blacked out, as the neglected machine finally gave up on life and put itself to sleep.

"Coming, Ry? Jesus, is that your third already?!"

Ryan drained the can he was holding and clambered to his feet, pleased to notice that his knees were already beginning to tingle. "It's been a long day. Come on, let's go. You've got some catching up to do!" Ryan pretended not to notice Ash's hesitation as his eyes flickered between the crunched up cans and the front door, but he felt it like an angry wasp in his chest. Jesus, what was wrong with the guy? He used to know how to have a good time, but since he'd started that job he'd become so bloody boring.

"Don't forget your keys, Ry!" Ryan jumped as the keyring clouted him against the shoulder.

"We're going out together man, why do I need keys?"

"Dude, that makes us sound like a couple. And you

need your keys because I'm not getting up at four o'clock to let you in again, I know how you like to wander off, and I've got a meeting in the morning. Come on, man! What's taking you so long to get your shoe on?!"

Ryan gave up on trying to untie his laces and rammed his foot into his trainer as his stomach rumbled. He felt much more light-headed than he should after three cans. But then when had he last eaten?

"Anyway, tell me, what happened to that bird who was hanging around the flat the other morning? Thought she'd be back again, or was once with you enough for her? Man, I love how close this place is to our flat. Pint?"

"Cheers. Nah, it was just a one nighter. Busy man like me can't be dealing with more than that, just want to do my own thing, you know? Had enough of all those ties, got to make the most of it all now, eh?!"

"Ah yeah, for sure." Ash handed Ryan a pint of Carling.

"Anyway, you've been a bit quiet on that front lately! When I first moved in you had a different girl round every night of the week, but I haven't met any strangers in the kitchen for ages now! You hiding anything?"

Ash took a sip of his pint then reclined against the bar, nursing his glass in both hands and briefly closing his eyes. "Actually, a bit. There's a bird in the office who's a bit different, know what I mean?"

Ryan didn't trust himself to respond.

"And I thought I might have a crack at it, see where it leads. Haven't actually spoken to her yet, though. But who knows?" Hey, two o'clock. I think we've found our entertainment for the night." Ash raised his eyebrows and nodded in the direction of two girls sharing a bottle of wine at a table by the window, who flushed and giggled as the boys looked over. "Shall we? What?! I can still look!"

49

Ryan followed as Ash led the way over to the table, instantly charming the girls with a grin, a wink and the offer of another bottle. Ryan felt his entire body slump as he sat down next to the girl with long brown hair and tiny tits, and played out the familiar old patterns and games, now ingrained as second nature yet still as superficial and insincere as ever. And that was how he met Kayla.

"Come on, get out! Don't you lot have homes to go to? You've got five minutes then you'll be out on your arses! Get a move on, lads!" Fred's eyes twinkled as he directed the end of his tirade at Ryan's table.

"He's a bit mad, isn't he?" Kayla snuggled into Ryan, so he slipped his arm around her as he finished his pint.

"Ah, don't mind Fred, he's always like this. Anyway, are you coming into town? Ash, you coming?"

"Nah, mate. I told you, I'm having an early one."

"Ah you're so boring man, you used to love a party! Come on, just come for a bit." Ryan turned to Kayla. "Ash used to be so much fun, then he got this job and now he's all like 'Oh no, I don't want to drink, I don't want to party, I don't want to have a good time. I just want to behave myself now and go to bed early'."

"Hey, chill out there man, ok?"

"Ooh, there he goes. Listen to him, 'I just want to work hard and be boring and suck my boss's cock and be a good little boy'."

"Hey, Ryan. Cut it out."

Ash's face was swimming in and out of focus, and just the sight of it made Ryan want to snarl. "No, man. *You* cut it out. Cut out that fucking crap and loosen up. Come on, Kylie."

"It's Kayla."

"Sorry, baby. I know. Come on Kayleigh." Ryan

grabbed her face and pulled her into him, vaguely aware of his teeth crashing into hers. He pulled her hair back from her face and grinned down at her. "You ok, baby?"

"Yeah. Jesus, I'm hammered." Kayla wiped a hand across her mouth and squeezed her eyes shut. "Oh shit, that's worse. What were you doing buying me all those shots? Come on, I need some air. Suzy, are you coming?"

"Yeah, sure. Let me finish this. Nice to meet you, Ash."

"Let's go," Ryan slurred, "and leave that boring sod behind." Ryan noticed Ash's face contort into a grimace as he lurched to his feet. Part of him experienced a flicker of remorse, but a greater part felt a wave of resentment. "Don't worry, *mate*, I've got my keys. You won't have to turn into a pumpkin." Ryan couldn't stop himself from sneering his parting words, but even through his muggy head he knew that Ash didn't deserve it.

## Chapter 4

"I'm back!"

Louise jumped when Amy burst through the door, bang on six thirty.

"It's so nice to come home and have you here! How was your day? How was your job hunt? And did you find a flat?"

Louise glanced at the clock. Shit! How could it be so late already? Hearing Amy approach in her nylon-ed feet she struggled back up into a sitting position and ran a hand through her hair, her veins starting to overheat as she struggled to bring herself back down from the rafters.

"Hey, Ames! How was your day?"

"Oh, same old. But I'm more interested in you! How did you get on?"

Louise looked blankly at her friend while her brain suffered a momentary whiteout. "Erumm…"

"Jobs? Flats?"

"Oh! Yes! Jobs and flats. Well…" A flicker of guilt swam through her belly.

"Louise? You've not just been lying here all day, have you?"

"No! I did, I, um, looked up some job schemes, had a browse at flats. I've even got a list of job applications to do tomorrow!" Louise idly waved her hand in the direction of the dining table, where a few papers were weighted down with a tannin stained mug. "And I set up some flat viewings, too. Then I went out and got some stuff for dinner. I was just having a nap, that's why I'm a bit dozy." Louise reached for Amy's hand. "Honestly, Ames, I'm sorted now. It's been an exhausting weekend and I just wanted to get five minutes while the flat was quiet."

Amy's shoulders slumped slightly, though she wouldn't redirect her gaze from Louise's face. Louise gave her friend's hand a squeeze, then withdrew her grip.

"You are sure, yeah? Lou?"

The back of Louise's throat wobbled as she felt her friend's scrutiny, but she forced herself to hold Amy's gaze. "Ames, I'm sure. It's over, honestly. But I do appreciate you looking after me." Silence ensued until Louise forced a smile and faced Amy square on. "Now, do you want some fajitas?"

Amy hesitated, then slipped into a grin and nodded. "Sounds good. But first, come here you," and she wrapped her arm around Louise's slender form. As Louise buried her face in the sweet scent of Louise's Ralph Lauren she crushed her eyelids together, pushing that concrete mushroom that was sitting in her stomach far back down into the depths of her body. Amy squeezed her tighter, which she found comforting. But at the same time it made her nerves start to tingle once more as she thought about how, in just a short while, Amy was going to leave her, too.

"Ok?" Louise sniffed and nodded as Amy loosened her grip. "Let's go cook. Well, you can cook and I'll pick at the avocado and make helpful comments. Yeah?"

Louise chuckled. "Come on then. But at the very least you can cut the onion, it make my eyes sting like crazy."

"Aha, you need contacts!"

54

"Contacts?"

"Yeah! Haven't had a problem with cutting onions since I got them. Or with cigarette smoke, smeechy cooking, anything like that. But walk me within ten feet of an onion without them in and I start crying like a baby. I've got tinted ones now!"

"Tinted lenses! I thought your eyes looked bluer, but then I thought I must be imagining it!"

"Hee hee! Yeah, they're really subtle ones but they do make a difference. I just wanted to go a shade or two bluer, so that I couldn't be described as 'grey-eyed'. It sounds so drab."

"Catch." Louise chucked the offending onion across the kitchen. "They look amazing."

"Thanks! Oh, by the way, I thought some of my friends could come round on Friday and we could cook here, sort of a goodbye thing, you ok with that?" The end of Amy's sentence got lost in a spoonful of salsa and sour cream.

"Ames! That's gross! And don't finish all that sour cream before the fajitas are ready! Anyway, yeah, Friday will be cool. It'll be wicked to meet some more people before you leave and desert me!"

"Don't try the guilt trip, it doesn't work!" Amy mopped at her lips with a piece of kitchen roll, while Louise feigned innocence with wide eyes and raised shoulders. "So where are these flats then?"

"Um, there's one in Islington, though I think it might be a bit cramped. It's a tiny little room. Then there's one in Clapham, and a couple in West Hampstead."

"Bloody hell, you're looking all over! How much are they? Salsa?"

"Um, no thanks. I know, but I don't really know what area I want so I'm just looking up cheap ones. Well, cheap-er ones. These aren't so bad. Anyway, hopefully I'll find somewhere soon. I really want to get settled in somewhere permanent before you go." A slight melancholy descended on the pair until Louise broke the silence with a shrill tone. "But I'm sure it will be fine!"

"It sounds very promising." Amy grinned. "Hey, I've got some Ben and Jerry's in the freezer, want some?"

"We haven't had the fajitas yet! And are you actually going to cut that onion?"

"Yes, yes. But first we need a starter, to whet our appetites!"

"Flipping heck, Amy." Louise caught her friend's eye. "Oh, go on then."

"It's Phish Food! And I have some extra toffee sauce! But I'll save that for later." A key crunched in the door to the flat. "Ooh, that must be Rachel. Hi!" she called out to the sound of stilettos clattering on laminate flooring. "Do you want some ice cream?"

"Oh yeah, thanks, that'd be great. I had a salad for dinner with Nisha and I'm craving something sweet and fattening!" Rachel rounded the corner into the lounge and came to shake hands with Louise. She was tall and thin with dark brown hair, carefully straightened and just sweeping her shoulders. Her olive skin was naturally highlighted by the sun, and huge sparkly brown eyes smiled out from behind what Louise heavily suspected to be false lashes.

"Help yourself."

"Hang on a sec, are you girls having ice-cream before fajitas?"

"Yes! It's a starter, flipping heck have you guys never had a three course meal before?!"

"Um, well yes. But not one that started with ice-cream. Hi, I'm Rachel by the way."

"Oh, Louise this is my flatmate, Rachel. Rachel,

56

Louise."

"Hi Louise, welcome to London! How are you finding it?"

"Hi! Yeah, so far so good!" Louise laid down the wooden spoon. "I'm really looking forward to being here, actually. I'm looking for jobs and flats already so hopefully I'll be up and running soon!"

"Sounds great! What jobs are you going for?"

The usual - PR, sales, marketing things. A few grad schemes. Just applying at the moment and seeing what comes back."

"Best way to do it, I reckon." Rachel paused to kick off her heels. "Mmm, this ice cream is so good! We need a bit of *Sex and the City* to go with it. And a glass of wine, that one still in the fridge, Amy?"

"Yeah I'll get that, you put on the DVD. Lou, are the fajitas nearly done?"

"No! I'm waiting for the onion! Pass it here, I'll do it while you go and finish your, um, starter. Here, take the sauces with you."

"Cool." Amy pottered off to join Rachel on the sofa as Louise turned back to her chopping and stirring. She was very glad of a few minutes to slip into her other world, where a scene very similar to the one that had just happened was being played out. Except in this one it was Louise who was coming home from work and kicking off her heels, before she started cooking up a meal for some friends who were coming over later. The table was all set and the wine was in the fridge, and she couldn't wait to catch up on the gossip and natter about her day. Oh, and tell them about her promotion, of course. And her hot date on Saturday.

Back in Amy's kitchen Louise's fajita mix simmered dry as the world around her shrunk. She leaned against the

57

counter in a little bubble and smiled down at her chocolate fish as she day-dreamed, flicking them out of the sea and chomping down on their fins to abruptly end their peaceful and innocent existence.

The following day, after an afternoon of yet more Carrie Bradshaw followed by a long hot shower, Louise slipped into a new dress then wandered into the kitchen to start prepping for dinner, flicking on the local radio station as she went.

"Because of you-ooo-ooo-ooo," she warbled as she imagined the lasers and spotlights dancing over the stage, the looks of approval on the judges' faces and the roaring of the crowd. But the final flourish of her microphone smashed into one of Amy's wine glasses - luckily the Ikea ones, rather than the crystal set - and sent it tumbling to the ground, where it shattered into a thousand diamond tears which spun out across the lino.

"Crap." Louise eyed the mess, willing the pieces to jump up off the floor and stick themselves back together. But when that didn't happen she accepted defeat, sighed, then retrieved the dust pan and brush from under the sink.

As Louise cleaned up she pondered on how she could meet more people in the city, picturing the groups of young professionals that hung out in the trendy spots in Swansea on a Thursday night. She transferred that image to London and tried to incorporate herself into the picture. She fitted. Almost. But as her mind drifted towards employment the increasingly familiar thought pattern surfaced: hope leading to disappointment, then failure and deflation. She tried to kick start herself into action by swapping the dust pan and brush for the laptop and opening up the job sites, but she just felt herself collapse and sag more and more with every unsuitable advert she read.

A short while later the slam of the door gave her an excuse to lower the laptop lid, so she closed her sites and logged off as Rachel came into the room. As Louise watched her remove heels and earrings and loosen her hair she experienced an emerald flash of jealousy in her gut. The twinge vanished almost as soon as it had appeared, but it left her insides squirming.

"God, I'm so glad to be home. What a hectic afternoon! How was your day?"

"Yeah, it wasn't too bad. I've just been having a look through the job sites and stuff."

"How's that working out?"

Louise sighed. "Not great. Everyone seems to want experience, and I haven't really got any."

"Ah, that old chestnut. No-one will give you a job because you haven't got experience, but you can't get experience because no-one will give you a job."

"That's the one." The girls lapsed into silence for a few moments before Rachel turned towards her room.

"Just going to jump in the shower cos I'm going out soon. You don't need the bathroom, do you?"

"No," Louise twiddled her hair thoughtfully. "Hey, are you not sticking around for tonight?"

Rachel popped her head back round the door. "No, I'd already made plans with a mate. I'd like to stay but he's bought tickets for some play so we can't really change it."

"Fair enough." Louise's phone suddenly burst into life so she rummaged around in the sofa cushions to find it.

"Hello?" It was an unknown London number and Louise held her breath as she prayed for it to be news of a job, already mentally accepting the position in her head as the MD told her she'd never met anyone more suitable, and was prepared to up her starting salary to £40K as she'd been so impressed. And throw in a company car. And a platinum credit card. And...

"Lou? It's me."

"Oh. Hi Amy."

"Sorry, were you expecting someone more exciting?"

Louise laughed airily. "No no no! Well, I did wonder if you were phoning about a job, but no worries!"

"Sorry! Any luck there?"

"No. Well I've done a few applications now but a lot of the graduate schemes I had my eye on aren't recruiting at the moment. Then I haven't got experience for a lot of the jobs that look good." Louise sighed. "I thought it would be easier than this, Ames! I really want a job, but I want to be a bit picky about what I take."

"I know, it's not easy. But didn't you know all of this before you left Swansea?"

"Well, a bit. But I think I hoped that once I got here something would, like, come along, you know?" She put her face in her hands and rubbed her eyes before emitting a groan. "Am I that naïve, Ames?"

"No, you're not Lou. A lot of my friends here have found that things aren't quite how they expected them to be. But I think it'll be fine in the end. It's just going to be something of a longer process than you may have expected. And it can take a while, you know, just to get through the application procedures and all that before actually getting started. It can take six months or so in some cases."

Louise flopped back on sofa and stared at the ceiling. "Damn. I hadn't really taken that on board. I guess I might have to get some other kind of job to see me through, bar work or something." Louise felt about ready to jump off a cliff at the mere thought of it.

"Maybe. But at least you got a flat sorted! West

Hampstead, yeah? And it's Tuesday you move in? That's so quick, even for London!"

"I know! Am I ok here until then?"

"Of course! Glad to have you for a bit longer. What's the other girl like?"

"She seemed ok. Pretty normal, I don't think she'll try and get into bed with me while I'm asleep or anything. And the flat was nice! I can't wait to do it up and make it all homely! And the rent isn't too bad." She drew out the final vowels of her sentence before sucking in a breath.

"And how is your money holding up?"

"Oh, don't Ames. I've got enough put by for my deposit and one month's rent, but after that I'm in overdraft. Was hoping I'd be earning soon. But then I think it's ok. It's a different kind of broke, isn't it, when you know you're going to have money coming in before long? It's not like absolute brokeness, when you don't know how you'll ever get out of it. Is it...?"

"I suppose not." Amy paused. "Have you got a big overdraft?"

"Mm-hmm."

"Well, kiddo, you're gonna need it! Anyway, I was actually phoning to say that I picked up a few things for tonight but didn't buy any wine as it's just so heavy to lug around, so would you mind popping down to Tesco and getting a few bottles? And also could you get some ice? Louise?"

"Huh? Sorry what did you say?"

"Can you go and get some wine and ice from Tesco for tonight?"

"Oh ok, sure. What are we having?"

"Lasagne. *Sans* charcoal, I'm afraid."

"Amy! Come on, they weren't that bad were they? And I've scrubbed the pan to death, it's gleaming now!"

61

Amy laughed. "No, they were yum actually. And just as good cold for lunch."

"Cool. So how many people are coming tonight?"

"Not that many. I think Kat is going to put in an appearance, so that'll be interesting. And Craig and Sarah are coming, and Martin and Jen, and maybe my friend Carl from work."

"So that means three couples, and me?"

Amy hesitated. "And Carl, hopefully."

"Is this a set up?"

"No! No, Carl's actually seeing someone. Although I'm not sure how serious it is…" Amy giggled sheepishly.

"I don't want to be set up!"

"Oh, I'm just kidding. He's practically taken. I think."

Louise held the pause in the conversation before shaking her head in mock exasperation, even though Amy couldn't see her. "Ok, ok. So I'll be the only single person there?"

"Umm, I guess so. Hadn't really thought about it like that. No-one's that coupley though, you won't be a raspberry or anything."

"Gooseberry."

"Look I've got to go, I'm being beckoned. See you later." And Amy put the phone down before Louise could even say goodbye.

As she wandered off on her chores Louise couldn't help but feel a bit intrigued by a mystery man, even if he was practically taken. Maybe Carl would be the perfect one for her; a cliched eligible bachelor, dark, intelligent and mysterious. And tall, of course, so she could wear high heels when he took her out for posh meals. He'd bring her gifts like chocolates and flowers, and she'd get all dressed up for him. They'd have a fun few years before things would get serious, then they'd move in together and before she knew it there would be the fairytale white wedding and the honeymoon in the Maldives…

"Ow! Sorry!" Louise had walked straight into a lamp post and on the rebound collided with a man struggling down the street, laden up with bags of shopping. He glared at her and she scuttled off into the safety of Tesco, reprimanding herself for yet again getting too deep into her fantasy when she really should have been concentrating.

"So, Amy, we're going to miss you loads, but we know you'll have a great time. And we'll be waiting here for you when you get back. So hurry up!" Martin smiled as the group clinked glasses, and Louise couldn't help but notice Kat eying Amy wistfully over the table, her gaze full of admiration and her smile sad. She wondered if Amy had noticed and concluded that she probably had, but was pretending otherwise; she hadn't paid much attention to Kat since disappearing off to the kitchen with her for ten minutes or so at the start of the evening.

"Ah, thanks Martin. That's so sweet! You'll bring a tear to my eye before the night is out! But let's chat now, or I'll become a blubbering mess. So, are you all going to Lena's wedding in the new year? I can't believe I'm going to miss it!" As the group moved on to talk about where they were staying and what they were wearing Louise noticed Amy take a deep breath and vigorously shake her head. She caught her friend's eye over the table and offered a supportive smile, before turning back to the conversation.

"Who's Lena?" She picked up another piece of bread and reached for the butter, as Amy headed off to the kitchen to check on the meal.

"Lena is Jen's friend from school, but we've all gotten to know her since we've been in London. How long have you known her now, Jen?"

"Sixteen years! Can't believe it!"

"She's lovely," Sarah turned back to Louise, "one of the nicest people. You know, I'm sure she wouldn't mind if you went along for the evening. What do you reckon, Jen? Do you think Louise could come to the wedding?"

"Yeah, I'm sure it'd be fine! Do you fancy it?"

"Oh, yes! I'd love that!"

"Well give me your number, and I'll check with Lena and get in touch."

"Cool!" Louise jumped up to find her phone, but as she was rummaging in her handbag Amy re-emerged from the kitchen, her earlier aura of excitement having returned with a vengeance.

"Lasagne's ready! Ta-da!" She triumphantly waved a Pyrex dish in the air, which slipped around dangerously in her mittened hands. "Jen? Do you want to do the honours?" Amy laid down the lasagne in the middle of the table as Jen picked up a spoon and dug in, making an appreciative sound as steam emitted from between the layers of pasta.

"Smells great! Thanks Ames! Here you go, Craig. Can you pass the salad?" As Jen started chatting to Sarah about a new type of salad dressing she had found in Whole Foods Louise hovered behind her chair, fiddling with her phone and feeling like the green fruit pastille in a tube full of purples. After a few seconds she laid it down and slipped back into her seat, trying to make her smile genuine as she waited for an entry point into the conversation. But it was hard, when inside she couldn't stop puzzling over how she could possibly feel so alone among a group of friendly people. What was it that she was always getting so wrong?

"So," Sarah topped up her glass of Chardonnay before lifting her fork and digging it into her lasagne. "What the hell was going on with Steve and Zahira last week?" At first Louise tried to follow the conversation, but so many names and rumours were banded about that she soon lost the thread. Her mind started wandering and her gaze flickered over the other girls. She noticed golden skin and styled, lightened hair. Make up had been carefully applied rather than slapped on, and they'd all used it to emphasise their eyes and lips and cheekbones, instead of purely as a cover up. Their clothes were colourful and sprinkled with funky belts, broaches and scarves, and Jen looked particularly stunning in her flowing turquoise maxi-dress. It clung to her curves in all the right places and the oversized scarlet pendant complemented the look perfectly, even if common sense screamed that it really shouldn't go.

Louise fingered her flowing, dark curls, wondering whether she ought to update the style she had been sporting since she was five. And perhaps she should revive her make up collection and maybe look into one of those St Tropez tans? The anaemic look surely wasn't doing her any favours.

As the conversation moved on to a discussion about the latest goings on between someone called Alex and her friend's boyfriend, Zac, Louise allowed herself to develop the vision of herself as she could be. She'd work out at the gym to build up some muscle and develop some curves, and would pay a trip to the hairdresser and a beauty salon. She'd go on a spree in Westfield to revamp her wardrobe and update her make up bag and then, once she put it all together, things really would all start to take off and be good once more. Louise sighed, then quickly covered it over with a cough. For now, before she could get started, she had a few more hours of 'fun' to endure.

"So you promise you'll send us a postcard from every place you go?"

Louise hovered on the outskirts of the group, watching as Sarah held Amy's hands and looked into her eyes as if her request was for something much deeper. She couldn't help feeling pleased when the night drew to a close; as much as she'd tried to join in and get in the swing of things she'd felt bored, although everyone else seemed like they were having a ball. If Carl had made it at least she would have had someone else to talk to who wasn't part of 'the group', but as it was she just wanted Amy back to herself.

"I promise." Amy gazed back in an equally serious manner, the sheen of tears having returned to coat her eyes once more.

Louise wiggled her big toe through a hole in her tights, then tried to flick it back the other way as the nylon started to cut into her skin. She felt a bit like she should leave Amy and her friends to the goodbyes, but then she wasn't sure if that would look anti-social. Plus she still wanted to get that number so she could go to the wedding; it would be nice to have at least some sort of social engagement on the horizon.

"And you'll call a lot, won't you?" Jen joined in as Martin and Craig shuffled their feet.

"I will. Oh, I'm going to miss you so much!" Amy reached out and enfolded both her girlfriends in an embrace. They pulled apart after a few minutes, sniffing and smiling wanly, then Amy turned to the boys.

"Guys…?" She held out her arms and the boys hesitated, looking at each other awkwardly, before Craig reached out to Amy.

"See ya. Take care." He gave her an awkward hug before leaving Martin in the limelight.

"Bye, Martin!" Amy put her arms around his shoulders. "Hey, I expect to see a ring on her finger by the time I get back, ok?" Amy nodded in Jen's direction and Martin's face flamed as he backed out of Amy's embrace, tripping over Craig's feet on the way.

"Sorry mate," he mumbled, and Amy laughed.

"I was only joking!" Amy poked Martin in his ribs and winked at Jen. "Anyway, off you go before this atmosphere gets so tense it cracks! Have a wonderful year and stay in touch. And I mean all of you." She waggled her finger at the boys and raised her eyebrows as they nodded in response. "Now, get out of here before I start to cry."

Louise watched them leave, still clutching her mobile tightly. She pursed her lips, resolving to ask Amy for the number later and make the move herself, then headed off to start on the washing up and see how her friend was holding up. It turned out her and Kat were doing just fine.

## Chapter 5

Louise opened her eyes, but closed them again as the summer sunlight streaming in through the window blinded her sight and sent a shooting pain through her brain. She went to pull the duvet over her head and catch a few more minutes of kip, but was properly woken up by the sound of someone hammering on a door. She was momentarily confused as the sound seemed to be coming from inside, but then Amy's voice rang out through the apartment and the haze lifted.

"Rachel? I know you're awake! Come out of that room now and tell me who that was creeping out of the flat! You may think you got away with it but I heard you come in last night, and I heard him leave this morning! Who was it? Was it who I think it is? Come on! Out you come! I'm putting on the coffee and I expect you out of that bed and in here by the time it has brewed. I mean it!" Amy banged on the door one last time then moved towards the kettle, groaning softly.

"Louise? You awake? Want a coffee? I'm making filter, far too hungover for a mug of milk."

Louise moaned in a manner which Amy managed to interpret as 'yes', then forced her eyes open and threw back the covers before braving the walk to the bathroom. She splashed her face with cold water then re-entered the living room to the revitalising scent of freshly brewed coffee, and saw that Rachel had emerged from her room and was sitting at the kitchen table, talking with a somewhat regretful expression on her face as Amy lapped up the gossip while grinning gleefully.

"Coffee, everyone?" Louise poured a stream of the strong, steaming liquid into a waiting mug, the intense scent of the beans wafting right up her nostrils and making her feel human again.

"Sorry, Lou. Are you alright there? I got distracted!"

Louise nodded and poured out a couple more cups before taking them over to the girls, then returning to the counter to collect milk and sugar. She poured a generous helping of milk into her coffee before focusing her attention on the gossip.

"So, what's going on?"

"Oh my God, you're never going to believe this. Fill her in, Rach!"

Rachel sighed and rubbed her eyes with her hands, before throwing a few heaped teaspoons of sugar into her coffee and taking a slurp. "God, I can't believe I'm such an *idiot*! Why do I drink? Why do I *do* it?"

"Do what? I thought you were just going to see a play?"

"Well, I was. But after that I went to meet some friends for a drink, then we ended up in this club and John, an ex, was there...no it was *not* planned Amy, I had no idea! And he was buying me champagne, and you know what it's like..."

"So, Rach, are you going to get back with John?" Amy teased as she massaged in some hand cream, while turning to look at a selection of evening dresses in the window of a boutique. "Oh Louise, look at that blue one."

"No, I'm bloody not! Oh God, how *could* I?" Rachel took another swig of Evian.

"But didn't you tell him you would see him again?"

70

"Yes, but I didn't mean to! It was that bloody champagne. Oh *God*."

"And he wants to get back together?" Louise asked.

'Yes!" Rachel bit her lower lip. "Actually, I think he thinks we already are..."

"Oh, Rach! Why am I going round the world when you provide me with so much entertainment right on my doorstep?!"

"Why are you not in Thailand yet?" Rachel glared at Amy before turning away and fingering a collection of 'Now' compilations on cassette.

"Ah, it's funny though, Rach! Isn't it Lou?"

Louise chuckled, although she felt somewhat in awe. What was it like to be adored by someone who wanted to be with you so badly? She couldn't quite imagine.

"Ooh, Now 28! That had some awesome songs on it, let me see! Rach, tell Louise how you got rid of him this morning. I can't believe you told him that you were going to camp outside the o2 for Boyzone tickets. And he offered to come with you! Why didn't you just tell him you had a doctor's appointment?"

"You said what?! You were going to camp out for Boyzone tickets?!" Louise echoed, as Rachel gave in to the giggles. A loud snort came out of her nose followed by a cackle the White Witch would have been proud of.

"I don't know! I don't know, I panicked! I never thought he'd offer to come along, with his tent!" She chuckled to herself. "I should have just said I'd meet him there. Oh God, how *could* I?" Her phone beeped but Rachel just closed her eyes and shook her head.

"Please, make him go away!" She fixed her gaze on Amy, clawing at her arm as if she feared desertion. "Can I come away with you? Shit, do you think I should change my number? Fuck, how *could* I?"

Louise tuned out as they came across a table strewn with old fashioned costume jewellery, sparkling and glittering in the sunlight. A silver bracelet caught her eye, and she picked away at the beads and chains that were covering it before holding it up to the light. It was pretty simple - slim but split, with the two bands engraved in a delicate swirly pattern. She turned it over in her hands and a marking inside caught her eye: 'To our future in London, 22 November 1963'. Louise broke out in goose pimples at the significance of the date: JFK's assassination or, as some historians would put it, 'the day the world lost its innocence'. She gripped it more tightly and waved her hand to attract the attention of the stall holder.

"How much is this?"

The woman took the bracelet and ran it through her fingers. "Real silver, that is. Twenty five quid, and that's a bargain."

Louise detected a Welsh twang to her tone. "Are you from Wales?"

"Yeah, Newport. Are you?"

"I'm from Swansea."

"Well, I tell you what, from one Welsh woman to another, have it for twenty. Wouldn't do it for anyone else."

"Thanks!" Louise handed over a crisp twenty and waited while the woman wrapped it in tissue paper and slipped it into a paper bag.

"There you go, love. Lucky find, that was."

Louise grinned and took the package. She had only walked a few feet from the stall when she broke into it, extracted the bracelet and slipped it over her slender wrist. She allowed herself to enter into a forgotten romance from a time gone by, imagining hopes and dreams that had long since died and been relegated to the history books. She gazed at the bracelet, stroking the engravings and marvelling at its past once more, then smiled to herself before heading off to find the others. It was easy enough; she just had to follow Rachel's plaintive self-laments and Amy's raucous belly laughs echoing back all the way through the stalls.

"Are you going to answer that?"

"Nope." Rachel picked up the last bite of salmon and cream cheese bagel. "I told you, I'm changing my number and moving to Cuba. And not necessarily in that order."

"Oh bless him! That was some good pastrami. But I need something sweet now. Ooh, look at those muffins!"

"Not 'bless him'! He's annoying and clingy and desperate!"

"Well, you'd know!"

"Hey!"

"Anyone else want a muffin? Rach! Is that him again?!"

Rachel threw her phone across the table. "Gimme one of them, God I need some sugar."

"So what shall we do tomorrow? Where shall we head? I want to make the most of you before you bugger off for distant shores!" Louise bit into her cake, briefly closing her eyes to the taste of the bittersweet chocolate.

"Oh, I can't tomorrow, Lou. I'm going to Basingstoke. Got a farewell dinner with my family, and I think some aunties and uncles are coming too." She paused. "You can come if you want?"

Louise hesitated. "No, no. I'll leave you to it. I'll get in touch with some of my mates from school, see if any of them want to catch up."

"Are you sure? Because you can come. I don't want to leave you in the lurch."

"No, seriously. It's fine. It'll be nice to catch up with

some people anyway. Will you be back in the evening? I could cook something, or we could go out, go to a film or something?"

"Actually, I'm going to be staying a couple of nights back home and come back Monday evening, as I've finished work now. But I'll be around to help you move on Tuesday!"

Louise has a sudden flashback to being six years old, when Bethan Jones had told her she wasn't her friend anymore and Louise had had to spend break time alone, picking daisies while watching the other girls play touch. It took a second to remember that that was then, and this was now. "Ok. I'm glad you get to see where I am before you go."

"Me too." Amy smiled. "And you're sure you'll be ok over the weekend? You can have my bed, by the way."

"Absolutely positive. Have a great time, and don't you worry about me."

"So, what kind of thing are you looking for, then?" Kate looked up from flicking through paperwork. "Have you made any applications lately? Had any interviews?" The recruitment consultant smiled encouragingly, and Louise relaxed a bit.

"Well, I had a couple of interviews a few years ago for marketing and PR, before I..." Louise inhaled. "Before I decided to go travelling. But I didn't get them. I don't have much experience, but my academic background is good." Her intonation rose at the end of her sentence as if she was asking a question rather than stating a fact, and her palms became sweaty as she thought back to the actual feedback she had received from those interviews, that she had never quite managed to let lie. Yet she refused to believe that she 'lacked the panache and initiative so important in the field of marketing' and 'alongside her lack of experience didn't display the interpersonal skills essential to a career in PR'. "So I'm feeling a bit lost now, and not quite as confident as I was when I started out." Her voice became small and she fiddled with her ring.

"Well, that's where we come in! Don't worry, I know exactly what it's like. It was the same for me when I got started, it's not easy to get your foot in the door and all that. But we'll sort you out with something, you can count on that!"

Louise felt her breathing stabilise as she listened to Kate's confident spiel, and the soft thud of that previous feedback, which seemed to have become stuck on a loop in her ears, finally started to lose its edge. "I wouldn't mind trying recruitment myself, either."

Kate nodded as she tapped away on her keyboard. "Right, so do you have a minimum salary in mind? And are you happy to commute across London? Are there any companies you are particularly interested in?" Louise paused again as she processed Kate's questions, and her silence prompted Kate to glance up from the monitor.

"Ummm...well, I hadn't really thought..." Louise trailed off. "I just wanted to get something sorted, really."

"Right, ok. Let's put your minimum salary at sixteen grand to start, that'll open you up to a nice lot of employers in the first place." Louise felt her eyes widen but she nodded in agreement, hoping that her visage didn't reveal her true sentiments. "And I'll say that you're happy to commute up to an hour and a half, that way you'll appeal to companies right throughout London. Don't panic, it's not as bad as it sounds." Kate chuckled gently. "Everyone commutes in London, you'll get used to it and you won't even notice it before long. It just becomes part of your day!"

"Do you commute?"

"Yep, I live down in Clapham. But it's not so bad. Anyway, so I'll say you're open to offers, which again will increase your chances of employment. Now, you do realise that you might not end up going straight into the job of your dreams, don't you?" Kate's expression had suddenly turned rather more serious and she leaned forward slightly over the desk. Her top hung low and Louise averted her eyes, embarrassed at the close proximity of Kate's generous breasts. She could smell coconut on Kate's skin, and noticed a tiny red mole positioned right in the middle of her chest. "You may find that you get something a little, well, less than what you're expecting, or hoping for, in the first instance. But stick with it, build up a bank of experience and contacts and you'll soon start working your way up. Ok?"

It wasn't, really, but Louise nodded and smiled and Kate seemed pleased with her response.

"Right, so we've got your details now and we should be in touch within a few days with something for you! Don't worry, we'll soon get something sorted out, even if it's just to get started."

Louise rose, smoothing the creases out of Amy's Planet skirt and picking up her bag. "Thanks, I look forward to hearing from you!"

"Bye now!" Kate held the door open as Louise walked through, catching another whiff of coconut on the way out and again noticing Kate's gold jewellery, dewy make up and glossy hair. Kate beamed once more and the edge of her confidence rubbed off on Louise, allowing a long overdue wave of optimism to wash over her and calm her like a cooling breeze on an overstuffed tube train.

"Wow, this is nice. Good work, Lou! And you've made it so homely already! I love the fairy lights and candles and things. I'm just so sorry I couldn't get back in time to help. I did mean to."

Louise shook her head. "Honestly, it's not a problem. It's not like I had much stuff, it was fine in a taxi. And it gave me some time to potter around Poundland and get some bits and bobs. Look at this candle, it smells so lush and it actually smells when it burns!"

"Isn't that the whole point of a scented candle, Lou?"

"Yes, it is the point, but they hardly ever actually do smell when they burn. But this one really does! Smell it!"

"Ok. How did you get on at the agency?"

Louise took a last deep sniff of berries then placed the candle back on her bedside table. "Alright. I spoke with someone called Kate, who seemed to think she could get something sorted out pretty soon."

"Cool!"

"Yeah! She warned me that I might not get exactly what I want straight away, but it would be just be good to get started. Especially now I have my own place!"

"It's a nice feeling, isn't it? And how is your house mate? What's her name again?"

"Anna. She seems cool. Quite busy though, but that suits me." Louise paused as all the changes of the past few weeks suddenly hit her, and her heart seemed to momentarily contract. "Oh Ames, what am I going to do without you? I feel like you're being untimely snatched out of my life!"

"Oh, don't be so dramatic!" Amy tapped Louise on her head. "You'll be fine, you'll settle in so quickly, you'll barely even notice I'm gone! Anyway, the year will fly. I'll be back before you know it!"

"I know, I'm glad you're going really. To do what you want, not because I want to get rid of you! It's just that it would be nice to have you around, just to know you're there. I'm going to feel lost without you!"

"Lou, get a grip." Louise jerked back her head as Amy

sighed. "Sorry, I don't mean to snap. I'm just a bit knackered with finishing work, moving out and sorting everything out for the trip. But you know, if we were both living in London we wouldn't see each other all the time. It's been different this week but usually I'd be at work, you'd be at work, we'd have our own friends and our own lives, we wouldn't be living in each others' pockets. This way you'll sort your own life out over the next few months, and that's better."

Louise sighed. "I know, Ames. Sorry. I just get a bit nervous but I don't mean to be clingy." She breathed in deeply, but the air didn't seem to fill her lungs. "I'm a bit scared, to be honest."

"Louise, you're going to be fine." Amy put both her hands on Louise's shoulders and stared deep into her pupils. "But it's not a picnic. You have to work for it all you know, it won't just come to you. But I know you can do it. Just don't lay off, don't get distracted. Real life is not easy, Lou. And it's not supposed to be. You've got to go out there and get it, but you can. But it's up to you to stay focused, stay on track and to deal with the shit as well as the good stuff. Ok?"

Louise tried to avert her eyes, but her friend's grip didn't leave much leeway. She sighed again, and met Amy's steely blue gaze head on. They'd been through so much together at Aber, Amy proving to be a pillar of support for Louise, always looking out for her and keeping her on track. But now Louise was going to be on her own, without the safety net of having either Amy or her parents in the next room.

"Ok, Ames. I know. Thank you."

Amy released her grip to brush a stray curl out of Louise's eye, then leaned over and kissed her on the cheek.

"You e-mail me anytime, ok? And I will get back to you as soon as I can. But you're on your own now Lou, you're doing it for yourself. No more cushions, ok?"

Louise nodded and gulped, then pulled her friend close into a tight embrace. That way Amy couldn't see her face.

## Chapter 6

"I've got it! The perfect job for you! It's in media PR, based just off Bond Street, with good pay and great prospects. I've shown them your CV and they're really keen to meet you! What do you think?"

"Yes! Yes yes yes! I'm free when they are, whatever suits them, wherever, whenever, just get me in!"

Kate laughed at Louise's response. "Ok, well they were thinking first thing Monday morning. Can you do that?"

"Yes, of course!"

"Great! I'll e-mail you the details, just make sure you do some research on the company before then so you know what they're about."

"I will do, thank you so much Kate! I'm so pleased!"

"No worries, Louise. Good luck!"

The shrill ring of the telephone broke Louise out of her revelry and she got a bit of a shock to find herself in front of the TV, Jeremy Kyle blasting out through the speakers and a cup of coffee going cold on the table on front of her. She shook her head and reached for the phone, her heart jumping as she saw Kate's number flashing up on the screen.

"Hi Louise, how are you? I'm just returning your latest call about work, I've got something I think you'd be interested in." Kate's tone had become a bit more strained recently. "I've got an accounts admin. assistant position at a company in Croydon, shall I put you forward?"

"Well...I don't...what's the pay like?"

"Seventeen thousand." Louise sighed. "Louise, I've been trying to tell you, you have to start somewhere. This really is a good opening, and it'll help you get your foot in the door. The big PR firms are just not recruiting at the moment, the economy is in a state and we're all having to make sacrifices. If you take a position like this, just for six months, then at least you'll have a starting base and somewhere to branch out from."

"In Croydon, you said?"

"I know it's not quite where you wanted to be, but as I've said you do have to start somewhere. Shall I put you forward?"

"I'll think about it."

Louise heard Kate's sharp intake of breath down the line.

"Louise, I'm really not going to be able to continue working with you if you keep rejecting jobs. As I said before, I don't think we're the right agency for you. Have a think about what you want out of this and I'll call you back tomorrow to discuss your options, because I do want to help you. Ok?"

"Sure." Louise made a mental note to screen her calls the following day.

"And Louise?"

"Yeah?"

"Please do think about it. It's really worth serious consideration."

"I will," Louise promised, but the line had already gone dead.

Louise dropped her phone onto the sofa and regarded it pensively until it burst into life again. When she looked at the

82

screen she sighed and considered rejecting the call, but felt too guilty, so found herself pressing the green button.

"Hi, Mum."

"Hiya, love! How did you know it was me? That's amazing!"

"It said on my phone screen, Mum, as I keep telling you. Whenever you call it says 'Mum', and that's how I know it's you."

"Well, I never did. Modern technology is marvellous, isn't it?" Louise could picture her mother shaking her head in wonderment and stifled a giggle, although Christine picked up on it. "Don't you laugh at me, just wait until you're my age. There's so much to keep up with!"

"Mum it's not that tricky a concept, and we've been through it time and again!"

Christine tutted down the phone. "Anyway, so how is everything? How's the flat? Thanks for sending those pictures on, it looks lovely! Are you all settled in? How's Anna?"

"Yeah, all cool Mum! Anna's hardly ever here so to be honest I feel more like I live on my own, but I like that."

"You must be missing Amy, though? It sounds as if she looked after you well."

"Yeah, I am. I can't believe she's been gone three weeks! It's weird, I mean I always knew that she would be leaving but at the same time I'd always imagined her here, almost like she could be gone but here at the same time. I know that sounds odd, it's just..." Louise's brain suddenly gave way to a sensation that made her think of a swallow swooping down to land, though she had no idea why.

"Lou? Louise? Can you hear me? I was asking about work, are you still in that pub?"

Louise sighed. "It's just a time filler, Mum. It's not like it's my career choice, it's just temporary to bring in a bit of cash while I get sorted out." Louise paused, but when Christine didn't say anything found herself continuing. "And anyway, I've got a job interview coming up."

"Oh love, that's great news! Is it in PE? Like you wanted?"

"Mum! PR! PE is what kids do in school to keep fit!"

"Oh, yes. So is it in PR? What is this PR again? There are so many new jobs around now…"

"Mum, I've explained this to you so many times! Anyway this job is in accounts…"

"Accounts? Well, that's just fantastic! Where will it be? Right in the City? Oh, love, that's so exciting, congratulations! At least they've realised your true potential now and they've stopped offering you those monkey work jobs, eh? You're on the up now love. We're so proud of you! I'll just tell Dad!"

And before Louise could stop her she heard Christine calling across to Mike, giving him a brief run down of her fabricated description of Louise's work. Louise heard a click and then her father's voice came down the line.

"I hear congratulations are in order! We're so pleased, Lou!"

"Guys! it's only an interview, I might not even get the job."

"Oh, don't be silly of course you'll get it, why wouldn't they want you? When is it?"

"Um...I'm not sure. They, um, have to confirm." Louise's head started to feel as if it was floating off somewhere, as she became more and more confused about where she really stood in the whole thing.

"Well, just let us know and we'll have the champers ready! Oh, this is such great news, isn't it Mike?"

"Yes! I..."

"Look, guys, I'd better go. I've got a shift..."

84

"You don't need to go back there now, Lou!"

Louise felt a stab of indignation. "Mum, I haven't got anything else yet, it's just an interview." And I'm not even sure if I'm going to go to that, she added silently. "So no, I can't give it a miss. I have a job to do."

"Sensible idea, Louise. We'll talk again soon."

"Ok love, well not much longer to go now. Speak to you soon, darling!"

"So how's the job hunt going? Got any leads yet? That'll be five pounds twenty, love."

Louise turned from where she was re-stacking the crisp display. "Well, my agent wants to put me forward for an interview. But I'm not sure I'm going to go."

"Why not?!" Bev's dark eyes sparkled with surprise. A layer of sweat covered her caked up face and her platinum blonde hair, complete with three inch long dark brown roots, was starting to curl up at the ends from too long spent leaning over the steaming glass washer. She was dressed in white jeans, which were a couple of sizes too small, with the regulation pub polo shirt tucked in at the waist. Three gold chains hung around her neck and big hoops dangled from her ears, practically resting on her shoulders. Her fingers were dotted with cheap rings and a faded tattoo snaked out from underneath her t-shirt sleeve. Bev seemed to walk around as if in a haze of cigarette smoke - she popped outside for a fag at every opportunity and subsequently smelled like an ashtray and looked about twenty years older than her (apparently) thirty nine years.

"It's just not what I want to do." Louise shrugged, starting to feel slightly awkward beneath Bev's scrutiny.

"What's it for?"

"Admin.' Louise screwed up her face as if she had just tasted corked red. "In an accounting firm."

"Well, it's a start! It's got to be better than this dump." Bev kicked the base of the glass washer and a few glasses clinked together in reply.

"Oh, you know you love it, Bev! How long have you been here now?"

"Twenty years this year." Bev's eyes drifted off before returning to Louise with a sparkle. "You'd never have recognised me back then, I was such a little punk! The men couldn't take their eyes off me, you know! Hey, you'd better believe it, time will catch up with you too. I had the most stunning boyfriend back then, did I tell you that he wanted me to move to Australia with him?"

"A few times. I still don't understand why you didn't go."

"I was attached, you know. I was established here. People knew me and I enjoyed it. I just didn't want to leave my life behind. Though I do sometimes wonder, you know, what if...? Don't end up like that." Bev flicked Louise with a tea towel. "You should go to that interview, you're too bright for a future behind a bar."

"But it's just not what I want to do." Louise shrugged, somewhat apologetically.

"And this is?"

Louise sighed. "No. I want to go into PR, and I'm sure it's just a matter of time before I get sorted out. And for the time being I'd rather hang on here for something better to come along than in some dull office in Croydon, to be honest."

"Oh, so we're not completely your reserve choice then, are we?" Bev took a packet of salt and vinegar crisps out of Louise's hands and ripped them open, a few loose flakes floating down towards the beer stained linoleum floor while the acidic tang of vinegar diffused out into the air.

"You know what I mean, Bev!" Louise leant over and

plucked a crisp out of Bev's packet.

"I'm only kidding." Bev sprayed Louise with a few nuggets of potato. "You need to go for what you want, but in the meantime I think you should think about that job. Would look better for your CV than being a barmaid, I can tell you that for nothing."

"I know. But I don't know! I just don't know if I can hack an admin assistant job. I wouldn't even be a dogsbody in charge, I'd be a dog's tail!" The metaphor was lost on Bev, who just frowned at Louise before tipping back her crisp packet to drink in the crumbs.

"Oi! Love! You serving or what? I'm dying of thirst here!" Louise turned round to eye her next customer; an overweight man with greasy dark curls dangling down into eyes that bulged. He winked as Louise crossed the bar.

"I'll get a pint of lager and a couple of bags of crisps. And one for yourself, while you're at it." He repeated his winking gesture but Louise still pretended not to notice.

"Six fifty, please." He pressed the cash suggestively into Louise's outstretched hand and she shuddered. His fingers were warm and damp, and she could smell his sour body scent beneath a layer of cheap lager. She sighed as she rang up his order on the old fashioned till and dropped the coins into the tray, wondering how she seemed to have ended up taking such a massive step back when she had been so sure that she was moving forwards.

"Hi Louise, thanks for calling in." Kate sounded weary and distant. "I appreciate that you want us to help you but I'm afraid I'm not going to be able to continue working with you. We're not the right agency for your needs."

Louise squeezed her eyes shut. "Kate, please. There must be something out there for me. It's just that Croydon is so far..."

Kate hesitated. touched yet irritated in equal measures by Louise's desperation. The girl reminded her of herself when she'd first moved to London; so naïve and full of hopes and expectations, which all too soon would be destroyed forever; shattered on the rocks of reality. "Ok! Ok. I have one more thing that might interest you. It came in this morning and I did have someone in mind, but it may suit you too. It's very close to you, not quite what you're holding out for but it's honestly worth taking something, just to get some experience in an office environment."

"Go on."

"'The pay is seventeen grand, possibly rising to eighteen before too long."

Louise gritted her teeth.

"It's covering maternity leave as a receptionist in a private doctor's surgery in the Swiss Cottage area. They're particularly looking for someone who's computer literate, as they need to update all their records and move everything from paper to screen. You'll be scheduling appointments and helping with the day-to-day running of the surgery, and I think you'll be able to turn quite a lot of the experience to your advantage when you get more PR interviews. More so than you will with bar work."

Louise sighed, aware that Kate was holding her breath; she could feel the tension even down the phone line. "Ok."

"Ok?" Kate exhaled in a rush. "You want to be put forward? And you'll go to the interview?"

"Yep. It's better than the pub, isn't it? And closer than Croydon."

"Oh Louise, that's brilliant! I'll get onto them straight away and arrange a meeting. Oh, I'm so pleased! I'll be in touch again very soon!" And then she was gone, as if worried that if she stayed on the line too long Louise might change her mind.

Louise stayed where she was, staring at the whitewashed walls of her kitchen and feeling her heart sink even lower in her chest. Then the phone rang again and she jumped in surprise.

"Louise? Tuesday at eleven suit you?"

"Um, yeah. Sure. That was quick."

"Great. Details will be in your inbox. All the best!" And the line went dead.

## Chapter 7

"So, Louise, it'll be great to have you on board. We'll look forward to working with you!"

Louise grinned at Tony. Despite her earlier reservations she had started to come round to the idea of working at the surgery. "Thanks, I'll see you on Monday! Have a nice weekend."

"You too, go out and have a drink to celebrate tonight, won't you?"

"Oh yes, I will." Louise laughed.

"Lovely, see you Monday." Tony shook her hand firmly as she exited through the door.

Riding the crest of her new found optimism Louise decided to get in touch with her old uni mates and arrange a meet up. She sent a few text messages to the Aber gang, then composed one to Rachel to see what had become of her on-off bloke. Finally - still hoping to curry favour for a wedding invite - she messaged Jen, whose number she had managed to get off Amy before she left. Louise slipped her phone in her jeans' pocket with a grin as she waited for it to start beeping with replies, then decided to act on Tony's idea of going for a drink to celebrate. Until it hit her that she had no-one to go with. Working anti-social hours in The Bat had temporarily alleviated her concerns over developing any kind of a social life, and it was only now she was aware of the free evenings and weekends stretching ahead that she wondered how she would fill them. And with whom. For want of a better option she decided to head down to The Bat and hang out with Bev. It wasn't quite how she had imagined her night of celebrating a new job, but then lately nothing had been going as expected.

"Here she comes! The top career girl! How did it go?"

"I got it!"

"Fantastic! She's in!" Bev swept Louise up in a hug and Louise almost choked on the smell of stale smoke that coated her peroxided hair. "Congrats! Though I knew you'd make it! Bet you're glad you didn't go to that interview in Croydon now, eh?"

"It was you who was trying to make me go, Bev!"

"Oh. Well thank God you didn't take my advice. What the hell do I know, eh? Now, have a bevy to celebrate. What can I do you for? It's on the house."

"Um, G and T, please."

Bev winked, "I'll make it a cheeky double."

Bev turned to push the glass up against the optic and Louise seated herself on one of the greasy, worn stools on the opposite side of the bar. She fiddled mindlessly with a hole in the fabric cover, poking and prodding at the cheap foam that cushioned the seat.

"So, your parents must be pleased! Here you go."

"Ta," Louise nodded in agreement, as it occurred to her that she hadn't mentioned anything yet. She wondered whether she should tell the truth. Not that she would lie, but she could say just enough to let them form their own ideas of the job that she was in. After all, they'd never have to know…

"Cheers." Louise slugged back the G and T, thinking how much nicer it would be if the tonic was actually chilled, then settled in with that day's issue of the *Evening Standard*.

She was half through the readers' letters when a dark stain started spreading out over the page, trickles chasing each other as if they were participating in some kind of race.

"Shit, I'm sorry! That was so clumsy of me, I wasn't concentrating!"

Louise looked up and smiled as she reached for a pile of napkins. The guy's cheeks were flushed, framed by scraggly dark waves and headed by anxious, emerald eyes.

"No worries, no harm done."

"Let me get you another, what was in there?"

"You don't have to…"

"I insist! What was it?"

"Um, G and T."

"On it." The young man caught Bev's eye and winked cheekily at her. She bustled across the bar in a fluster, ignoring the poor middle aged man who had been waiting a fair while longer than the younger new arrival.

"Hiya, love." Louise smiled to herself as Bev draped herself over the ale pumps and fluttered her eyelashes; she was such a cliche it was unreal. "What can I, *do* for you?" She raised her eyebrows and shifted on her hips, and the poor lad shuffled his feet while blushing once more to the roots of his jet black hair.

"Um, a pint of Smooth, and a G and T for the lady." He indicated Louise with his head, at which point Bev's eyes widened and her smile deepened.

"Coming right, *up!*" Louise almost laughed out loud as Bev glanced suggestively at the guy's crotch, and his face turned an even deeper shade of crimson.

"One gin and tonic." A few seconds later the guy handed the fresh drink over to Louise, who smiled bashfully and accepted it, her fingers brushing against his as she took the glass. "I'm Steve."

93

"Louise." Louise placed her hand in Steve's and he shook it firmly.

"Well, I must say, Louise, I'm quite glad I knocked your glass over. Now I have an excuse to talk to you!" He grinned and Louise briefly wondered whether he had knocked the glass deliberately. "Are you from around here?"

Louise quickly glanced downwards before looking up again and meeting Steve's gaze. "Yeah, just around the corner."

"Ahh..." Steve drawled, holding her gaze until Louise looked away. "So what do you do then?"

"Ooh, she's just got a top job! We're celebrating now!" Bev, who had appeared back behind the pumps at that opportune moment, turned to Louise and nodded her encouragement. "She's on the way up you know lad, she's way too good for the likes of you, lazy layabout!"

Louise was rather surprised at Bev's bluntness, but Steve just laughed.

"So, what are you doing? You working down in the City?"

"Yep!" Bev answered again for Louise, with a rather proud tone as if she was solely responsible for Louise's fantastical success. Louise did open her mouth to right her now ex-boss, but on second thoughts decided to leave it.

"Wow, good work." Steve appeared pensive for a moment before Louise felt she should return his interest.

"What do you do?"

"Not much!" Steve laughed so uproariously Louise physically recoiled. "I'm not a worker, me. I do a bit for my mate's dad every now and then and spend the rest of the time getting drunk or smoking weed!"

At that point Steve's phone rang, and as he wandered off to answer it Louise turned back to her sodden paper, the balloon that had inflated in her stomach losing air rapidly. She felt her spine curve as she lost her support and slouched back into the bar.

"Louise?" Steve was slipping his phone back into his pocket and signalling at Bev. "I have to go, got a session to get to!" He winked and Louise cringed. "But I'd love to meet you for a drink! Can I have your number?"

"Um..."

"Of course you can! Give him your number, love."

Louise glanced at Bev - who winked unsubtly back at her - before hesitatingly typing her number into Steve's phone. Her fingers tapped away despite her brain instructing them otherwise, then she handed it back as he stood up and slipped on his coat.

"And a lager for the road, love! Cheers, see ya soon." Steve pocketed his change and took a swig out of his fresh bottle, then winked at Louise before taking off.

"There you go, eh? He seems like a catch! If I was twenty years younger..." Bev trailed off as she gazed wistfully at Steve's departing back. "Hang on, don't you have a boyfriend? Oh well, no harm in browsing is there. I'm coming, love!"

As Bev bustled off Louise's insides crumpled further still. Her city life seemed nothing like Amy's had been. But where had she gone so wrong? She drained her glass and, with something of an effort, stood up and reached for her jacket and bag.

"You off already? That wasn't much of a celebration."

"Yeah, I know. I'm just a bit knackered. Going to get an early night I think, need to call my folks too."

"Ooh yeah, break the exciting news to them! Ok love, I'll see you soon, eh?"

"Yep, see you soon." Louise shrugged into her denim

jacket. "Bye!"

"So, do you want to come over tonight? We can have a nice night in, watch a DVD, have a bottle of wine and a bit of a snuggle. Help ourselves relax after a busy working week…"

Steve chuckled softly down the line. "Sounds good to me, but are you sure you don't want to go out? My mate's going to an opening of a new bar in Hoxton and he said he can get us in, you don't fancy that?"

"We did that other bar opening last week; I'd rather just chill. And anyway, we've got your company charity ball next Saturday. Hey, I got a dress for it today!"

"Is it revealing?"

Now it was Louise's turn to snigger suggestively. "Well it's long, and black, and quite low cut and slinky."

"Sounds perfect to me…"

"But there is a bit of a problem with it, though."

"What's that? Will you need to change it?"

"I don't know. See, it's rather clingy, so I get a bit of a VPL."

"VPL?"

"Visible Panty Line. So I don't know if I'm going to be able to wear any underwear. I mean, I wouldn't want to spoil the effect of the dress. I don't really know what to do…"

"Keep it. Wear it. And I'm on my way over." Louise smiled as the phone went dead, and ran her straighteners through her hair to give it an added touch of gloss. Her phone beeped with a text message and she glanced down to see that it was from Steve.

*You're amazing. Can't wait to see you. And perhaps you should try that dress on for me? Just so that I can make sure it's ok…*

96

Louise hugged her phone to her chest before dropping it back down on her duvet, slipping out of her underwear and into the Gucci dress that was draped over the door of her cupboard.

But Steve wasn't like that. Not that she was ever going to see him again, despite the plague of text messages she'd already received. Louise exhaled loudly then hauled herself up off the sofa to prepare for bed, pondering on the fantasy Steve as she brushed her teeth. He must be out there somewhere, waiting for her. But why couldn't he just get a move on and come and find her? Surely it was her turn by now?

But then, once in bed, she could almost feel Steve's breath on her neck, and her skin began to tingle as she imagined his contact. As she touched herself her fingers became Steve's, and as she climaxed she saw his face above hers. It was only once her heart rate slowed and her breathing returned to normal that Louise came back to earth with a bump, surprised to find herself in bed alone. She pulled the duvet up right over her head, rolled over and staggered into an uncomfortable, broken slumber.

## Chapter 8

"Right, deep breath. You'll be fine, it's not going to be hard and you're a good learner. Ok, calm it down butterflies. It'll be..." Louise broke off her self-directed pep talk as a blond man with a golden tan, in an open necked shirt and dark grey trousers, exited the building and sparked up a cigarette. A few curly hairs peeked out from under his collar, and when he crooked his arm to flick the lighter the muscle in his forearm winked at her.

"Hi!" He called out as she reached the entrance. "You the new receptionist?"

Louise nodded, clutching the paper coffee cup so tightly that the lid popped up and a trickle of boiling liquid rolled down her hand. She ignored the pain.

"Nick, nice to meet you." He extended his hand in greeting. "I'm one of the doctors here. And this is Chase, my colleague."

Louise shook Nick's hand then turned to see an even brighter blonde woman emerge from the building, also with a cigarette in hand. Sparking up next to each other Chase and Nick looked more like a glamorous Hollywood high school couple than a pair of doctors at an inner-London surgery. They couldn't be much older than Louise but they seemed worlds apart.

"Chase, this is our new receptionist. Sorry, what was

your name again?"

Louise found herself cringing inwardly at 'receptionist', and resisted a huge desire to add 'but I do have a degree, you know'. "Louise," she muttered, eying Chase's gleaming, poker-straight ponytail and hating her own loose curls.

"Hi Louise, nice to meet you. Please excuse the cigarettes, such a bad example, I know! But we only have this one a day. Promise! Anyway, I hope you enjoy your new job and you're not too nervous! Mavis will take good care of you, she's been here since dinosaurs roamed the land and knows exactly what's what." Chase chuckled and Louise smiled back politely. But she didn't want to work with Mavis, who had been there since dinosaurs had roamed the land. She wanted to work with Chase and Nick, with their glossy hair and snazzy clothes. She wanted to go out and drink cocktails on Friday night and talk intellectual talk, not sit in and sip tea with Mavis while discussing blue rinses and knitting.

"You coming?" Chase stamped out her cigarette and turned to Nick, who followed suit.

"Yep, busy day ahead - better get cracking." And they turned and walked back into the surgery together, leaving the air behind them smelling of careers, drive and achievement (as well as the more pungent scent of Marlboro Lights). Louise sighed, feeling the heavy nugget of her heart sink yet again, then followed the young doctors' path into the building to look for Mavis.

"So, dear, this is how you start the computer. Just wait for it to warm up, dear. Now, see this box here? This is where you need to type the password, which is pass, with a capital p. So you press this one first," Louise stifled a scream as Mavis demonstrated how to use caps lock, "and then you type pass, but don't forget to turn the capitals off after you've typed the p, or it won't work!" Louise exhaled and tried to slow her rushing pulse as Mavis painstakingly typed in the password. "Ok, so now you're in. Shall I close it down so you can have a go and we can check that you know how to do it?"

"No!" Louise spoke sharply and Mavis looked up in surprise.

"Alright, dear, as you wish. But any problems and just give me a shout, I'm always happy to help."

Louise tried to smile without grimacing. "Thank you, Mavis."

"Right," Mavis was peering at the screen intently. "Now, we need to open up Exit so we can get to the spreaders."

Louise wondered what that medical jargon meant when translated into English. She waited expectantly, pleased to have a new challenge, when a familiar view popped up on the monitor.

"Aha! Here we are! Now this is tricky, so listen carefully…"

And Louise sat through Mavis's hour-long demonstration of how to enter data into an Excel Spreadsheet.

"So, now that you know how it works I can give you your task. What I need you to do is check all these contact numbers here, no here, no hold on, where are my glasses?"

"Here?"

"Ah, yes. Now, you need to take one of these questionnaires here, that we sent out to all the patients to check their details were correct. Got that? And if you look carefully you can find the contact number. Now, see this one? They've put in a mobile number and a house number, so you need to put them both in. Put 'm' before the mobile number and 'h' before home. But if they only have one number that's ok. But put the 'h' or 'm' anyway, just so we know. Now, you'll know a mobile number because they all start with '07', let me show you, here you are."

Louise turned her eyes down to the paper, but she couldn't be bothered to focus them.

"And the house numbers start with '02', or sometimes '01', but that's not very common here. Shall I write that down for you?" Mavis reached for an envelope and scrawled Louise's instructions across the back.

"Ok, dear, do you think you've got that? It's a bit tricky with all these different numbers these days, but if you get stuck just give a shout! Right, let's start with tea. How do you take yours?"

"Um, milk no sugar. Thanks."

"Right, I'll go and do that and while I'm gone..." Mavis tottered around to her desk and pulled open the bottom drawer. "Here, Tony said you were starting today so I bought a box of Roses to celebrate. Take your pick."

"Oh! Thanks, Mavis! That's really nice of you!" Louise slipped her fingers under the opening, feeling her eyes dampen as an irrational sense of gratitude at Mavis's gesture welled up inside her. Squeezing her eyes shut and sniffing she flicked out a couple of strawberry creams, then settled herself at her desk.

"Here you go dear, now is it all clear? All making sense?"

"Yes, thanks Mavis. I'll give you a shout if I get confused." Louise took a sip of her tea.

"Oh yes, you do that dear. Right, well I'd better turn the phones on, I was meant to do that about an hour ago. Tony will go mad if he finds out they're still off! Ooh, give me a fudge to be going on with."

As Louise fell into her work she felt strangely calm. The rhythm was soothing and it was nice just to be directed for a change. And the work was so simple that she could check her e-mails from time to time, or nip onto Facebook to update her status and let her friends know that she was now a fully fledged Londoner, with a job and a flat and everything.

"Right, dear, now you can go and get some lunch. Did you bring something? We have a microwave up in the staffroom, I could show you how to use it if you like?"

Louise jumped at the sound of Mavis's voice. "Um, that's ok. I need to go out and get a sandwich, I didn't bring anything with me." The soup that Louise had stashed in her bag would do for dinner; she couldn't cope with another one of Mavis's technology lessons.

"Ok, dear, well come upstairs when you get back and we can have a nice cuppa together."

Louise nodded and smiled, but Mavis's attention had wandered.

"Have a nice lunchtime dears! Are you going to your posh lat-tay cafe?" Nick and Chase turned to talk to Mavis briefly, regarding her rather fondly, then Nick lifted his hand in greeting at Louise before they wandered out through the door.

"So clever, those young doctors." Mavis was shaking her head thoughtfully. "They've been to such good universities, you know, and they're going to go a long way. They're a different breed to us lowly types, aren't they dear?" Mavis looked up at Louise and had the grace to blush as she took in what she had just said. "Not that you're a lowly type, dear! Oh no, but you know what I mean. Some people are just in different leagues to others, aren't they? Isn't that what they say on the tele? But you obviously have lots of talents too, dear! I mean, you're great on the computer! We'll let you take the phones for a bit tomorrow, maybe even get you booking a few appointments by the afternoon. That'll be something nice and new to look forward to, won't it dear? I can see you having a bright future as a receptionist!"

Louise picked up her bag and headed off; she needed

103

some fresh air. "See you in a bit, Mavis."

"Oh yes, I'll have that cup of tea waiting for you. Now, do you watch *Emmerdale*? Because I missed the last episode and I need to know what happened with the baby!"

Louise pretended not to hear that, instead just waving cheerily once she had safely reached the external side of the glass door.

"Hey Babe, good day at work?" Louise threw her keys onto the kitchen table and rooted in the fridge for a bottle of white. "What do you fancy for tea?"

"You."

Louise squealed playfully as Steve came up from behind and caught her in a tight embrace, then proceeded to drop slobbery kisses over the back of her neck. She spun around in his grasp to kiss him full on the lips then regarded him thoughtfully for a few seconds, absentmindedly fingering his floppy hair while thinking, once again, how lucky she had been to find him.

"How was your first day?"

"You know," she shrugged. "A first day as a receptionist. Nothing to write home about! But I guess it'll do for the time being. It kind of has to."

"Well, pour yourself a glass of wine, then come and join me on the sofa. I'll help you forget all about it..." Steve winked then backed away from her. She paused only to fill her glass, before going through to the living room to find out exactly what it was that Steve had in mind.

But in actual fact Louise walked into a cold, dark, empty chamber. Anna was out, as per usual, and Steve, well Steve didn't exist. She switched on the light then plonked herself down on the sofa before flicking on the TV. *Emmerdale* was playing and someone was having a barmy because they

104

had just found out that her sister had been sleeping with their boyfriend, who had turned out to be married to someone else who was pregnant with his child. Or something like that. Louise put her feet up and sat back to lose herself in a pretty bog standard day in the Dales. At least she'd have something to talk to Mavis about in the morning.

**Chapter 9**

"Good morning, dear! How are you today? Pop the kettle on, will you dear? I still haven't recovered from last night! Isn't *Emmerdale* exciting?"

Louise really wanted to say that she wouldn't know as she had been out gallivanting round the bars of Mayfair. But she had already resigned herself to the fact that she was going to have this conversation, while feeling incredibly resentful that, in fact, she knew exactly what had been going on in the Rovers last night. She silenced a sigh and mooched into the little kitchen to flick the kettle on.

"Now, dear, some good news. I was really impressed with your skills yesterday! And I told Chase all about you and she wants to recommend you to her sister, as she has her own PR firm and is looking for an assistant right at this moment! And Nick was wondering if you had a partner, you know he looked like he might be interested in courting you!" Although, of course, Mavis didn't actually say that. Well, she got as far as 'yesterday', but continued somewhat differently. "I've never known anyone to be such a whiz on the computer! So, I was thinking that instead of training you up for front of house, we would have you as Head of Computer Operations! What do you think?"

Louise hesitated. Head of Computer Operations actually sounded like a reasonable job title, but she couldn't quite see where that fitted into a quiet little doctors' surgery. She wondered whether Tony had seen something special in her at interview and had decided to promote her, and then her heart fluttered as she realised that could mean a pay rise.

"So? What do you think, dear?"

"Well, umm, I guess I'm pretty flattered, actually."

Mavis beamed at Louise. "We thought you would be, dear! We talked about it last night and we thought that role seemed much more suited to you than what we originally had in mind."

"We? You discussed it last night?" Louise fiddled with the Primark pearl in her earlobe.

"Oh yes, dear! I wouldn't just make a decision like this on my own!" Louise felt herself blush as she imagined Tony, Nick, Chase, Mavis and the others sitting around in a boardroom meeting, discussing and evaluating her talents and skills, then coming to the conclusion that she was overqualified and over experienced to settle for a basic receptionist job. "I talked to Priya about it!"

"Who's Priya? Another doctor?"

"No, Priya! The lady you're standing in for! You know the doctors said it was quite a miracle that she had that baby, and that there were no complications for either of them. She's no spring chicken, you know! And she was hopeless on the computer, she's glad you're here to do the work for her. She was worse than I am!" And with that Mavis erupted into a volcano of chuckles, emitted simultaneously from her nose and mouth. Louise was glad that the tsunami of laughter prevented Mavis from noticing the involuntary flinch that she couldn't withhold. "She suggested you become Head of Computer Operations, and I said what a great idea! We decided it last night while we were watching that fight in the Rovers Return over a sneaky sherry! Well, I had a sneaky sherry. She had to

108

have juice."

"Oh." Louise deflated. "So, Tony..." She wasn't really sure where she was going with that, so she waited for Mavis to continue the sentence.

"Oh, Tony doesn't know anything." Mavis gave a dismissive wave. "Don't you worry about him, he doesn't care what goes on down here as long as we keep the practice running. This is just between you, me and Priya! Now, can you put some milk in these - just a drop - and remember to take the tea bag out, while I pop to the little girls' room. Don't forget to use the semi-skimmed milk - that's the green one, not the red one which is skimmed and is just a bit too much like water - and I'll see you back at the desk!"

Louise had never taken longer to finish off making a couple of cups of tea. She made a game of seeing how slowly she could squeeze out the tea bags and how long she could take to unscrew the bottle of milk - green cap, of course - but when she checked barely two minutes had gone by. She predicted that much of the day would pass in the same fashion, but then suddenly her head snapped up and her whole soul seemed to lift. So what if her body was stuck in this place, doing dreary jobs and repetitive tasks hour after hour, day after day? It didn't mean that her mind had to be. She just needed to programme her limbs to carry on unaided and then she could slip off to join the life that she really wanted, for up to eight hours a day! Of course it wasn't an ideal way to live, but if it meant that she could get through the work and make a bit of cash then that was all that really mattered. And it wasn't the same as wasting time at home when she could be doing other things, or slipping away on the tube and missing her stop. Plus it wasn't like she'd be doing it if she was in PR, or any other job that she actually wanted to do. That would be a completely different situation; then she would be working solidly and giving it her all. She

109

wouldn't be so bloody bored.

Despite the sense that a guilty shadow seemed to have attached itself to the left hand side of her body, the prospects at the surgery were suddenly looking a lot more appealing.

"Here she comes! Our new Head of Computer Operations!" Mavis clapped as Louise wandered back into the room with the tea. "Come here, dear, I'll tell you how to do your new job!"

Louise attempted a smile to humour Mavis, but it became somewhat stilted as Nick walked in the door. His puzzled, amused frown made her cringe and blush as she inwardly cursed Mavis's announcement; Nick must think she'd elevated herself to that ridiculous title, or that she truly believed she had been given some big promotion. Head of Computer Operations, in a Doctors' Surgery that had two outdated PCs and a laptop that no-one used because they couldn't remember the password! Louise placed one of the mugs on Mavis's desk then took a sip from the second one, appreciating the burning sensation on her upper lip. It reminded her that she was still alive.

"Now, this is what I need you to do, dear. See those files?" Mavis indicated a collection of cardboard boxes absolutely stuffed to capacity with cardboard wallets, from which protruded sheet after sheet of paper covered in hand written scrawl. "Well, all of those need to go onto the computer. So, as you're now Head of Computers - and you're so good at using Exit - I thought you could focus on that and I'll just do the front of house work. Then you won't even need to be disturbed! Doesn't that sound great? You'll really be able to get your teeth into it! I thought it'd be right up your street!"

Louise didn't trust herself to answer, as she gazed dolefully at the masses of paper folders and felt her heart contract. An invisible weight pressed down on her chest as she

110

imagined how the next few weeks, or even months, were going to progress. Day after day of sifting through those outdated - and probably disused - records, just putting all that information onto the computer, where most probably no-one would ever look at it again. She couldn't quite comprehend how everything in her life had suddenly arrived at this single, soul-destroying moment.

As she knelt down in front of the first box Louise's mind was already fluttering off. Then, as her hands removed the first of the files, it left the room completely to take up residence in a spangly office in the City. She was just leaving for the night so she could meet Steve, who was taking her out to celebrate her recent promotion. Louise felt her energy levels lift as the fantasy gained momentum and within a few minutes she was miles away from the surgery, despite her physical body monotonously carrying out her designated tasks in the office.


"So, how's it all going? How's the accounting? I was looking it up on the line and I found out about that Big Four, you know with all the top accounting firms. Are you going to be doing one of those graduate scheme things? We've been telling everyone about your big success!"

"*No!* You've got it all wrong! It was a crappy admin job that needed no qualifications, and I didn't even take it! I'm now working in a shitty receptionist job and slowly going mad as I try not to give up on my dream of becoming a PR queen!"

But Louise couldn't bring herself to burst her mother's bubble, even if it was so dreadfully misinformed. Instead she just mumbled something incoherent, which Chris evidently took as modesty.

"Oh, don't go all shy on us, it's brilliant! You deserve to be proud of yourself, you should enjoy your success." Chris paused. "Ok, well if you're going to be all bashful about it let's

111

change the subject. Now Lou, now that you're a successful career woman you may notice that men start paying you a bit of attention."

"Um, yes. Ok, Mum." Louise bit her lip, unsure whether she was about to laugh or cry.

"Now, it may all seem a bit odd and new but you just hang in there, and the right man will come along. You know before I met your father I was a right one! I'd been round the block a few times, believe it or not, and even…"

"Mum! Stop!"

"Ooh, sorry love, was that a bit much?" Christine giggled coyly and Louise felt the colour rush to her cheeks. "But yes, you will meet a nice young lad soon, I think, and if you ever need any help or advice then you know where to come. And, you know, that first time, well it can hurt a bit. But you have to get beyond that and then it can get really great…"

"Mother! Have you been drinking?!"

"Oh no, love, I'm just excited about your new life, and excited about bragging to everyone! But as I was about to say, that first time…"

"Mum, for God's sake! I have had sex before, you know!"

"Oh, love! That first time is so special. When was it? Have you met someone in London?"

"About six years ago! In my mate's parents' bed with that spotty kid from school who you met once and hated!" Although Louise's fuelled reply remained silent as she reasoned that sometimes a white lie was necessary in order to protect loved ones.

"Err…yes." Well, that wasn't a complete fib. She'd met lots of people since she'd been in the city.

"Who?! What's his name? What does he do?"
"Steve!"

"Steve! I like the sound of him! Tell me more!"

"Mum, I have to go. I think someone's at the door."

"Ooh, maybe it's Steve! Have a great evening love, and next time we talk you can tell me all about him! Bye!"

Louise flopped back on her bed and eyed the ceiling, which felt as if it was starting to close in on her. She took a few deep breaths before heaving herself up off the mattress and mooching into the lounge, where she proceeded to slouch on the sofa and resume her activity of ceiling watching. There was more light in this room, bigger windows and greater space, so she didn't feel quite so claustrophobic. But she felt bored. Beyond belief. And everything felt wrong. She was in London! Arguably the greatest city in the world, a sprawling metropolis with a plethora of bars and clubs and theatres and sights and shops and people. Millions and millions of people. So why did it all feel so flat?

It seemed so easy, in theory. Just get out there and get on with it, make new friends and try new things. But where to start? Work seemed the obvious place, but no matter how desperate she got there was no way she was going to take Mavis clubbing with her. Then there were flatmates, but as Anna was rarely around that wasn't going to be easy. She needed to network but first she needed people to do it through, and everyone she knew always seemed so busy with their own lives. Yet she knew it was time to get some balls rolling, and not with weedy pushes but great big shoves with lots of momentum behind them.

She wandered back into her room with a little more bounce in her step and grabbed her phone. Neither Jen nor Rachel had replied to her earlier messages, and only two of her old mates had got back to her. They had both essentially said that they were just too busy at the moment, but now Louise decided to take matters into her own hands. She typed out a text instructing her old university crew to meet her at seven o'clock on Saturday night, at a pub she knew in Covent Garden, no excuses. She sent it to Paddy, her Irish next door neighbour from her first year in halls; Ollie, Paddy's best mate; Shereela, Ollie's fiancee; Maura and Natalie, who Louise had lived with in her third year and Ryan, who had moved into the spare room of their house when he'd had to resit his final year. Aside from Amy, Louise actually viewed most of her uni mates as friends by circumstance, rather than anything deeper. But she remembered Amy's leaving speech, and knew that if she wanted to meet people it was up to her to make an effort and get out there.

After that she moved on to Rachel and Jen. She decided to give Jen a ring, as she had been so friendly the night of Amy's leaving meal, but the number had been disconnected. Feeling somewhat disheartened Louise tried again but reached the same monotonous dead tone, so accepted defeat and tried Rachel. Rachel's phone rang through to voicemail, so Louise left a message then went off to make a cup of tea, now feeling a couple of pounds lighter as she congratulated herself on her efforts.

## Chapter 10

"Ash, man, I've been trying to catch you for days! Listen, I'm sorry about the other night. I don't know what came over me but I know I was out of order. I can't really remember it, to be honest, but I know I was being a cock..."

"Huh? For fuck's sake!" Ash picked up his golf clubs and tried leaning them against the wall again. "No worries, mate. I know what you get like when you're hammered – you're one of those angry drunks. Like I'm one of those drunks who just loves everybody. Then there are those ones who have to get naked, like Chris at work, then those ones who have to have a fight, then those ones who retreat into themselves and just sit. I'm well experienced in this field mate, I've seen it all!"

"Thanks, Ash."

"Just make sure you always take your keys. So what happened after the pub?" Ash threw himself down next to Ryan.

"Oh, nothing special. We just went out in central, found a few bars and clubs. Nothing much to report. Well, I don't think so anyway..."

"And the bird?"

"Got her." Ryan reclined into the sofa and let himself smile smugly.

"Nice. Thought you would. Seeing her again?"

"Yes, tonight actually. Going out for dinner."

"Aha! Where are you taking her?"

"Pizza Express."

"Oh, you are a classy date aren't you?"

Ryan laughed. "Something like that. All just a gesture, really, isn't it?!"

Ash slapped the back of the sofa. "I like your style. Listen, I'm going for a run, have a good night. Don't do anything I wouldn't do."

"That doesn't leave much, does it?!"

"Exactly!" Ash hesitated. "Ryan, man, umm...is everything ok?"

"Hmm? Yeah, why?"

"Well, it's just that you've been, um, drinking a lot lately. I mean, I'm all one for a party, but...it's just...you seem to be hungover most mornings these days and, you know..."

Ryan snorted. "Ah bugger off, you old man. You really are getting boring. Listen, go and have your jog and only come back when you're ready for a can, *capiche*?" He grinned light-heartedly at Ash, despite the churning feeling in his stomach and the headache thumping away at the base of his skull.

"Alright, mate. Catch you later."

Ryan held the smile until he heard the front door slam, then he fell back against the sofa and closed his eyes. He knew he should be getting on with some work, but surely five minutes wouldn't make a difference. And it was the weekend, after all.

Ryan awoke with a start, and it took him a while to work out where he was. It was already dark, and he was cold. His neck ached and his mouth felt like he had swallowed velvet. But he still felt a whole lot better than he had a few hours earlier.

His Blackberry was flashing on the table, among the

116

debris from Ash's run: i-pod, water bottle, energy bar wrapper - how had he not woken up when Ash had come back? There was a text from Kayla asking if they were still on for later, a few junk e-mails and a Facebook notification, telling him that a friend of Ash's had invited him to a party. He tapped out a reply to Kayla then stretched out for the glass of water on the coffee table. Downing it felt like a gift from heaven.

But as he lay there a cloud settled over him, and his insides started churning once more. His breathing quickened as the somersaults took over his whole body and spread to his heart, which started thumping as if he had just done a 400m sprint. Ryan started to panic and struggled into a sitting position. He tried to take a deep breath, but that only made it even harder to breathe. His rasping gasps scared him further and he felt his internal body temperature soar, like a vehicle that was overheating. He flailed about for a glass, grabbing one off the coffee table and shoving it up his t-shirt, where he pressed it against his chest. The cold shock brought him down somewhat, though the sense of panic rose up once more as he realised he was all on his own. But through the sheer force of will he managed to force his brain to override his body and told himself that he was fine, everything was ok and he was going to get through. He just had to calm down.

Ryan moved the glass over his skin and focused on breathing properly. As his heart rate began to reduce, his limbs slowly started to reconnect to his body and regain some semblance of strength. He moved the glass upwards to roll it over his forehead and his breathing became deeper once more, but his legs still wobbled and his heart was sending out aftershocks.

Ryan replaced the glass on the table and lay back down, just as his message tone went again; Kayla was looking forward to seeing him and wanted to know what time they were meeting. Would 7.30 be ok? He replied to say that something had come up and he would have to cancel after all, but that he would make it up to her next week. He dropped the phone between the cushions, and when it beeped in response he couldn't even muster the energy to pick it up. He flicked on the TV and sat in front of it until midnight, yet he couldn't have told anybody what was actually on that night. Not if he been under oath, not on pain of death.

"See you tomorrow, guys." Ryan raised a hand before turning and stepping out of the office and into the mild early autumn evening, grateful for his brief respite from data entry before nine o'clock would come round once more and it would start all over again. Turning his face to the sun he plucked his phone from his pocket, more out of habit than necessity, and saw that he had a message from a random number. Frowning, he opened it up.

*Hey, I just felt I should let you know that I'm with somebody else now. I'm not telling you to hurt you, I just didn't want you to find out on the grapevine. I loved you so much, Ryan, and I hoped we could work things out and move on. But if this is how you want it then so be it, I guess. Zoe xx*

As Ryan re-read her message something stirred in his stomach. Turning off down a side street he slipped into the doorway of what appeared to be a deserted building and vomited, over and over. Once he was feeling nice and empty he collapsed onto the doorstep and sat gazing at the paving slabs, his throat stinging and his mouth sour. He stayed that way for an hour, and when he finally was able to pull himself to his feet he headed straight for the pub.

118

*　　*　　*

Later that night Ryan slammed down the lid of his laptop, a part of him really wanting to damage the machine. He breathed heavily as he imagined hurling the computer against the wall, ripping the lid off its hinges or stamping on the keyboard. He just couldn't get the words right, and he was so tired and such a failure. There wasn't any point in anything; especially not now that Zoe was with someone else. He wished he had stayed in the pub to drink through the pain, but he had stupidly thought that his tortured soul might inspire his work, the way it had so many greats before him. What a load of bollocks.

Although his mind checked his desire to smash up his Macbook a destructive urge still invaded his veins. He picked up a mug, empty but for a crystallised lining of coffee stained sugar, and threw it against the door. The mug jeered at him as it refused to even crack, rebounding off its target and landing in a pile of t-shirts that lay on the floor. Taken over by an immense sense of exhaustion and futility Ryan put his head in his hands and flopped onto his desk, pressing his fingernails into his scalp so that it felt as if ten little daggers were piercing his skull.

Ryan's phone beeped into life and he grabbed for it, hoping upon some miracle that it would be Zoe again, but at the same time praying it wouldn't. He was surprised to see Louise's name flash up on screen, then felt his heart sink as he read her message. He just didn't feel ready to go back to his old friends yet, not when everything was so tentative and, to be honest, crap. It seemed like everyone else was doing so well and to have to explain himself…not that he had to justify his life but he just wanted to have something exciting to say, something to take people's breath away and make him stand out from the crowd; he wanted to feel he was making something of it all. But he'd made so many excuses, and Louise wasn't the only one pulling him up on it. Somewhat reluctantly he tapped out a reply, then grabbed his jacket and went out to meet Kayla.

Ryan knew things would look better once he had a pint inside him. And Kayla was ok; they could have a laugh together, at least. And she was hot. He thought about how her long brown hair hung straight until the ends curled in around her nipples, and how her concave stomach sported that little constellation of freckles right above her pubic bone. He felt himself begin to harden.

She was waiting for him outside the pub, and without saying anything he marched right up to her, pushed her hands together behind her back, shoved her up against the wall and kissed her. If you could call it that. He ran his free hand up her side before pulling down the zip on her jacket and slipping his fingers under her top, feeling her wince as her flesh hit the night air. At that point he felt her struggle to try and pull away. At first he wouldn't let her go, but then he released his grip and took a step back as she took a deep breath and ran a hand through her hair. She had scarlet streaks down her cheeks, and when she pursed her mouth to exhale it looked like a bullet hole with blood smeared around the edges.

"Bloody hell, Ryan! What's got into you?"

It made his stomach churn to see her looking like that. But he smiled and shuffled forward again. "I just find you so hot," he muttered, kissing her more gently this time. "Come on, let's get out of here."

"Hmm...wait..."

"Come on!"

"Where are we going?"

Ryan shuddered as she slipped an arm around his neck; it felt like a boa constrictor wrapping him up and waiting to squeeze him to death. Ryan imagined a boa constrictor would take a long time to kill its prey, getting pleasure from watching the life being squeezed out of it drop by drop, second by second.

"Don't care. Anywhere we can be alone." He kissed her again. "Over there."

"What's over there?"

"Bushes."

"Ryan! No! We can't!"

"Why not?" He smiled the lopsided grin that he knew she found irresistible.

"Because!" Kayla looked into his eyes, then broke into a mischievous smile. "I don't know. Come on, then!" And she grabbed his hand and led him off to the back of the car park. Ryan was pretty sure that when she brushed her hand against his erection it wasn't accidental.

"So, what now?"

"What do you mean, what now?" Ryan adjusted his boxers and buttoned up his jeans.

"What shall we do now?"

"Well, I don't know about you, but I need a drink." Ryan watched as Kayla rolled up her tights and pulled down her skirt. Although he knew that her actions were sexy he suddenly felt more disgusted than turned on. "Let's go back inside."

"I can't! Not looking like this!"

Ryan pulled Kayla into the street light and laughed.

"Don't laugh! Have I got panda eyes?"

Ryan laughed harder. "You look like a doll from some weird horror film!"

"Ryan! That's a horrible thing to say!"

"No! No, no! I didn't mean it like that. I just mean that

you have black all round your eyes and your lips look as though they've been bleeding. And in this lighting....!'" Even to himself Ryan's laughter sounded manic, and out of proportion for the joke.

"Oh, cut it out. Let's go back to yours, it's closer."

Ryan steadied himself. "Come on then, Chuckie's waiting for you anyway."

Kayla thumped him as he flung his arm around her shoulder. Then as she fell into him he let himself pretend, just for a second, that he was really holding Zoe.

"So, how's your writing going? You were telling me about it the night we met but I can't really remember. You said you were temping too, right?"

"Yeah, that's right, temping while I build up a portfolio. Bloody painful it is, too."

"Yeah, I know. I temped for a while before I started with the council. It was like dying a slow death every day. Actually, there were times when I thought a slow death might be preferable; that can only happen once. But how's the writing?"

"Ok, yeah. I do some work for Music Mania, do you know it?"

"Yeah! I do, actually. Wow, that's pretty cool."

Ryan suddenly felt about six inches taller. "And I'm working on a novel too! Where's my bloody key?"

"Really? That's awesome! What's it about?"

"Um, I'm not really telling people yet. It's still forming, you know." Ryan moved aside to allow Kayla into the flat, then shut the door behind her.

"I do, actually. Yeah."

Ryan turned to look down at her. "Huh?"

"Yeah, I wrote a novel out once. Just a silly romance thing, never got anywhere. But I wanted to try it, so I did."

"Really?" Ryan felt as though Kayla has just stolen something precious from him and kicked him in the stomach as she ran off with it. It was ridiculous, it wasn't like he was the only person to have ever thought about writing a novel. But it was meant to be *his* thing, not something anyone else anywhere near him had ever done.

"Yeah. It wasn't that great though, I'm sure yours is better. How long is it? Mine turned out at about 100k."

"Well, um, I haven't actually started yet." Ryan kicked himself for being caught off guard. "But it's all planned and ready to go, I'm just waiting for a time to sit down and give it a good bash to get going. I want to clear a few days, rather than just try and do it in an afternoon or something."

"Fair play. Hey, I meant to ask you, do you fancy coming to a party with me on Saturday?"

"Saturday? No, I can't. Here."

"Thanks." Kayla took the can of Strongbow. "How come?"

"I've got a thing, a reunion type thing. With people from uni."

"Urgh, I hate those things. Come sit here."

"Yeah, I don't know. It should be good though, there'll be a lot of people there I haven't seen for a while and they were mates, it's not like it's just a load of people I never really spoke to. And it'll be interesting to see what everyone's doing."

"What are they all doing?"

"I don't know. I'll find out on Saturday!"

"Do you want to come join me afterwards?"

"Yeah maybe, I'll see how things go. Where will you be?"

"Somewhere round Old Street, I think. I'll let you know. Hey!" Kayla jumped up and thrust her can at Ryan.

"What?"

"I've just remembered what I look like! Back in a sec."

As Kayla hurried off to the bathroom Ryan knocked back his can and thought about the reunion. Now that it was coming around he was quite looking forward to seeing everyone. Especially Maura. But he just had to make sure he had his veneer in place. As in superglued on so tightly there would be no chance that anyone could budge it; there was no way he was going to let any of them see how shit things really were.

## Chapter 11

"See you later, Anna!" Louise threw on her jacket and rummaged around in the shoe rack for her left ballet pump.

"You off out? Going anywhere nice?" Anna's voice drifted out over the strains of someone warbling their heart out on TV, and Louise tried not to take offence at the note of surprise in her tone.

"Yeah, going to meet up with my old friends, haven't seen them all in so long!" She called back, before adding 'See, I *have* got some friends,' under her breath.

"Cool, that'll be good!"

"Yeah, I'm all excited actually. Will be good to see everyone! See you later."

"Laters."

As Louise wandered into the Prince of Wales, scouting around the bar for a familiar face, she felt her stomach fizzling. She went to get herself a glass of white then had a better look round, and it didn't take long to spot Paddy's dark black mop and Ollie's golden curls through the gathering crowds. Just as Lou was reaching their table a gorgeous model-type girl with long blonde waves, big sparkling eyes and a tiny waist slipped in next to Paddy, who momentarily stopped in his tracks and gave her a peck on the lips, before resuming his monologue to Ollie as the girl slipped her arm around his shoulder. Then Shereela appeared on her way back from the bar, clutching wine and a pint and Louise instantaneously gasped, unable to contain her surprise and glad that she was still far off enough to be unseen and unheard.

Shereela had completely and utterly transformed. Back in their uni days she'd always been a generous size fourteen, more of a sixteen really, and had hidden herself away in jeans and sweaters. She had scorned make up and hair products, instead preferring to spend her money on CDs by bands with obscure names that would never make it into the Top 40, and books with sinister covers and bizarre storylines. But this girl was someone else entirely. She was definitely Shereela; there was no disguising the purpley scar that haunted the side of her cheek, the result of an unfortunate incident with a bike when she was a toddler. But today the scar was much less visible, hidden away by a perfectly applied coat of foundation topped off with an expensive looking face powder. Shereela had lost about three stone, at least, and couldn't have been bigger than a size eight. Her hair was gleaming and had been cut into a style which shaped her face, and very faint golden highlights peeped out from between the strands of dark brown silk that fell to her shoulders in an elegant curtain. She was dressed in skinny jeans, spiky boots and a lacy cream top which emphasised her slender figure, topped off with a black shrug. Little diamond earrings glittered from earlobes that had previously sported cheap silver hoops, and her teeth appeared suspiciously whiter than they had been at graduation. Indeed, without that tell-tale scar Louise would have been hard pushed to have recognised this graceful, beautiful swan her old friend had become.

At that point Shereela turned around and spotted Louise, her face lighting up with her familiar, radiant smile. Louise felt surprisingly relieved to see the old Shereela grinning across at her, as if she had just received confirmation that nothing had really changed, and hurried across the floor to greet her mates.

"Lou! Babe, it's so great to see you!" Babe? Shereela never said things like 'babe'. "How are you doing? How are you finding the Smoke, isn't it fabulous?" Fabulous? Really?? Shereela swept Louise up in a big hug (another new part of her transformed persona) and a cloud of designer perfume before turning to Ollie and getting him to shuffle up so Louise could squeeze in next to them. "So, tell me all about it! Where are you working? Where did you end up living?"

"Hey, Lou!" Ollie offered Louise his cheek over the table as she grinned over at him. "How's it going? What are you up to?"

"Good! Yeah, really good. I'm still looking for work at the moment so I'm biding my time in a bar, but I'm loving being up here!"

"We've all been there, eh Dav?"

The blonde girl who was draped over Paddy looked up with a questioning expression on her face.

"Bar work, temping. By the way this is Louise, Lou this is Davina, Paddy's girlfriend."

Davina smiled and proffered her hand over the table top. Louise shook it and grinned back, rather struck by how Paddy had managed to attract such a beauty.

"What do you do now, then?"

"PR. Media PR."

Louise felt her eyes widen as her mind jumped to attention. "That's what I want to do! Where are you working?"

"Just off Piccadilly. You?"

That wasn't exactly what Louise had been asking but she didn't push it; she felt slightly intimidated by Davina.

"Swiss Cottage at the moment, but it's only temporary. I'm desperately looking for PR jobs though, any thoughts?" Louise giggled lightly but her heart was going at a rate of knots.

"It is, like, impossible to get a job in PR at the moment. Everyone had stopped recruiting, there's no money. Hopefully it'll pick up again though in the next few years." Next few *years*? "Best thing you can hope for at the moment is getting an internship or some work experience. But obviously all that stuff is in high demand too, and unpaid."

"I can't do unpaid."

"It might be the only option." Davina raised her perfectly plucked eyebrows at Louise, whose heart plummeted right down into her toes. She sighed, then changed the subject; this was her first proper night out in ages and she didn't want to spoil it.

"So, how are things going with you?" She directed her question at Shereela, who beamed back at her.

"Really well! I'm on a retail graduate scheme and I love it! Things are great with Ollie, and I'm hoping we can get on and plan this wedding now! We've been waiting long enough!" She added the last part in a whisper, grinning smugly over in her boyfriend's direction as she played with the diamante band on her left hand. "We've got a great little flat down in Pimlico, and he's done with law school and has a training contract with one of those big City firms. It's all working our perfectly!"

Louise smiled at her friend, desperately trying to be happy for her but finding it difficult to make the feeling genuine. She could feel envy rising up and consuming her insides, closely followed by guilt.

"Hey, there's Maura and Natalie! Hey guys!" Shereela jumped up and waved manically across the pub, a welcome reprieve for Louise. She used the break in conversation to give herself a stern talking to, reminding her to be happy for her friends, and then followed suit.

Maura and Natalie spotted them and grinned, heading

across the pub to join the gang, and Louise breathed a silent sigh of relief as she saw that both girls looked much as she remembered them. Maura was dressed in a short flowery skirt with black tights and an oversized black cardigan, finished off with chunky boots. Her chestnut hair was pulled back into a loose ponytail with a few wispy tendrils framing her pale, slender face, which had been made up in Maura's classic 'less is more' style; just enough concealer to hide her minor blemishes and a touch of mascara, topped off with a slick of lip gloss and a sprinkling of copper coloured powder brushed over her cheekbones.

Natalie was wearing boot cut jeans with Indian style silver slippers and a glittery white top. Her mahogany hair had been straightened, as per usual, and hung down just below her shoulders. Her face was rather heavily made up but that was how Louise remembered her, and the familiarity of it suited her, despite the pale orange line that rimmed her visage.

"Hey! So good to see you all!" Maura arrived at the table first, with Natalie just a few steps behind. Shereela repeated her enthusiastic hugging routine, which Louise was pleased to see appeared to surprise the other girls as much as it had herself, before grabbing a few extra stools so the newcomers could sit down.

"So, what are you guys *up* to?"

As tales of successful careers and passionate relationships continued to flow Louise felt the fog that had recently lifted off her shoulders start to settle once again. She tried to remind herself that it was just a matter of time before her life would emulate the others', but she couldn't be at peace.

"So, you've been keeping very quiet Lou! What's going on with you? Don't tell us you're still single!" Shereela elbowed Louise in the ribs and giggled, but Louise felt her hackles rise.

"Oh well, you know, there's always someone in the game, eh?" She adopted an unnatural tone, and the response it caused encouraged her to continue. Suddenly she had the attention of the whole table as they all paused in their conversations to lap up the gossip.

"See, the job may be crap but at least you have a nice man to take your mind of it! Who is he?"

Louise felt her jaw clench. "Well, he's called Steve. I met him in a pub recently." Again, not a *lie* as such.

"Oooooh!! Lou's got a boyfriend!"

Louise clouted Paddy on the arm.

"He's not my boyfriend, as such..." (still not a lie...) "He's just..." Louise trailed off, at which point Natalie finished her sentence for her.

"A thing. We understand. But he'll be more than that soon, eh?!"

"Hey! Look who it is!"

Louise was thankful to see Ryan ambling through the pub towards them - extremely late, as to be expected - and as casually as a surfer on Bondi Beach. Apart from the welcome interruption to the current conversation Louise was glad that, knowing Ryan, his life would be about as much in order as hers.

"So, you are now looking at the latest contributor to Music Mania Magazine, with my own review page, probably soon my own column and with a view to interviewing real live bands before too long!" Ryan stood with his arms above his head as if in victory, eyes closed, awaiting the praise.

"Oh my God Ryan, that's amazing!"

"Nice one mate!"

"Congrats!"

"Yay! I'm so glad it's all working out for us, life after

130

uni is good!"

Louise faded into the background as Natalie's last comment rang in the air. She was happy for her friends, she really, really, was, but why was she so far away from where they were? They'd started out from the same point, after all, but now the others were steaming off miles ahead.

"And…" Ryan waited until he had the attention of the table once again. "I have to break the rather grievous news to you that I am now off the market. And it's looking pretty serious…!"

"Ooh, Ryan! Tell us more!" As Shereela led the others in clamouring for details Louise slowly closed her eyes and took a deep breath. This wasn't meant to happen; Ryan wasn't the settling down, working 'properly' and getting his life in order type. He had been her last hope that she wasn't getting completely left behind while life moved forward for everyone else. Now she really did feel all at sea.

## Chapter 12

"So what happened with Zoe, then?" Ryan's heart flipped as Maura mentioned her name. "I thought you guys were really serious? I mean, all through uni you had all those girls, but I'd never seen you with anyone like you were with her. What went wrong? Shit, sorry. Have I overstepped?"

Ryan sat up taller and took a slug of wine. "No, no not at all. No worries. It just, you know, didn't work. I guess these things happen, what can you do?" He caught his old friend's eye but quickly looked away. Maura always did have a knack for hitting the nail on the head and seeing through his bravado, and it always made him feel self-conscious.

She was another one, like Zoe, who was different to the others. He'd noticed it in her when they'd first met in the union, though he'd never had a crush on her. Actually, he had her to thank for having met Zoe in the first place - if she hadn't hooked up with that Aussie rugby player in the local Wetherspoons he'd never have got talking to Shanay, and then she'd never have thrown her glass of wine over him for snogging her mate while she was in the bathroom, so he'd never have gone to ask that barmaid for a towel to mop up the worst of the damage. The barmaid who was in the year below him, who had accepted his friend request on Facebook and then vanished out of his life for the next year or so. Well, physically. Because there was just something about Zoe that Ryan just couldn't get out of his mind.

"Ry? Are you ok?"

Ryan realised that he had been staring at the tabletop for quite some time. "Yeah, sorry Maura. I don't know." He sighed. "We were just young, you know? I guess that's the thing about first love - it just doesn't last."

"Love?" Maura echoed, arching a brow. "Were you in love with her? Bloody hell! I thought you were just, you know. Messing around and that."

"Well, yeah. But, you know. It's complicated, Maura. There was stuff..." Ryan thought about that photo he had tucked away in his sock drawer. He'd told Zoe that he'd destroyed it ages ago, but in truth he couldn't bring himself to part with it.

"Ry?"

"Huh?"

"I said, what stuff? I mean, you don't have to tell me. But, you know. If you need someone to talk to, or anything?"

Ryan felt as if he'd stepped off a steep cliff and was about to plummet to the rocks below. But, like a cartoon character, he had a split second to decide which way to go.

"It's fine, Maura. You know what it's like!" He attempted to smile jovially. "Life happens, shit happens. And what can we do about it? Anyway I've got Kayla now, I've moved on."

"Ryan..." Maura began, but Ryan cut her off with the slightest shake of his head. "Ok. Listen, I'm going to the loo. I'll be back in five."

Ryan poured himself another glass of red, catching Davina's eye as he replaced the bottle on the table. She seemed to flush slightly before glancing pointedly at the empty bottle then looking away, and he felt a wobble of indignation in his stomach.

"Alright, Dav?" He deliberately slurred. "Did you want a glass? 'Fraid I've polished this one off but there's more behind the bar. Don't worry, I haven't had it *all*." He made a point of eyeballing her.

"Oh! No, thanks Ryan. I'm fine, don't really drink too much actually. I'm fine with the water." She half-smiled at him but he raised his glass to his lips, deliberately putting a barrier between himself and what he saw to be her accusatory stare. Once he had finished knocking back half the wine she was deep in conversation with Shereela.

"Back in a sec..." He muttered to no-one in particular, stumbling to his feet and seeking out the bathrooms on the other side of the pub. As he undid his flies and slipped his cock out of his boxers he thought back to the conversation in the bar. Why had he made such a big thing about Kayla, when it was nothing more than a casual relationship at best? And what about Music Mania? Ok so they'd published a couple of his reviews, enough so that he was starting to get used to seeing his name in print, but not nearly enough to be able to call himself a 'writer'. He'd intended to bend the truth but hadn't quite meant to lie outright, and now it all felt like the start of a web he was spinning that he was already getting stuck in. But everyone else seemed to be doing so well, with everything, and he couldn't bear to be the failure of the group.

Zipping himself up he ran his hands under the tap and went back out to the bar, stopping before he reached his old friends to drop a message to Kayla.

*I'm coming to see you, want to get smashed?*

It beeped with a reply just a few seconds later:

*Yep!*

135

Good. That was another night down.

*     *     *

By the time she got home Louise had a cracking headache. She was rooting around in the drawer looking for some paracetamol when she came across the silver bangle she had bought at Portobello Market with Amy, so recently but at the same time so long ago. She pulled it out of the drawer and studied it pensively. It seemed unbelievable to think that a few months ago she had been so confident, so full of optimism for the upcoming future and feeling so positive about her life.

She wandered into the kitchen to get a glass of water for her pills, then stopped in the bathroom to eye herself in the full length mirror that adorned the far wall. She regarded herself critically, plucking at her clothes, pinching her skin and fiddling with her hair. And then it all started to fall into place. She'd been faffing around for too long, moving sideways instead of forwards. Now, all that was about to change. Like Amy said, she needed to make it happen; no more sitting around and waiting for it to come to her. In a flurry of triumph - and with an underlying sense of rebellion - Louise sat down and wrote a courtesy resignation e-mail to Tony, conveniently glossing over the fact that the very reason she was at the surgery was because it had proved so hard to find a job she actually wanted in the first place. She triumphantly clicked 'send' then stripped off and crawled into bed, without bothering to take off her make up or clean her teeth.

Once her eyes were closed she reached for Steve, wrapping her arm around his chest and gently dropping a kiss onto his broad shoulders. He stirred in reaction to her touch but drifted straight back to sleep. Louise pressed herself up against

136

him, enjoying the sensation of his warm skin on her bare nipples, and feeling his breathing slow down as he returned to the land of dreams. Her muscles relaxed, her heart beat slowed and her eyelids began to droop as she relished in the freedom to become whoever she wanted and do what she pleased. Until that old anxiety started flooding her limbs, weighing them down until she felt as if she were sinking into a mattress of quickmud. She fought to blank it out but it wouldn't go away, so she pushed it down into the back of her calves, as far as it would go. Even though it lingered at least then she could contain it. And, on the plus side, that way she knew where it was. That wasn't half as scary as wondering where and when it would pop up the next time.

# The Denial

# Chapter 1

"Louise? Worthington? Gosh, you've changed a bit! You looked completely different at the interview!"

"Hi, Shirley! Yeah, I felt it was time for a re-vamp!"

"You can say that again! You're all tanned, your hair has gone platinum and poker and that fringe makes your whole face look different. And your eyes! They're so bright! Gorgeous turquoise though, where did you find those lenses?"

"Oh, just online. And it's Skye, actually. Louise is my, um, formal name. But Skye is what I go by." Skye smoothed out her pencil skirt, enjoying the feel of her new name on her tongue. It had come to her last night when she had glanced over at her special shoebox, all covered in blue paper with fluffy white clouds, as she was admiring her new look.

"Ok, Skye. You look very smart, by the way. And you found us ok? Apologies again that we had to interview you at head office. What's your route?"

"Jubilee line to Finchley Road, then Metropolitan into Liverpool street. It was fine and you were right, you can't miss the 'Edwards, Greenwood and Benjamin Media PR Agency' sign!"

Shirley snorted. "Indeed. Anyway, you ready to get started? Let's take you through to meet everyone else."

As Shirley walked off Skye took a deep breath, ran a hand through her hair and briefly closed her eyes. This is just the beginning, she thought. But who knew where it might lead? She shook her head, inhaled again and strode off behind her new boss.

As the train from Liverpool Street pulled into King's Cross that evening Skye studied the commuters, identifying a woman in a purple trouser suit as the most likely candidate to vacate her seat. She was shuffling her bags and sitting up on edge, her eyes sharp as she marked out her route to the doors through the maze of passengers. Skye sidled around her fellow *Standard*-reading sardines to hover close by, then as the doors slid open and the woman rose she slipped in behind her and smugly settled into the seat, closing her eyes as she finally relieved her feet of her weight.

As the tube trundled on once more Skye momentarily marvelled at how it was able to heave such a mass of people along with it, before she left the overstuffed people-container for the duration of the cramped, overheated journey to reflect on her day. She embellished the good and minimised the bad until she got the balance just right, then stayed in that place until the train reached Finchley Road, where she whipped out her mobile to call her parents before the early evening slump kicked in.

"Hello, love! How are you? How was your first day? Tell us all about it, we've been so excited! Are you at home now?"

"No, just walking back from the tube, Mum. And remember, it's Skye now, ok?"

Chris hesitated. "Why are you changing your name? I don't really understand. And why to Skye?"

Skye pretended not to notice the unusually sharp edge to her mother's tone. "Oh Mum, it was just a nickname I picked up in uni, and the guys started using it when I met up with them here. It's just kind of stuck, but now I really like it!"

At Chris's silence Skye pressed her mobile more firmly to her ear. "Mum?"

Chris sniffed down the line. "Well, if that's what you want. But I think we'll stay with Louise, ok? That is what we named you, after all."

"Alright, Mum." Skye paused. "Anyway, shall I tell you all about work today?"

"Oh, yes! What did you do?"

"Oh, Mum, it was amazing, it really was. It was so nice, to get all dressed up this morning and set off for work with the commuters!"

"How exciting!" Chris squealed slightly manically. "Tell me about your office! Is it one of these modern glasshouses? And what are the people like? Do you have a nice boss? And what do you do all day? These HR jobs are such a mystery to my generation!"

"*PR*," Skye stressed, a hot sweat suddenly spidering across her forehead as her heart skipped a beat. She poked around in her handbag for a tissue but that only got her more flustered, so she aimed a few exhalations upwards which temporarily cooled her off. "It's *P, R*. It stands for Public Relations."

"Oh. I see."

"So anyway, the office is beautiful, it's one of those glass fronted buildings, all spacey and minimalist, with sparkling floors and transparent lifts…"

"So, talk me through your morning! I want to know exactly what happened, where you went, who you met!"

"Mum, that's what I'm trying to do! So I got there and…"

"Ooh! Maybe we could look it up on Hotmail! I'll get your dad to set it up!"

143

"Google, Mum. Hang on, I need to find a tissue." Skye tucked her phone under her ear and balanced her bag on a traffic cone while she rooted around, finally managing to locate a scrap of kitchen towel that had slipped through the hole is the lining. Chris's voice echoed down the line as Skye mopped her brow.

"'Mike! Get the computer fired up! We can giggle Louise's new office."

Skye smothered a giggle herself as she rested a cooling palm against her forehead.

"He's on it now! So tell me how your day went."

"Well, I got in at about eight forty-five as I wanted to be early for my first day, and I was met right away by my boss, Shirley. She was very friendly and showed me to my workplace where I met my new colleagues."

"Colleagues! What are they like? Are they nice? Are they young?"

Skye vacillated as her trail of thought was pulled in opposing directions. The middle part of her brain was fluffy and vacant and she felt her eyes narrow, but then her vocal chords took charge of the situation. "Well, there are, um, twelve grads on the scheme. Yeah, twelve. Seven girls and five guys."

An image of Dan appeared on the pavement before her, tall and muscley with sparkling blue eyes and a cheeky grin. At the start of the day he had been clean shaven, but by five o'clock stubble was beginning to peek through on his jawbone. He had golden blonde hair swept back and fixed with wax, although again by late afternoon a few sections had begun to droop forwards. Skye had been dying to brush them back off his forehead. At one point she had bumped right into him and caught a whiff of Hilfiger aftershave mingled with washing powder as he turned around and caught her eye. He'd smiled to reveal a set of almost perfect pearly whites bar one slightly crooked front tooth, which also sported a tiny chip, and she'd felt herself turn beetroot as she'd mumbled something incoherent and scuttled away. But in her mind it hadn't finished there.

"Louise? Are you still there?"

"Oh! Sorry Mum, I drifted off! Yeah so there were two girls who seemed really nice, called Di and Suki. Di's from the Southwest and Suki is from Hong Kong. They were so pleased to have got to Edwards, Mum!"

"I'm not surprised! It's the best in the country, isn't it?"

"Well, one of them, yes. They seemed really friendly so hopefully I'll get to know them better. Di's gorgeous, Mum! She's tall and slim with long blonde hair, and she was wearing this beautiful trouser suit. Actually, I think I might buy one with my first pay packet. And then Suki is so smart, she's tiny and so trendy. She had these cool scarlet glasses, I think they were Osiris. It kind of made me wish I needed specs! And she has stunning black hair. Do you remember when I was little and I wanted black hair, Mum?"

"Yes, how could I forget that, Lou? You coloured in your hair with a permanent marker!"

Skye chuckled.

"Anyway, the girls sound great, love. I'm feeling a little bit jealous, it's all so exciting!"

A wave of tiredness swept over Skye as she approached her front door and slipped the key into the lock. "Look Mum I'm sorry, I've got to go. I've just got home and I'm absolutely shattered. Today has just been a blur and I didn't sit down once."

"Ok, love, well thanks for telling me all your news! What are you going to do tonight? Are you going out?"

Skye dropped onto the sofa and gazed at the blank TV.

145

"Um, yeah maybe. But I might just stay in. I think Anna's out and it's nice and quiet here."

"Ok, love. I suppose you've got a busy week ahead of you. Have you got plans for the weekend?"

"Umm..." Skye blinked as the black screen won out. "Not yet. Maybe I'll arrange something, but I might just have a quiet one."

"You should go out, love! Make the most of it all!"

"I might. Anyway, I'll speak to you soon, Mum."

"Ok, bye love."

"Bye, Mum."

Skye flicked on the cable menu to find that she had a choice between yet another programme on obesity, something about the Scottish Lochs, multiple repeats of American comedies or *Emmerdale*. She opted for the latter, in remembrance of Mavis, though it didn't really matter; the TV was just a security measure in case Anna happened to came back early. If so Skye wanted her to think she was doing nothing more than just lounging on the sofa watching the tele, after a long but satisfying first day as a graduate PR Account Executive.

A bell tinkled as Skye pushed open the door to the vintage clothing shop on West End Lane on Saturday afternoon. She hesitated as her eyes adjusted to the dim lighting, then noticed a familiar figure on the other side of the boutique. She was flicking through a rail of skirts, holding some out before frowning and returning them to their hangers, and looked quite different in jeans and a sweater. But her scarlet glasses were unmistakable.

Skye inhaled a lungful of damp dust then headed over and tapped Suki on the shoulder. "Hey! It's Suki, right?"

Suki nodded and Skye noticed her eyes narrow slightly

146

as she re-hung a cord skirt.

"I'm Skye! I'm working at Edwards, too! Hasn't it been a long week? I had such a long lie in this morning, then a nice brunch. I feel so much better for it! I bet you're knackered too, and Di and Dan. It's been manic!"

Suki's frown faded slightly but the flicker of recognition Skye was waiting for failed to materialise. A wibble of embarrassment tickled her tummy. "You're one of the new grads, right...?"

"I am, I'm so sorry. It's been such a long week and we've been meeting so many people. I feel so rude, can we start again? Skye, you said?"

"Yeah. Actually I bumped into you in the toilets the other day - you dropped an earring in the cubicle and I chased after you to give it back! Umm...I..." Skye's cheeks felt hot as she silently berated herself for saying too much.

"Oh! Right! Skye, yes I'm with you. Listen, um, it's great to see you but I really have to head off and meet a friend. Do you live around here?"

Skye nodded.

"Me too, I'm further up off West End Lane. I'll probably see you around!"

"That'd be lovely! Maybe we could go for a drink sometime? I'm really keen to meet more people around here."

"Umm, sure! Anyway I've got to go." Suki raised her hand before turning and tip-tapping her way out of the shop.

Skye gazed after her then drifted across to a rack of colourful jackets, running her fingertips distractedly across the mixture of wool, corduroy and denim before trailing over to a selection of flares and drainpipe jeans. But although she tried to stay upbeat she could feel her shoulders slump and her heart become heavy as her lighter mood faded, to be replaced with an increasingly desperate sense of isolation at facing yet another

Saturday night alone.

For want of anything better to do Skye left the clothing store - which was out of price range anyway - and popped into the newsagent across the road, where she picked up a paper before mooching back home. She settled herself down on the sofa with a cuppa and became absorbed in the news, until a flashing red light caught her eye. She laid down the paper and picked up her phone to check her e-mail, and her heart skipped a beat when she saw the incoming address.

*Hi Skye,*

*It's Suki, from Edwards. I hope you check your work e-mail at home, it's the only way I can think to contact you! Anyway, I hope I didn't seem a bit off earlier, I just have a lot on my mind at the moment. I'm going out tonight with some friends and I wondered if you wanted to join us? Just a few girls heading down to The Alice House for a couple of cocktails and a natter, but it's a good excuse to get dressed up for a Saturday night! We'll be there about seven thirty.*
*E-mail me back, or give me a ring - 07468 4624934*
*Hopefully see you later!*

*Suki xx*

Skye immediately grabbed her mobile and entered Suki's number, then on second thoughts decided to send a breezy text. She typed out a message, thanking Suki for the invite and saying she would definitely be in The Alice House later, and within a few minutes her phone beeped and vibrated with a reply.

*Great! Look forward to seeing you. Have a nice afternoon, S x*

148

Skye blinked rapidly and shook her head from side to side. She picked the Weekend section of the paper off her lap and carried on reading where she had left off, a smile creeping over her face and that increasingly familiar glow reappearing, but this time in her stomach.

*　　　*　　　*

"Hey! Oh my God you look amazing, did you buy that dress in the shop we were in earlier?"

"Mm-hmm!" Skye nodded and laughed, pulling a few model poses to show off her frilly 1920's dress, teemed with black patent heels, a matching handbag and a string of plastic beads. Every hair on her head lay in its rightful place, her cheekbones were highlighted with bronzer and her eyelashes black as treacle. They sent shadows across her cheeks every time she blinked.

"Freezing outside, isn't it? You look stunning, Suki!"

Suki was dressed in an incredibly short black satin dress which flared out at the waist before coming into a tight hem around her thighs. Her hair hung down her back in a glossy velvet waterfall, and even from a couple of feet away Skye had been able to detect the scent of strawberries.

"Thanks! Hey, I'm glad you could make it tonight. The others are over there," she waved towards the back of the pub. "I got you one of these, hope you like fruity ones!" She handed over a glass of pale yellow liquid with half a passion fruit floating on top, then turned back to pick up the others. "Would you mind carrying this one? Cheers, let's go." And she glided off across the pub with Skye in tow, sipping on her tart yet mellow fruity cocktail and looking forward to a night of gossip, cocktails and dancing.

149

Skye jumped as she rolled over and her duvet slid off, exposing her naked body to the cold night air. The return to full consciousness caused a pulsation of guilt to punch at her insides. But didn't everyone have a vice? She didn't smoke (often), drink (excessively), swear or do drugs, and she had to get her kicks from somewhere; that uncomfortable five minute interlude with Suki had been the only thing of note to happen that day.

"It's just escapism," she whispered to the darkness. "It's just a place to go, where I can be who I want and do as I please. It's my sanctuary, where everything is good and safe and where there's nothing scary and no uncertainty. Where's the harm in that?"

Only silence replied.

## Chapter 2

"So when are you coming home to visit your old Mum and Dad? Have you forgotten all about us now that you're a top career girl? It's been months since we last saw you!"

"I know, Mum. I'm sorry. I've just been working a lot, and there's so much going on!" Skye sighed and rolled her warming tea mug across her forehead before taking the last sip. She put down the cup in the sink, eyeing the growing pile of dirty dishes guiltily.

"Oh, I know love, and I do understand. But we just miss you. What have you been doing today? Have you been out with your new friends?"

Skye squeezed her eyelids shut. "I've had a busy weekend actually, Mum. I went shopping yesterday and then out for drinks with some of the girls from Edwards. And today I went up Parliament Hill on Hampstead Heath. There was an awesome view, Mum! I could see right down into the City. I tried to find the Edwards office but obviously I couldn't, though I could see the Gherkin! It was really cool."

"Oh, that sounds lovely! Who did you go with?"

"Umm, I went by myself actually."

"Oh. Well what about those girls you've been talking about at your new job?"

"They were busy, Mum. And I wanted to go for a walk so I just set off on one. I'll see them next weekend."

"Oh good. I wouldn't want to think of you all by yourself up there."

Skye's eyes moistened as she mumbled something inane in response.

"Now listen, you are coming home for Christmas, aren't you?"

"Yes, of course."

"Good. Because that's our special family time isn't it? For just the three of us. We've got the sherry in already!"

Skye relaxed into a giggle, but then she caught sight of her cloud box and her mood sobered once more. With Christine's monologue about sherry, Baileys and Christmas pudding streaming out of the speaker Skye reached out and took off the lid. She slipped a hand inside and her fingertips brushed over a few leaves of paper before coming to rest on the cold metal of her silver bangle. She pulled it out and re-read the inscription, running her fingers over it as she was wont to do from time to time. She loved the mystery of that engraving and thrived on dreaming up possible stories and scenarios behind their significance. And she also loved knowing that she would never actually find out the truth.

"Are you listening to me, Louise?"

"Yes! Yes, Mum. Of course I am!" She dropped the bracelet back into the box, closed the lid and replaced it on the shelf.

"So, what do you reckon then? I need some help you know, this isn't an easy decision to make. Tesco or Sainsbury's?"

"Umm, Tesco...?" There was a pause.

"Yes, I think you might be right. Tesco is closer, after all. Let's get the Christmas pudding from there this year. Right I'd better go and have a look at them. Call us again soon, love!" And then she was gone.

Skye twiddled her phone in her fingers as she wondered what to do with the rest of her evening. She automatically scrawled down to check her Facebook account before remembering that she had deleted that when she had deleted Louise. She re-read through the last few text messages she had received, then did the same with her e-mails. She idly opened her browser to check the weather forecast but the connection was too slow, so she returned to the main menu, tickling the screen for a while as she gazed out the window into the oppressive white sky. The silence hummed in her ears.

For want of anything better to do she scrolled through her contact list and came to Shereela, which reminded her that Shree had sent a message a while back about some dinner or something. Skye reopened her inbox and searched for the message, then started typing out a reply before deciding that it would be nice to hear someone's voice.

"Shree? Hey! It's me!"

"Hey! How are you? I'm so glad you called, I've been wondering if you could make Saturday?"

"Yeah, sorry I completely forgot to reply, I've been so busy. It just came back to me so I thought I'd give you a ring. It's been a long time!"

"I know! So can you come on Saturday? I can't believe we haven't seen each other since the summer. We have to catch up before Christmas! Everyone'll be there and we really want to hear all about your new life!"

Skye coughed a few times. "Well, it's a bugger but we've got some work thing that night. But I'm going to try and come afterwards."

"No! That's not good enough! You have to be there, you've been AWOL for ages now and we want to be brought up to speed!"

Skye exhaled. "Ok, I'll be there! I'll just have a couple

of drinks and then head over to you lot."

"Great! Listen I gotta run, I have a late Skype meeting with the New York branch, you know what it's like!"

Skye made a sympathetic noise in the back of her throat.

"See you on Saturday! And you'd better be there!"

"I will be," Skye replied, but she spoke to a dead line.

Skye sank back into her pillows, exhausted from the hours she had been working. She felt her eyelids start to close but hauled herself up off the mattress and went into the kitchen, where she set up her cafetiere for the morning, and made a lunch of salad and couscous. Once that was ready and boxed up she returned to her room where she laid out her clothes for the following morning, then had a quick shower before sliding under the covers. One last glance at the clock showed that it was 21.37. Good, that still left plenty of time.

"Hold the lift!" Skye charged across the shiny white tiles at five to nine the next morning, clutching her grande latte and chocolate croissant and ignoring the smirk she received from the receptionist at the front desk.

"Made it!" She gasped, as she sucked leaking coffee off the plastic lid and bit into her breakfast, then she looked up and froze. Panic took over as she caught Dan's eye and swallowed hastily, wiping the back of her hand across her mouth to rid her lips of any crumbs or milky bubbles.

"Morning work out?"

He smiled, so that Skye became fixated on that tiny chip, imagining her tongue sliding over it and feeling the roughness of its edges in contrast to the smooth marble of his other teeth.

"What floor do you need?"

"Umm…third. Edwards." Like you, she added silently.

He leant over and pressed the button, brushing past Skye so that she could smell his citrus aftershave alongside the scent of fresh coffee.

"Want a mint?"

Skye shook her head, watching as he reclined against the side of the lift and extracted a tin from his pocket, then slipped a tiny white stone into his mouth. By the time they exited at the third floor she could smell the fresh scent on his breath. It made her knees knock like a starstruck schoolgirl.

As soon as he was out of sight Skye exhaled noisily, suddenly aware of how little oxygen she'd taken in during that short ride. She closed her eyes and collapsed against the wall, ramming her heel into it. She cursed at the dull pain that spread across the back of her foot, but at the same time relished in its distraction. Why the hell hadn't she spoken to him? She'd had her chance, after all those subtle looks and all that gentle corridor brushing, and she'd completely blown it. Idiot! Slurping on her coffee, which by now was lukewarm, she decided to pop back down to the ground floor and use the plush bathrooms there to pull herself together; she didn't want to face the Edwards lot while feeling so fragmented.

After splashing her face with cold water and patting her skin dry, Skye dusted on another layer of face powder and slicked on some lip gloss, then just about felt ready to face the day. She took a last glance in the mirror, breathed in deeply and wandered through the door. And couldn't believe it when she walked straight back into Dan.

"Hey, I'm glad I've caught you again! It's Skye, isn't it?"

"Um, yeah. Hi!"

"Dan."

Skye smiled.

"Hey, I'm on my way to a meeting but I wanted to ask

you if, um, if you'd like to go for dinner or a drink next week? I just, um, would really like to get to know you better."

Now he was the one flushing scarlet, and his nervousness enabled Skye to relax. She felt like she had gone up a dress size as she released her stomach muscles, but she also felt a lot cooler and more together.

"I'd love to. Take my mobile number and just drop me a text." Skye smiled coquettishly as she recited her number while he tapped it into his phone.

"Thanks, I'll be in touch." He grinned his sideways grin, his eyes reminding Skye of the sun reflecting on the sea on a bright summer's morning. "You like Thai food, right?"

Skye chuckled and nodded, as her thoughts briefly flickered back to that night with Amy. "I do. Look, I have to go and make a few calls now, sort out a few contracts. I'll see you soon, though."

"Oh yeah, you will." Dan winked as Skye turned on her heel and strode off down the corridor, feeling his gaze lingering on her rounded buttocks in her fitted skirt. She was pleased that she hadn't put on tights that morning, so he had the naked view of her spray tanned, toned calves rising up out of her new scarlet stilettos.

Later that day Skye was finishing off the photocopying, working on autopilot while letting her mind slip forward to a time when she would be the one waltzing off to expensive business lunches while the graduate dogsbodies did the monkey work. Her thoughts oscillated between her fantasy and what to have for dinner when she heard soft footsteps approaching from behind, and she turned to see Dan wandering up with a sheaf of paper covered in official looking print. Her heart jumped; who said 'be careful what you wish for'?

"Hey." His voice was gruff and sexy, much more

gravelly than usual. He blushed, clearing his throat. "I just need to..." he waved the wad of paper in the air.

"No worries, this is my last lot." Skye pressed the button to start her final bit of copying and picked up the warm leaves that had already come through the copier. But as she was shuffling the sheets her fingers slipped, and she watched in horror as they cascaded downwards before coming to rest on the deep blue carpet in a mass of giant, unruly snowflakes. She closed her eyes and sighed deeply, hoping that once she opened them it would all have been a mirage.

"Don't stress, it's ok. Let me just stick these in the copier and I'll give you a hand. Are they numbered?"

"Yes, thank God!" Skye exhaled loudly as she knelt on the floor, while Dan set up the copier.

She heard a few beeps, and then the shuffle of expensive materials rubbing together as Dan bent down to join her. He held her gaze for a few seconds, before reaching out for the first pile of paper.

They collected and collated to the rhythm of the machine, the sound of their breathing becoming more and more amplified; Skye was sure Dan would be able to hear the increased speed of the beating of her heart. Being the end of the day his personalised musky scent was breaking through his token citrus tang, and every time she caught a whiff of perfume she was glad she was sitting on the floor. Otherwise her legs might have given way.

"There, all done." Dan handed her the last few pages and she slipped them in behind her pile, thanking him for his help.

"No worries." He paused and she held his gaze, losing herself in that secretive smile that drew her to him. They seemed to stay there for ages, but it could only have been a few seconds before the copier beeped to announce that it was out of

157

paper, and Dan jumped up to sort it out. Skye tried to compose herself by running her hand through her hair and taking a few deep breaths before rising slowly, clutching her papers tightly to avoid a repeat performance.

"So..."

"Hold on a sec."

Skye waited until Dan had finished loading the paper tray, then he stood up straight and faced her properly.

"Listen, I was wondering if you fancied that drink tonight? If you're free. Don't worry if you're busy, I understand. We'll sort something else out for another day..." he trailed off and she picked up on the hope emitting from his eyes, relishing in the power she held over him for those few moments.

"Yeah, sure. I'll just go and dump this on my desk. Swing by when you're done and we'll head off." Her coolness retrieved, her demeanour composed, she turned on her heel and sauntered away.

Skye pulled herself out of her thoughts and back to the real world, feeling refreshed after a few minutes away from everything. She hauled herself up off the lid of the toilet, picked up her bag and wandered over to the sinks. As she struggled to break from the draw of her dreams she touched up her make up and forced herself to focus, and when she had asserted herself firmly in the building once more she headed off to get on with her day.

## Chapter 3

"Hey, wel...oh my God, Louise is that you? What have you done? I'd barely recognise you!"

Skye chuckled at Shereela's bulging eyes. "Hey! Let me in, it's freezing out here! And it's Skye now, remember? Everyone at work has adopted it, and it's just kind of stuck." She flicked her hair out of her eyes. "My feet are fucking killing me. I just need to...ahhh..." Skye exhaled in pleasure as she flicked off her heels then massaged the flaming ball of her right foot, winching at the icy touch of her fingers. "Have you got any blister plasters? My heels are messed up! Smells great, by the way. Garlic always smells so homely!"

"Yeah sure, I'll go grab you some. But Lou...Skye..." Shereela hesitated. "I mean, you look great. But you're completely different. Even your eyes! What's going on?"

"I just felt like a change, Shree." Skye hesitated under her friend's scrutiny, then returned her attention to her feet. "Anyway, can I get those plasters? I'm in agony here!"

"Yep, course. Everyone else is through there, except Ryan. I hope he's coming. Grab yourself a glass of wine on the way in! Oh, and hang your coat here. And Skye?"

"Mm hmm?" Skye paused in rubbing her feet, looking up to meet Shereela's gaze.

"You look amazing."

Skye returned Shereela's broad smile, hugging herself

tightly once she was alone in the corridor.

"Louise is here!"

Skye heard Shereela bellow down the hallway.

"Sorry, I mean Skye."

Skye paused as she picked up on the mockery underlying Shereela's tone, her heart racing and a chill shooting through her. She suddenly had an urge to crawl under the low level shelving, that boasted an impressive collection of nostalgic photographs, and hide. Perhaps never come out. But instead she shook her head briskly, pasted on her grin and headed towards the lounge.

"So what's with this Skye thing? Why have you changed your name? Isn't that a bit weird, after being Louise for so long?" Paddy frowned at Skye, before jerking in his seat as Maura delivered a rather obvious kick to his shins. "Ow! I was only asking!" His frown deepened to a scowl, which he aimed at Maura.

"It's ok. It's nothing, really. It just came about, as nicknames do, and I like it so I thought I'd adopt it properly!" Skye took a slug of her chilled glass of white as Paddy shrugged and went back to his Bolognese.

"I like it." Maura asserted, while Natalie nodded in agreement.

Skye smiled gratefully across the table, pleased to have their acceptance, yet annoyed that it mattered so much.

"Anyway," Nat continued. "You haven't filled us in on what's been going on with you lately. I know you've got so much to tell us!"

Skye eyed the scarlet tablecloth, suddenly feeling shy. They'd already covered Ollie and Shereela's wedding ideas, Paddy and Dav's summer holiday plans and Maura and Natalie's latest career developments, and Skye had been waiting for her chance to shine. She felt a rush of adrenaline as she launched into her tales of a new life in London, appreciating the captive audience and relishing her space on centre stage. She finally felt as thought she belonged, and it felt so good.

"You should be proud of yourself, I'm really pleased for you! It's all working out so well, and you've come so far since the summer! I'm even a little bit jealous!"

"Jealous, Nat? Of me? Why?"

"Yeah!" Maura piped up. "You just seem to have it all together, while the rest of us are trying our hardest but can't quite get there."

"What do you mean? You're all doing really well! I'm the late bloomer!"

"Not really," Maura curled her lip and poked at an overcooked corner of garlic bread lying on her plate. "It sounds good but underneath it all I'm just a glorified admin assistant, Natalie's pretty much a shop girl and neither of us are having an iota of luck on the man scene."

"I'm thinking of doing a PGCE next year."

The group turned to look at Paddy in surprise; he seemed the least likely person to become a teacher.

Paddy just shrugged. "There must be something else out there that pays well and leaves me feeling fulfilled. Dav's considering it too, actually. Can you pass the water? Ta."

"Really? But I thought you were doing really well in your job?' Skye turned to look at Paddy's girlfriend, noticing Dav recoil slightly from her almost accusatory gaze.

"Well, yeah. But like Paddy I just feel I could be doing something more worthwhile with my life. It's been a few years now and it's just not, you know. Not doing it for me, really."

"You and Ol are doing well though, aren't you? Where is he tonight, anyway?" Skye turned to look at Shereela, and

161

for the first time noticed the dull glaze to her eyes and the shadows underneath them. "Shree...?"

Shereela shook her head as her eyes filled up, and when she brushed them away Skye noticed her ring finger was bare. She felt her eyes widen and caught Natalie's eye over the table, but Shereela just sniffed and started clearing plates.

"He got held up at work, you know what these law firms are like. Anyway, let me just get rid of these." She tottered off into the adjoining kitchen and the group lapsed into silence.

"It's not quite how we hoped it would be, really. Is it?" Skye spoke tentatively, with a slight tremor in her voice.

"No." Maura and Natalie responded in unison, shaking their head dispiritedly.

"But you're doing really well, L - Skye!" Skye turned as Shereela came back into the room, the redness of her eyes having faded slightly to be replaced with a distant gaze. The corner of her mouth kept twitching. Skye was struck once again by how incredibly thin her friend had become since finishing her degree and examined her face, trying to detect her true emotions. "Aren't you? You and Ryan. Shame he didn't show up. He sent a text, by the way. Said he had some big gig to go to, or something. VIP list, after party, the lot!" Shereela smiled and placed her hand on Skye's arm. "We just wish we were as sorted as you guys, but I'm sure we'll all get there. Eventually. For now you can just enjoy being on top. Make the most of it and show off as much as you like! We are really happy for you, and we do hope your success continues." Shereela grabbed her glass of red and waved it dangerously over the white table cloth. "To Skye. May her career and man success continue!"

"To Skye!" The table echoed, before knocking back their glasses in sync.

Skye also took a gulp of wine, although this time it

didn't flow quite so smoothly down her throat. It seemed to have developed a bitter taste, so she knocked it back, then placed the glass on the table and slipped off to the toilet.

In the bathroom she eyed herself in the mirror. She smiled and the girl in the mirror smiled back. She looked happy, but Skye knew there was something restless flitting around in her stomach. She stared the girl out, daring her to flinch. Then, telling the girl in the mirror to stop worrying and to just enjoy her recent success and her friends' praise, Skye gave her hair a final toss before turning and heading back to the party.

## Chapter 4

"So, yeah. That's it really. We had a good time though, eh?" Ryan flinched as Kayla's elbow stabbed him in the ribs. "But, you know. I wanted to tell you straight away."

Ryan picked up his pint and held it to his lips, keeping it there until he had formulated an appropriate response. As he paused he felt as if he was being sucked away down a long tunnel, further and further away from the pub, until he was watching himself and Kayla from a distance. His body became a shell, fooling the outside world into thinking that he was present while the real Ryan hovered somewhere up in the corner of the lounge.

He fixed his eyes on Kayla and spoke slowly and deliberately. "You bitch."

Kayla's eyes widened, and Ryan felt adrenalin surge through his system as he watched the procession of expressions cross her face – confusion, disbelief, hurt and indignation, before she finally settled on anger. His hackles rose in preparation for an outlet. "You bitch! You were carrying on with him the whole time, weren't you?" Ryan had planned to stop there but he was enjoying the power trip far too much. He raised his voice. "You always knew you were going to go back to him, but just used me for a bit of fun on the side while you waited, eh? Eh?"

"Ryan!"

"No no, no no. Don't try and make it ok for me. I know I'm better off without you. Slut." He added the last word with a particularly cruel sneer, feeling a sense of satisfaction as Kayla started gathering up her coat and bag, turning to face him once she was free of the booth. But as she stood over him Ryan noticed how the look on her face had changed from one of pain to one of pity, and he felt his jaw shudder. He wanted to curl up into a tight, little ball and stay there for a very long time.

"You're a dick, Ryan." Kayla's voice was calm and each word clouted him like a breezeblock. "I thought you were a decent guy, but this! We only went out a few times! And you weren't exactly the most attentive date. I don't know what your problem is but deal with that yourself. And do not ever, *ever* speak to me in that way again."

"Oh, don't worry about that. I won't be speaking to you ever again, at all." It was the best he could do; suddenly he hated Kayla more than anything for rendering him so powerless and small, but now his poisonous energy exhausted rather than energised him. He picked up his pint and turned away from her. He was aware of her hesitation, then heard her stilettos trip-trap across the stone floor.

He only put his glass back down on the table when he was sure that she was gone - he couldn't risk her witnessing the tears that stung his eyes, or the solitary one that slipped down his cheek. As he went to brush it away he realised how much his hands were shaking, so he downed his last inch then stood up and strode out of the pub. It was only when he had got a few hundred yards down the street that he remembered he had forgotten to pay his tab. Fuck it, he thought, and carried on striding.

"So what's happening with that girl then? The one from The Horse?"

"Dumped her." Ryan muttered, without dragging his eyes away from a re-run of an old Simpsons episode. He could sense his face start to radiate as if his skin was lined with hot coals, and he gritted his teeth as he prepared for a ribbing. He felt the muscles in his throat tense, to stop the lump in his chest from reaching his mind. If they conjoined he might combust.

"Mate? Are you ok?"

Ryan looked up to meet Ash's eye, and his stomach quivered as he clocked the creases of concern etched into his housemate's forehead.

"Yeah, fine. Wasn't that into her anyway." He shrugged and turned back to the TV, but he didn't think he could keep face for much longer. His eyes were stinging and his throat convulsing. "I gotta go write an article, catch you later." It took more effort than usual to stand up, and when he started walking he felt as if he had a hundredweight pushing down on his shoulders.

"Hey, Ry," Ryan paused, but didn't turn round. "Um, do you want a pint later? Or a pizza? Or, um, something?"

Ryan squeezed his eyes shut. "Sorry mate, I've got to get this piece done tonight. Another time, maybe."

Once he reached his room Ryan checked that the door was closed, then slumped down on the carpet. A ball of fluff lay about 6 inches from his mouth, so he exhaled extra hard, watching it skip and dance across the fibres. The room started to blur as he let his eye muscles relax, and the last fragment of himself that had managed to linger in the wake of his conversation with Kayla slipped away, to leave his body as hollow as the tree he used to play in as a child.

After an indeterminable amount of time Ryan jolted out of a revelry and was surprised to find himself in the middle of his room, the Bournville curtains drawn tight and his angle poise providing a limited circle of light. The compass fell to the floor with a gentle thud, and Ryan stared down at the criss-cross pattern of red streaks he had carved into his forearm as if they had been made by someone else. Yet despite his inner horror he wanted to finish what he had started. Picking up the compass once more he found a fresh spot and placed the spike on skin as pale as milk. He relished in the feeling of life as he pressed down until he felt a pop, then he drew the compass down his arm, feeling the endorphins flooding into his system and allowing his muscles to relax. He threw back his head and inhaled deeply as he withdrew the compass, which still had the remains of 'Ryan 8T, hands off' tippexed on the side, then glanced down to watch the blood bubbling up to form little shiny pearls on the fresh opening in his skin. He brushed his right index finger over the graze, squashing the pearls and spreading the crimson ink. But when he saw the bloodied mess of his arm and the stain on his fingertips his heart started racing with shock and disbelief. He momentarily froze, before grabbing a damp towel that was strewn across the floor and scrubbing vigorously at the scratch. Then he wrapped the towel tightly around his forearm until his cuts were well and truly hidden, got into bed and wept until his body shut down.

The next morning Ryan felt surprisingly light. It was almost as if last night had happened to someone else in some other time, or perhaps the release had purged his system of the toxins that haunted it. At least for the time being.

Pushing back the curtains he felt a sense of calm emanating from within as he gazed out onto the clear sky, and a whisper of chilly air snaked in from between the single glazed panes. He suddenly felt inspired to move his body and feel the fresh winter morning kiss his skin, so he jumped out of bed, pulled an old pair of joggers up over his boxers and grabbed a wrinkled long-sleeved t-shirt off the floor. He nipped into the bathroom to sponge the browning-red smears off his arms - squashing down the nauseating sense of guilt that always boiled up the morning after - then covered up once more and bounced out of the flat.

Ryan managed a couple of miles before his lungs forced him to slow down. He had enjoyed the feeling of his feet pounding on the pavement, his leg muscles stretching and his lungs burning as he gulped in air as if he had been locked in a cell for the past year. He could feel the iciness trail through his system, and for the first time in far too long he felt like he was alive.

He hummed as he walked, trailing his hand across the side of slatted fence and dodging the cracks in the paving. Kayla slipped into his mind but he pushed her out again; he wasn't going to let anything spoil his rare moment of bonhomie.

"Hey! Excuse me, have you got a minute? Hello? Excuse me? Can you help a sec?"

"Um, yes? Me?" Ryan thumbed himself in the chest and looked around, but there was no-one else in sight. When he turned back to the woman she smiled and nodded so he stepped off the kerb, and straight into the path of a black Polo.

"Shit! Sorry!" He waved in apology as the driver ground to a halt, glaring and gesticulating through the windscreen, and scuttled across to the other side of the road, where a slim yet curvy brunette was stranded in the middle of a pile of carrier bags. He ran a hand along his brow in a lame attempt to wipe off the sweat, cursing himself for not having done so on the inside of his t-shirt when he had the chance, then took a few deep breaths as he approached her. She was only wearing a vest top with a pair of leggings, and as Ryan got closer he noticed that the hairs on her arms were standing on end, rising out of batches of tiny pimples. He glanced towards her chest to see if the effect was replicated there, then cursed under his breath and pulled his gaze away when he realised how obvious he was being.

"Hi." She smiled warmly and her eyelids lowered slightly. He wasn't sure if it was a reflex or not. "I'm sorry to bother you, I've just had this online shop delivered and the guy said he was running late and couldn't bring it upstairs. Would you mind helping me?" She started poking around in the groceries, and Ryan had to avert his gaze and count to ten as she bent down to reveal the perfect c-curve of her buttocks. "There's loads of cans and bottles and boxes and things. I'd be here all day!"

She turned her face up to his and he couldn't help but notice that her t-shirt was ballooning forwards, leaving a gulf between her neck and chest. He could just see down into the dark valley beneath, where he glimpsed a slither of crimson fabric.

"Can you manage a couple?"

"Uh, yeah. Sure." He took the bags she was proffering and followed her as she turned into the flat. He could smell a zingy, flowery scent trickling back in her path and couldn't stop himself from hardening as it diffused throughout his body. He dumped the bags in the hallway and ran back down for a few more loads.

"Last one!" Ryan called out, while hauling a bag of flour and sugar up the stairs.

"Thanks so much, I never could have moved that all by myself. I didn't even catch your name! I'm Cindy."

Ryan dropped the last bag in the kitchen, turning to grin at Cindy as she blew a few strands of hair out of her eyes.

"Tom's such a useless pillock, and I can't believe those delivery men wouldn't bring it up. And they pack it so badly that all the heavy stuff is in the same bags. I'm definitely going back to Ocado next time. Anyway, do you want a cuppa?"

"Lovely, thanks. I'm Ryan, by the way." Ryan turned and wandered back towards the hallway. "Let me just get that bag of detergents, where do you want it?"

When there was no response he hesitated, suddenly acutely aware of an increased tension in the room; it made the soft skin on his upper inner arms tingle. He turned around slowly and Cindy was stood right behind him, her piercing green eyes gazing daringly into his and her full lips only centimetres away. The tang of fresh sweat overrode the flowery scent of twenty minutes earlier, and the self-consciousness that Ryan had managed to quash during the rhythmic lifting and carrying resurfaced with a vengeance. He felt his face flame, while inexplicable itches broke out over his body like chicken pox.

"In the bedroom." Cindy replied, and before he could think she had grabbed him in a steely grip and planted her lips on his. He felt her tongue prise its way into his mouth, and at that point his senses returned. He swung round to gather Cindy up in his arms and they stumbled down the hallway, and into the bedroom at the far end.

A short while later Ryan lay staring at the ceiling, fixated on a tiny patch of damp in the corner. He couldn't quite connect up the course of the morning's events in his mind, and every now and then would experience a brief moment of confusion when he would temporarily forget who was next to him and run through a few possibilities before it all came back. When Kayla entered his mind he felt flooded with guilt, but that was far more bearable that the emptiness that arose when he thought of Zoe and imagined, just for a second, that Cindy was her. The void in his belly was like a relentless hunger, a million times worse than the physical emptiness he experienced after a night on the tiles. And that one could be relived with a Big Mac, some crisps and a few black coffees. But he couldn't think about that now.

"That was amazing." Ryan propped himself up on his arm and gazed down at Cindy, sprawled naked and sweaty on the mint green duvet. "You are amazing." He leant over and kissed her nipple, running his tongue over the ridges of her areola while turning his head to meet her eye. Cindy grinned back, before pushing him away and pulling herself up on her elbows.

"I know. But you have to go now. Tom'll be back soon."

"Tom?" Ryan reached out to brush his fingers up her leg, but she batted him away. "Who's..." He trailed off as his eyes finally took in the ties, aftershaves and loafers dotted around the room, and his mind flickered back to the Tom Cindy had mentioned earlier, that he had conveniently repressed to the back of his mind. "Hang on. You have a boyfriend. And he lives with you?"

"Well, not a boyfriend as such. More of a...well...a husband."

"A husband? You're married?!"

"Well, yeah." Cindy shrugged. "Didn't you notice the ring? Most men do."

Ryan glanced down and clocked the gold band on her finger, wondering how he possibly could have missed it. Then he looked up and frowned. "Most men?"

"Yeah. They usually know the score, or at least work it out. I mean, it's hardly rocket science, is it?"

As she spoke Ryan noticed the crow's feet around her eyes. They weren't too dramatic, but definitely present. Her visage had a kind of heaviness to it that Zoe and Kayla's lacked, and her neck was saggier than he had realised. And

172

then a thought struck his stomach like the judder of a ferry across the English Channel.

"You checking me out?" Cindy chuckled. "I'm not quite what you're used to?"

Ryan flushed. "No, no. You're great. I mean, you know. But, um, does that mean…do you have children?"

Cindy held his gaze for a moment and he felt his blood run cold, while his stomach trembled again. Then she threw back her head and laughed. "You're sweet. You're just what I need, you can come again. Ooh yes, you sure can." She winked at Ryan, who felt his face heat up even more.

"So…?"

"No. I don't have children. That a relief?"

Ryan breathed out and felt his gut begin to settle. "Well, yes." He attempted a grin. "But is this, um, what you, like, do?"

Cindy sat up properly, her stomach creasing in the middle and her hair settling just on the top of the ridges of her breasts. "Look, kiddo. I'm bored. My marriage is a mess and I've just lost my job. I saw you down there and thought we could have some fun, which we did. If you're freaked out then just go, if not leave your number and go." Her face softened into a grin. "And maybe we can catch up sometime."

She leaned over and kissed him ever so softly, and Ryan took the opportunity to cup her breast. He brushed over the gentle flesh then tweaked her nipple, at which point she pulled away.

"But now you have to leave. Right now. But come back soon. And next time take your shirt off." And with that she walked into the bathroom and turned on the shower.

Ryan dressed his lower body and sat on the edge of the bed, wondering whether he should wait for Cindy to come out of the shower or just head off. He fiddled with the satin edging of the duvet cover, then caught sight of himself in the mirror.

His hair was matted down and his skin paler than he had realised. A cluster of spots has broken out in the corner of his mouth and his eyes were ringed with dark shadows. He caught his own gaze in the mirror, but barely recognised the person staring back at him. The eyes were empty, the alien euphoria of the past few hours having drained right out the back of them, and as if on cue the inner hollowness returned as quickly as it had vanished. With it came a growing sense of dislike for the person he was staring out. As he heard Cindy turn off the shower taps he stood up quickly and slipped out of the bedroom door, but not before scrawling his number on top of a pile of post-its perched on top of her dressing table.

Once he arrived home Ryan sat down at his desk and opened up his laptop. He had a couple of reviews due and was running late with one of them, which was not a good look having only written for Music Mania for a short while. But, despite his inner ambition, he was struggling to make himself really care; it was like there was a massive boulder resting on top of his creativity, and until he shifted that rock his spirit couldn't be released.

'Bolts and Vaults: great band, shame about the name,' he wrote, then instantly hit delete.

"Bolts and Vaults, a band for...no that's shit too," Ryan twirled a pencil around his fingers. "Bolts and Vaults: The Band for the New Year." He sighed. It was completely unoriginal and would never stand out in a crowd, but at the moment it was the best he could do; he'd try and come up with something more catchy for the re-edit. He started typing and banged out 300 words in no time. They were far from his best but at least they were on screen, and that was the absolute best he could hope for right now.

## Chapter 5

"Shall we go and surprise her? I want to see where she works! We could just pop in, say hi, give her a plant and then leave. I think she would love it! We could make a short break out of it, and get our Christmas shopping done in Harrods while we're there!"

Mike rolled his eyes as Chris took the paper out of his hands, the soft skin under her chin wobbling as she created her plan.

"What? Expand."

"Well," Chris laid a pale hand, scented with lavender and showing the coffee coloured stains of ageing, on Mike's thigh. "I think we should go away to London for a few nights, stay in a nice hotel, get the Christmas shopping done and pop into Lou's - or Skye's - office and give her a plant!"

Mike felt a cloud of irritation descend over him. "I don't know why you insist on playing along with that," he snapped, placing his weathered hand on top of Chris's so that he could feel her soft down beneath his dried cracks. "Why change her name? And why to Skye, of all things? We need to talk to her properly about all this. Anyway, you said you were going to stick with Louise."

"Mike, leave it. You know what we said. If it makes her happy then that's enough for us."

"I just think...I don't know." Mike sighed. "Don't you

think…?"

"No, Mike! She just wants something a bit more trendy, everyone out there now is called Skye, or Breeze, or Tree…"

"Tree? Really?" Mike raised his eyebrows but restrained from further comment when Chris eyed him sharply.

"No-one wants a regular name anymore! That's just the way of the twenty-first century, things are different now." Chris got to her feet and picked up a couple of empty tea cups that were scattered across the coffee table. Mike hesitated then sighed again, feeling trapped between the two walls that just kept closing in on him.

"Ok, ok. We'll leave it there. But why do we have to take a plant?"

"It's what you do! When someone starts in a new job! She'll like a nice potted flower for her desk, it's what every young career woman starting out needs. Now, shall we get a cyclamen or a little fuchsia? She always loved that fuchsia as a child. Remember how mad you used to get when she popped all the buds? Perhaps we should get her one of her own now, so she can pop the buds as often as she likes without having her pocket money taken away from her!"

"What? What are you talking about?"

"Oh, never mind. Fuchsia it is. Come on, let's get down the garden centre. We can go up in the morning!"

"Ooh here we are Mike, look - Edwards, Greenwood and Benjamin Media PR. That's the one! Gosh, doesn't it look smart?"

"Is it *all glass*? You can see everything that's going on in there! Look at those people having a meeting. Look at that man scratching his behind!" Mike guffawed as he gazed up at the post-modern construction towering over him. "And does anyone ever walk on those floors? They're gleaming!"

He eyed the constant stream of people dashing in and out of the complex, carrying laptops and disposable coffee cups. A rally of police cars screamed past as a continuous stream of taxis pulled up at the pavements, bored drivers watching office workers rummaging around in wallets filled to bursting, hoping that payment would be succeeded by those heavily sought after words 'you can keep the change'. Scarlet double-deckers roared along the street, their fits and starts interrupting the underlying buzz of murmuring interspersed with cries of vendors distributing free papers. But despite being in the middle of the city the air smelled surprisingly clean - gone were the days when buses would announce their arrival and departure with a puff of black smoke - and the bright mid-winter sun added to the clarity of the atmosphere.

"But it certainly is smart," Mike concurred, nodding in appreciation, and in truth feeling rather overawed. Of course he'd known that his daughter was all grown up now, but to actually be stood outside this building made the situation hit home. His little baby girl, once just a helpless bundle in his arms, was now living a real adult life. And where did that leave him?

"Well, come on then. Let's go in!"

Mike jerked out of his revelry as Chris pulled at his arm, dragging him up to the front doors - again, glass - of the block.

"Chris, are you sure this is a good idea? She might be busy. I'm still not sure she'll appreciate us turning up unannounced in the middle of the day to give her a pot plant."

"Oh, she'll love it. You know how much she used to love that fuchsia!" And before Mike had time to reciprocate she was pushing on the glass panel and poking her nose into the foyer. "Come on!" She turned and hissed at her husband, before striding in through the door and tapping over the tiles

177

towards the reception desk. Mike took his last breath of outside air and followed his wife, wishing he was back at home, slouched on the sofa with a beer.

But the heated foyer was a pleasant contrast to the chill outside, and the scent of freshly brewing coffee and toasting croissants coming from a snack counter in the corner made Mike feel marginally more relaxed. Until the Receptionist looked up as he followed Chris across the hall; he couldn't miss the look of bemusement that flashed over her face before she arranged her features into a welcoming smile. Although if Mike been watching the scenario he knew that he, too, would have found the whole thing rather entertaining: two old biddies strolling into this flash office in their winter coats and walking shoes, Chris clutching her potted fuchsia and Mike with his khaki Karrimor slung over his shoulder. But being there and actually living the scene was incredibly uncomfortable, and he had a sudden flashback to the secondary modern where he'd never quite felt that he fitted.

"Good morning, can I help you?" The receptionist had long, sleek black hair tied back in a low knot. It contrasted with her white trouser suit, while matching the black shirt under her gleaming jacket. Her skin was pale, though her lips had been painted blood red, and it looked as if she hadn't had a good meal since she exited her teens. Which, on reflection, was probably only about six months ago. Now if that had been part of the secondary modern the whole experience might have been a lot more bearable. Mike shook his head brusquely and reminded himself of his seniority.

"Yes, we're looking for our daughter. She works for Edwards, Greenwood and Benjamin. In PR." Chris added the last part with a confident nod of the head, and Mike hid a smirk as he thought of their conversation on the train, where he had spent at least an hour just getting the correct abbreviation into

Chris's head. He'd sidestepped the explanation of what Louise actually did for a living by going to the buffet car, as he wasn't really sure what Lou's days comprised of himself, but wasn't quite ready to admit that.

"Ok, can I take her name? I'll call through to the third floor and ask her to come down. Please take a seat over there."

Chris frowned at the Receptionist. "I think you'll find it's the eighth floor. That's what she told us."

The girl smiled her toothy smile, but this time it didn't reach her eyes. "I assure you it's the third. I'm very well acquainted with some of the Edwards staff, and they are certainly on the third floor. Now, if you'll just wait over there. What's her name?"

"Louise. Worthington. Now come on." Mike aimed the instruction in his wife's direction and led her away by the arm, making soothing noises as Chris muttered on about how she was sure that Louise worked on the eighth floor, and why would her own daughter lie to her?

They sat down tentatively on the plush white sofas, and Mike worried about leaving marks or creases in the expensive leather. Why did everything have to be so *white*? It was almost clinical. If he worked here he'd live in constant fear of trailing mud through the halls, spilling his coffee or scratching a surface. What was wrong with those normal office blocks with grey carpets, wooden furniture and fabric covered seats?

But Mike was interrupted in his internal rant by the black and white receptionist, who came over with her fake smile pasted on once more. As she approached Mike noticed that she had a badge pinned to her lapel, and with a squint he managed to read her name: Eve.

"Hi," Eve's grin widened further until it looked set to take over her entire face. "I spoke to Khadijah upstairs, and I just need to confirm your daughter's name. She's a bit too tied

179

up at the moment to come down herself. Is she a graduate?"

"Oh, yes," Chris replied, "she studied in Aberystwyth, you know. She did History with Geography and she did really well. We were so proud of her. She was working as an accountant before she came here, and we were so pleased that she got the opportunity to do what she really wanted..."

"That's great! I was just wondering really whether she was on the graduate scheme or not, so I know where to look for her."

Mike took over as Chris flushed scarlet. "Yes she is a graduate, and her name is Louise Worthington. Thank you, Eve." He inclined his head towards her name badge and she smiled a natural smile this time. Her sharp veneer fell away like a snake's disused skin and she suddenly looked like a sweet, young girl.

"I thought that was what you said. I'll phone through for you." As she strode off towards her desk Mike prided himself on not gazing after her, but instead turning back to his blushing wife and placing a comforting hand on her thigh.

Mike and Chris watched as Eve dialled a number into the phone and waited for someone to speak. They saw her talk confidently and cheerily, then watched as she paused before turning back to the older couple, a quizzical expression on her face. She frowned in their direction, then nodded her head assertively. After a few more shakes of the head and a deepening frown she hung up the phone, stood and walked back over to where Chris and Mike were waiting.

"That was Khadijah on the phone, and she doesn't know of a Louise Worthington. You're sure she's a new grad, yeah?"

"Oh, yeah." Mike blinked a few times. "She's, um, going by Skye these days. I didn't realise that name had spread to her professional circle. I assume she's still using

180

Worthington, would you mind checking again?" His scalp seemed to tighten up so he shook his head to release it.

"Of course not, I'll go and call through."

The Worthingtons watched once more as she picked up the internal phone and re-dialled the extension number for Edwards. A repeat of the earlier conversation ensued, only this time Eve appeared more agitated than before. The call ended with her slamming down the phone and lowering her head into her hands, before she brushed a few loose strands of hair out of her face and once again got out of her chair.

"Um, Khadijah doesn't seem to know of a Skye either. We're a bit confused actually, I think we must have crossed wires somewhere along the line. Anyway, she's coming down now to talk to you. She won't be a minute."

Mike smiled as Eve retreated behind the desk, pulling herself up to her full height and opening up a file rather grandiosely.

"So what's going on?" Khadijah's abrupt tones easily reached Mike's ears though the echoes of the foyer and he watched Eve jump, even though she'd been expecting Khadijah's imminent arrival.

"Well, that couple over there say that their daughter, Louise Worthington, is one of the graduates in your department. Only she's started to go by the name of Skye, so they're not sure which name she's using now. Do you know her?"

Khadijah frowned but ignored Eve's question, instead turning and striding across the glossy surface to the sofa.

"Hi, I'm Khadijah. From Edwards." She extended her arm and shook hands with Chris and Mike. "How can I help?"

"Look, I'm sorry to cause you any bother. Our daughter started working here a few months ago and we're down in London doing some shopping, and we just wanted to pop in

181

and say hello."

"And give her this fuchsia plant. It's her favourite, you see, when she was a child…"

Mike elbowed Chris and she abruptly swallowed her words.

"Look, it doesn't matter. She's probably busy. Could you just tell her that we came by? Louise Worthington is her name, but she also goes by Skye." Mike spoke confidently but eyed Khadijah warily. It didn't feel right to be in the presence of such an evidently powerful woman, who yet again appeared young enough to be his daughter.

"I'm not actually sure I know who you mean. Are you sure you're in the right office?" Khadijah's coffee coloured skin wrinkled up above her glasses.

"Yes." Mike answered with more conviction than he felt, as something else came back to him. Hadn't Louise said her boss was called Shirley? He could have sworn she had, and 'Shirley' sounded nothing like 'Khadijah'. Although who knew how many bosses Louise had in this place? "We've looked up the office on the internet, and it's definitely this one. I think she has a friend called Suki, and she once mentioned someone called Di. And a young man I believe, called Dan."

Khadijah had started blinking too frequently, and her mouth had become a line; Mike was acutely aware that she must have a thousand better things to do with her time than this.

"Yes, I know Suki, Di and Dan, they started working for me recently. I do apologise, I must have got some names muddled up. I'm afraid the graduates are all busy at the moment. Can I just take a message?"

"Yes, that would be great, thanks very much." Mike went to stand up but as he was gathering himself together Chris sprang to her feet, holding out the fuchsia towards Khadijah.

182

"Can you give her this? Just to put on the corner of her desk to remind her of us. Please? And just tell her that her parents came by and that we are *so* proud of her!"

For the first time in a very long while Mike wished that the ground would open up and swallow him whole, as Khadijah rather rigidly reached out towards the proffered pot plant. She assured Chris that she would pass it on - although Mike wasn't convinced it would reach its destination - shook hands with the couple again, and led them to the door. With a huge sigh of relief Mike stepped out the futuristic bubble, and back into the something vaguely resembling familiarity once more.

*      *      *

"So where were you the other day? Did you get the message? We came in to surprise you and no-one could find you! You must have been so busy."

"What?"

"Did no-one pass on the message? We brought you a plant for your desk, a fuchsia like you used to love…"

"You did *what?*" Skye's breathing got shallower and her heart felt as if was about to implode.

"Yes we met Eve, the receptionist, and we met your boss Khadijah, though she was being all weird and claimed she didn't know who you were. We were a bit confused but then figured it must be something to do with staff security, after all we could have been terrorists or anyone! Anyway she took the fuchsia and said she'd pass it on to you, did you get it? Skye?"

Skye finally managed to inhale deeply, feeling her anger manifest itself in the tense muscles at the back of her neck and the jelly-like sensation at the pit of her stomach. Her muscles contracted until they felt too small for her body while her veins became flooded with a chomping and restless stream

183

of energy.

"Don't you ever, *ever* do that again, do you hear?"

"What? Louise! We just wanted..."

"No! Don't you *dare* come into my office, my workplace, in the middle of the day, without even telling me that you're going to call." As Skye raised her voice she could sense Chris drawing away from the receiver.

"Louise, I mean Skye, I'm sorry." Her mother's voice sounded distant. "We didn't mean to upset you, we just wanted to see where you worked. We've been so excited about your job and we haven't seen you for ages. You never come and visit, and we miss you."

Skye dropped her shoulders, suddenly feeling ready to collapse into bed. "Ok! Ok. Listen, I will come home soon. It's nearly Christmas, anyway. Just don't ever, *ever* call on me unexpectedly again. Clear?"

"Yes. I'm sorry." Chris spoke meekly. "And L...Skye? You are coming home for Christmas, aren't you?"

Skye rubbed her fingertips over her eyes, pressing them into the brow bone and taking comfort in the pressure and support. "Yes. I'll be home for Christmas. But I have to go now, I'm at work." She hung up without saying goodbye, gathered up her things, grabbed her coat and headed down to the foyer.

As the lift doors slid open she caught sight of a familiar looking male draped over the reception desk, chatting to that perfectly preened receptionist, Eve. Skye set out across the tiles to the sound of a tinkling laugh, and turned just in time to see Eve flick her jet-black sideways fringe out of her eye and smile flirtatiously at Dan. Skye felt a bubble of jealousy form in her stomach while a wobbly sensation spread to her bowels. After a second of deliberation she scurried towards the main doors, praying that she would be able to slip out unnoticed, and made for the safety of Starbucks. She ordered her standard skinny latte with a lemon and poppy seed muffin and went over to her usual window seat, attempting to stem the wobbles that continued to unsettle her stomach. But she couldn't manage a crumb. Instead she gazed out of the window, feeling her mind drift away from her body as she allowed herself to slip off from her boring and disturbing morning and into her realm of safety.

She'd only been there a few minutes when she heard someone approach from behind, and felt a tap on her shoulder. Jumping out of her revelry she glanced upwards and saw a handsome blond man towering over her, smiling a twinkly smile and revealing a crooked and chipped front tooth. Her heart warmed in spite of itself.

"Hey, mind if I join you?" Dan plonked his espresso down on the table and pulled out a chair, lowering his tall body into it before leaning back with a contented sigh and placing his hands behind his head. "Why didn't you wait for me?"

"Hmm?"

"When you were leaving? I was just in the foyer, I thought you saw me but you walked straight past!"

"Oh! Well, you looked kind of busy. You were chatting to Eve, or whatever her name is." She waved her hand dismissively.

Dan chuckled. "Chatting to Eve? Don't tell me you're jealous!"

He looked so pleased with himself. Part of her wanted to punch that cocky, arrogant face, but a larger part wanted to jump on him and stick her tongue down his throat.

"No." She turned to look out of the steamed up window, breathing in deeply so that the scent of coffee tickled the back of her throat.

"You are! You're jealous!" He turned his taunt into a song and leant over the table to chuck her chin, but she pushed his hand away.

"Oh, fuck off." But she failed to hide the grin that insisted on creeping out the side of her mouth, the relief washing over her like a wave of warm water.

"You're smiling!" He sang, before taking a swig of his coffee. She tried to glare at him but couldn't keep a straight face. Instead she picked up her napkin, balled it up and threw it at his face.

"I said fuck off, you." But she spoke without conviction, and he just grinned cheekily back.

"Listen, Skye, I was asking Eve to update my personal record. That's it."

She looked up and this time his eyes were serious.

"I've just moved, so I had to change my address. Look, I've got to go. I just wanted to come and snatch a quick coffee. With some good company." His face crinkled into another grin as he stood. "See you back at the office?"

Skye nodded in response.

"Oh, and I was wondering, are you going to the Christmas drinks this weekend?"

"Um, yeah. I think so."

"Great! I'll look forward to seeing you there, then." He raised his hand and was gone.

Skye blinked as her eyes focused on the empty seat opposite her, then reality struck her jowls like a dead weight and her eyes misted over.

That night, despite the glaring truth in the scene that she had witnessed between Dan and Eve earlier that day, Skye couldn't stop herself from slipping over to the other side. She lay in bed wide awake, picturing a single yellow rose perched on her dresser, and before she knew it the flower had become real. She leant over and sniffed it before flopping back on the pillows and hugging herself in happiness. Once again she re-read the card in her head, and when she finally turned out the light she could still make out the shape of the flower through the haze of orange shining in through the window. She closed her eyes and as she slipped into a deep slumber felt Dan's arms wrap around her. She snuggled into him as he dropped a soft kiss on the top of her head and laced his fingers through hers, and listened to his breathing slow down before she drifted off to sleep herself.

## Chapter 6

Ryan frowned at the screen as he tried to decide which question was the most pressing to answer: whether he had descended from vampires, had a hidden penchant for cannibalism or if he was gay. As he felt pretty confident about the answer to the last two questions he clicked on the link that would tell him whether or not he was related to Dracula, then flicked onto Facebook while the page loaded up. An old friend from sixth form had shared a video of an obese man doing the haka in a mankini, but it wasn't as entertaining as he had hoped.

"Want a coffee, Ry?"

"Shit, Ash! You scared the crap out of me, I thought you were at work!"

"Sorry man! I'm starting late, finished late with a client last night and seeing another one tonight. Coffee?"

"Yeah, cheers." Ryan wandered into the kitchen where Ash was fiddling with the coffee machine. The room smelled toxic with the scent of undigested vodka. "Good night?"

"Yeah, alright. You get your work done?"

"Uh-huh, yeah. Bit last minute but got there in the end!" Ryan joked as he took the coffee from Ash, but he didn't really find it funny. He had just about managed to get his articles in by the deadline, but Lara had said that the one on The Tyres wasn't up to scratch, which worried him. Not so much because the work wasn't good enough – that feedback hadn't been a surprise – but more the fact that he still couldn't bring himself to care. His motivation levels were at an all-time low, and whenever he tried to write he would end up watching nonsense on Youtube, reading ridiculous articles or pissing about on Facebook, before garbling out a review at the eleventh hour and getting it in right before the bell.

"Ryan? You there? I said have you got any mate's rates for your gigs then? Or are you giving them all to your new woman?"

Ryan grinned smugly. "Nah, she's not fussed. But I have tickets for Arena this weekend if you fancy it?"

"Yeah! Cheers mate!"

Ryan's phone beeped across the room.

"Is that her? Look at you go! She's got you whipped mate, you need to watch that!"

Ryan opened the message from Cindy, which was the first thing that had happened that day to make getting out of bed worthwhile. The thought of her lying out on the bed next to him, her breasts glowing in comparison to the tanned skin around her bikini marks and her pubic hair waxed into a tiny narrow strip, sent him scurrying off to change, downing his coffee as he went. "Catch you later mate! Gig is on Sunday."

"Laters." Ash called out. "Whipped, you wanker!"


"And then where would we go?" Ryan nuzzled Cindy's hair and ran his hand along her abdomen. Her roots were scented with chemicals and he could see a tiny smear of chocolate-brown dye behind her left ear. "Mmmm, I love holding you like this afterwards."

"Well," her voice was husky and drew him into the middle of a cocoon. "From the coast we would drive down to Paris, and spend some time there in the cafes and plazas, and do the sites. You could write that novel you're always banging

190

on about and I would learn French, then I could get a job in a pension."

Ryan chuckled, although the dig about his unwritten novel triggered a ripple of irritation at the base of his spine. He shifted uncomfortably on the laminate flooring. It was the first time he had experienced that kind of animosity towards Cindy, and he had a flashback to that irrational cloud that had cast such a shadow over his relationships with Zoe and Kayla. But he opted to smile through it. "Sounds like something out of an old novel. Paris in the1920s...would we drink champagne and go to the Moulin Rouge?"

"*Bien sur!* Maybe we'd just stay there. We could get a holiday house in the country and share our time. I have savings, they'd keep us going."

"Hmmm...sounds amazing." Ryan slid his hands up her body, starting to relax as physical sensations took over from the emotional. "Let's do it!"

"Hey, your scratches have healed well!"

Ryan froze as Cindy lifted up his left arm. He allowed his eyes to glaze over as he stared at the handle of the front door, too tense to even blink.

"I can't believe you got yourself so fucked up falling into a holly bush on the piss. I thought you'd been slashing yourself or something!" Cindy laughed before wriggling around to face him, her coarse pubic strip brushing against his penis as she righted herself. The friction caused a bolt of lightening to dart through him, despite every single nerve ending in his body already standing to attention. He squeezed out an awkward chuckle and turned his head away, gasping in a breath before turning back to face her.

"Hey Cind, I wanted to ask you something."

"Yeah?" She entwined her fingers in his hair.

"Do you want to, like, *do* something some time? Go for

191

dinner, or drinks? Or maybe come out with me and my mates or come to one of the gigs? I've been meaning to ask you for a while but I keep getting distracted..."

"No." Cindy kissed him but for the first time Ryan pulled away.

"Why not?"

She sighed and sat up straight, her fingers now scraping back her own tendrils. "Ryan, we're not like that. Come on, look around you. I'm married!"

"But..."

"And I'm nearly old enough to be your mother. We're doing something now, and this is just fine. I don't want a boyfriend, I don't want a full on affair. Just your standard, dirty fling on the side between a bored housewife and her sexy toyboy. Those are my cards, and there they are on the table." She raised her eyebrows and licked her lips. "So, do you still want to play?"

Ryan held Cindy's gaze for a few seconds, although it felt like an age. Once she broke his gaze he reached for her once more, ignoring the part of his mind that screamed out for Zoe and her tender love-making. He told himself to man-up; he was living the dream, banging a hot housewife who didn't want anything more than a brusque, passionate fuck when her husband was at work, without any strings, drama or commitment. But, the problem was, Ryan wasn't sure exactly whose dream it was.

"Hello?"

"Ryan, it's Maura!"

"Maura! Your number didn't come up. How are you doing?"

"Yeah, you know. Same old, just plodding along. Thought I'd give a ring and see how you are, we missed you at

Shereela's the other night."

"I know, sorry about that. Something came up. Good night?"

"Yeah. Well, kind of. A bit half-hearted, actually. Everyone seems a bit low at the moment. And I think Ollie and Shree and breaking up."

"Huh?"

"Yeah, I don't know, but he wasn't there, she wasn't wearing her ring. She said he had to work late but she was practically crying. No-one's been able to get anything out of her though, and we're all worried."

"Shit. I never saw that coming."

"I know, we all thought they were solid, eh? Anyway. How are you holding up? How is the writing?"

"Yeah, good! Still doing my reviews, though not quite as many as I'd like. I'm trying to scout out some paid freelance stuff as well, and I've made a start on my novel! Well kind of. I have a title." Ryan thought back to how his screen had looked when he left the flat, the title of his novel and his name sitting in the middle of a glaringly empty page, double-underlined, italicised and in bold, while Facebook and Youtube flashed away at the bottom of the screen. He'd told himself that it was a start, and that he could take a break now that he had something on screen. But Cindy's jibe had taken the sense of achievement out of getting even that far. Who was he really kidding?

"Cool! What is it?"

"I can't tell you that! If I did I would have to kill you!"

Maura chuckled. "Ok. Well, I must say you sound a lot happier than you have in a long time." She hesitated. "There's something I need to tell you, though."

"Go on."

"I saw Zoe the other day."

"Mm-hmm." Ryan that wobble in his gut that had been dormant for some time now.

"She's moving to New Zealand."

Ryan stumbled into a lamp post, wrapping his free arm around it to enable him to carry on standing.

"Ryan? You still there?"

"Yeah, I'm here."

"I'm sorry to have to say this, I just thought you'd want to know. She said she wanted a fresh start, after everything that had happened. I'm not sure what she meant by that, though...?"

Ryan remained silent. A fresh start, eh? That sounded like a good idea.

"Anyway, I think she misses you. I'm not convinced this is what she really wants. Maybe you could...I don't know."

Ryan cleared his throat, feeling his arms tense up and his eyes glaze over. "Too late, I'm afraid. I've moved on, I'm with someone else now."

"I know, that Kayla girl. I just didn't get the sense that you were that bothered by her and I thought..."

"Maura, due respect and all that, but I don't need this. Zoe and I are over, that's all there is to it, and it doesn't concern anyone else. I finished with Kayla a while back, when she got too clingy, and I've met someone wonderful now. So it's all ok, and I hope Zoe will be very happy down under. I don't need you to mediate between us, ok? There's nothing to say, and if there was then we would say it ourselves."

"Ok Ry, I hear you. Let's catch up soon, ok? I have to run now."

"Yeah, sure. See you soon."

"Bye, hun."

"Bye Maura. Love you."

"You too. Take care."

"Bye." Ryan cut the call, felt in his back pocket to

194

check that the envelope was still there, then turned off down Cindy's road.

## Chapter 7

Eve sat at her computer, staring at the fuchsia plant which still sat where Khadijah had dumped it, and puzzling over the morning's events. She felt drawn to the older couple, who were so warm and loving - granted also a little bit quirky - and triggered happy memories of her own family life, and she wanted to deliver their gift to their daughter; she'd love it if her parents would walk in out of the blue and deliver a pot plant for her desk. But Chris and Mike must have wandered into the wrong office, and Eve could hardly trawl all the PR offices in London until she came across this Louise/Skye Worthington. Though how did they know about the others on the graduate scheme? Eve picked up the pot and fingered the cerise bells as she turned on her computer.

A few moments later, with a furtive glance up and down the sterile corridors, she clicked on the internal staff database icon, chewing anxiously on her scarlet lower lip and tapping her perfectly manicured nails on the desk as she waited for the page to load. As soon as it was ready she typed 'Louise Worthington' into the search bar and hit the button, but nothing came up. Frowning she changed the forename to 'Skye', then struck enter again and waited.

There was a Skye Worthington listed. She hadn't been there long and her mailing address was still down as Swansea, although her home address was in London. So why had

Khadijah been so weird about it all? Although she was a renowned bitch, after all, and probably got a kick out of giving out wrong information. Only to people who didn't matter, of course. But as she went to close the database something on Skye's page caught her eye. Eve frowned and peered closer, thought for a second, then reached for her handbook. She flicked to the relevant page and ran her finger down the crinkled, well-thumbed paper until she reached the right section. Comparing the information in front of her with that on the computer screen she frowned deeper, checked the screen and the book again, then heard the sound of approaching footsteps. Snapping the book shut and quickly logging out of the database she flicked back her hair and turned to look out from the counter. And her breath caught in her throat as her stomach simultaneously somersaulted.

Dan was coming towards the desk wearing a confident smile, his eyes shining and his swagger verging on arrogant. Though she'd be lying if she said she didn't find that attractive.

He walked right up to the counter, leaned casually on the top and grinned down at her, so that she felt her insides twist and turn as they always did when he was around. She hoped her external appearance wasn't so flustered. He was so close that she could smell what he had eaten for lunch - a strong coffee and a cheese croissant; a tell-tale speck of flaky pastry lingered at the top of his collar. He was wearing a dark grey suit with a sheen, teamed with a crisp white shirt and a grey and black chequered tie. Up close Eve spotted one or two residual pock marks, then felt her gaze drift towards that one front tooth which was wonky and chipped.

Eventually he spoke. "Hey."

"Hi," she picked up a pen and threaded it through her fingers. "Uh, can I help you?"

"Eve, isn't it?" She nodded. "Dan. Listen I hope you

198

won't think me too forward, but I was wondering if you'd fancy a drink sometime?"

Eve remained a prisoner to the adrenalin running through her body, and his self-assurance faltered.

"Unless, of course, you don't want to. Or you're taken. Sorry, I didn't mean to offend you, it's just that I've noticed you every morning and evening, and we chatted the other day, and I've been building up to this. Oh God, you're taken, aren't you? I'm so sorry, please forget I spoke." He skin turned crimson as Eve finally managed to find her voice.

"No, it's fine, I'm not with anyone. And yes, I'd love to go out for a drink with you."

He smiled at her, and this time it was a genuine smile, not a cocky one. "Great. Can I take your number?"

She scribbled it down on a post-it and handed it over, smiling bashfully and feeling a lot more relaxed now he had shown something of his real self.

"Thanks, I'll be in touch." He winked at her before turning and striding off towards the lifts.

After that Eve needed a cup of herbal tea to compose herself enough to carry on with her work. She quickly closed the window and removed the fuchsia from her lap, then noticed that the soily pot had marked her trousers. Cursing under her breath she brushed away at the crumbs, causing the soil to streak across her sparkling pants before fluttering onto the virginal tiles. She attempted to rub it in with the heel of her stilettos, before rolling her eyes and heading for the kettle.

As the tea brewed Eve focused on the steam warming her nostrils, the sweet scent of raspberry and echinacea and the purpley-red colour spiralling out from the tea bag to turn the entire mug of water deep maroon. She had been reading a book about mindfulness and was trying to put it into practice, but keeping her mind 100% focused on the present was a lot harder than it sounded. Sighing, she picked up the mug and let her thoughts about what had just happened with Dan, what she would have for dinner, who Skye Worthington was, what she would put on her status update and whether she should get another tattoo all pool together once more into a haze of activity. It all felt a whole lot more natural.

Back at her desk Eve re-opened the database to double check her sources, and pondered the meaning of life a little more as she finished her tea. Then she picked up the plant and headed for the same lift that had taken Dan back up to the third floor just twenty minutes previously.

Once the lift doors pinged open Eve headed out into the corridor, and walked slap bang into Dan. He was carrying a glass of water which emptied itself all down the front of his shirt, pooling out into a dark stain at his crotch.

"Shit! I'm...shit!" Eve felt her eyes widen in horror and her mouth fall open. Her free hand flew to her mouth and before he had time to confront her she ran back into the lift, desperately pressing all the buttons in her haste to get the door shut. As the lift started its descent she sank back into the corner and closed her eyes. The fuchsia would just have to wait for another day.

## Chapter 8

"Hi girls! Good to see you all! Di, you look even more stunning than usual, I didn't realise that was even possible!"

"Oh Skye, you're such a sweet-talker!" Di nudged her playfully. "Thanks, though. And you look pretty stunning yourself, you know. Mr you-know-who will not be able to take his eyes off you!"

Skye was wearing a blue satin dress, with matching stilettos and contrasting silver accessories. She'd taken time to apply her make up flawlessly and had straightened her hair to perfection, after getting her roots topped up at the salon a few days before, and prayed that she was looking good enough for Dan's eyes to remain solely on her for the entire course of the night. She stifled a grin and tried to appear laid back. "We'll see. So who's about?"

"We haven't seen Dan yet, but the others are all here."

"That's not what I was asking! I just meant in general."

Suki raised her eyebrows at Skye. "Ok, if you say so! But you do realise that your eyeballs have been on stalks since you walked in the door?"

Skye allowed a grin to slip out. "Ok, ok, give it a rest. Hey, is that Eve girl from Reception coming along? I thought I heard someone mention it the other day?"

"No, not now." Di shook her head. "She's broken her ankle! She's ok though, just not really up to partying."

201

"Oh, that's a shame. I haven't really spoken to her yet and she seems nice." Skye congratulated herself on how genuine she sounded.

"She's alright, nothing special. Nice place this, isn't it?"

"Mm-hmm," Skye glanced around the bar, her eyes lingering on the massive Christmas tree covered with soft golden lights perched at the end of the room. She was always a sucker for the decs this time of year. "I stayed around here when I first moved to London, with my mate Amy. It was a good place to be!" At the mention of her friend Skye realised that she hadn't heard off Amy for a while, but now she wondered how she was getting on. She'd also never heard back from Rachel or Jen, and until now had forgotten how eager she had been to get to Lena's wedding. Ah well, none of that mattered anymore; she'd found her niche now, as Amy had predicted, and she could catch up with those girls once Amy returned.

"Ooh, he's here! And he's looking hot…" Di sang her final word and clawed at Skye's arm.

"Ow! Jesus, ok! Stop it! Stop it!" Skye manhandled Di off her and shook her head to allow her hair to fall naturally.

"Hey girls! How's it going? Anyone want a drink? Skye? White wine spritzer?" Dan strode into the middle of the group. "Anyone else? You're all ok? Cool, I'll be right back."

After presenting Skye with her glass Dan led her over to the dance floor, seemingly oblivious to the winks and glances that Skye exchanged with her friends as they went. They chatted and watched their colleagues become progressively more confident on the dance floor, in direct correlation to the amount of alcohol they managed to put away, and once they had finished their drinks Dan offered her his arm.

"Come and have a dance!"

"No way! I told you, I don't do dancing."

202

"Come on, it'll be fun! Everyone's hammered anyway, they won't care what we look like. Come *on!*"

Skye felt his fingers slipping between her own as Dan attempted to pull her off towards the dance floor, just as the opening strains of Mariah's 'All I Want for Christmas' reverberated out of the speakers.

"Ok, but after this one, let's get another drink first!"

"Are you crazy?! It's Christmas! Get into the spirit!" He yanked her off her stool, grabbed her waist in a solid grip and spun her round so fast there was no way she could escape.

"Ok! I'll dance! Just slow me down!" Skye shrieked, batting at his hands and covering up how much she was enjoying the faux scrap. But he only tightened his grip, yelling along to the words and jolting around the dance floor as if possessed, until he suddenly came to a stop. Unfortunately Skye didn't, and she felt her full weight smack into him as she continued spinning. Laughing, he steadied her and she looked up into his sparkling face and burst into giggles. And then he kissed her. She could taste lager and smell the fruity scent of his hair wax, and then she was aware of nothing except his mouth on hers and his hands in her hair. When they finally parted he looked deep into her eyes, kissed her again then offered her his hand.

"Shall we go?" He asked, and she nodded. They slipped out of the party without saying goodbye, and into the crisp night air.

Back in West Hampstead they lay together in Skye's bed, Dan dropping light kisses onto her pale pink nipples and Skye running her fingers through his hair, brushing out the wax so that it flopped down onto his forehead, where it stuck to his skin with the layer of sweat that coated his face. Afterwards he spooned her, and all night she was aware of his fingertips dusting her breasts and his cock pressing into the soft flesh of her buttocks. She could feel his warm breath on his neck, and smell his residual aftershave mingled with the salty scent of sweat. She didn't sleep a wink all night.

The following morning Skye sipped her tea and glanced over at Dan lying curled up under the covers, and a lump appeared in her throat as she recalled what he had shared with her when they had lain awake in the early hours. Her heart ached as she wished she could make it all better, but at the very least she could make sure she was always there for him. She blinked a few times, then picked up her phone and crept into the kitchen

"Mum? It's me. Listen, I'm really sorry. But Dan's mum still isn't well and he really wants me to be there over Christmas."

"What? But you said you were coming home!"

"I know, Mum, and I know I haven't known him very long, and I know I promised, but he needs me. I'm going to come home this weekend and see you and give you presents. I'm so sorry Mum, but I just need to be with him."

"But Lou, Skye..."

"Mum, my mind is made up. It's just what I have to do."

"Well, ok. I suppose if she's really that ill."

Chris sounded so downhearted that Skye felt tears prickling the backs of her eyes.

"We'll just see you next weekend, and have our celebration then."

"Thanks, Mum." Skye whispered, rolling her eyeballs upwards to stop the tears from falling. Her gaze landed on her special shoebox and she couldn't stop a drop trailing its way down over her cheek, but she brushed it away. "I've got to go now, Mum. I'll see you on Saturday." She gently replaced the receiver in the cradle while eying the shoebox, then stood on her bed and reached into it. She pulled out the bracelet, and relived that time back in the summer with Amy, when everything had seemed so promising and shiny. She could almost feel the kiss of sun warming her skin, and smell the barbequed food lingering in the air, as she transported herself back a few months.

Skye's face became numb and her eyes started to sting. Her breathing was shallow; if she breathed too deeply that woolly thing with teeth that was residing in her stomach might invade the rest of her body and take over completely. It was already seeping into her arms and infecting them with its deadness. She wished she could rip it out and throw it away, but that was impossible; it was too deeply entwined with her cells. Skye rose and stumbled to the bathroom where she leant over the toilet bowl, stuck her fingers down her throat and retched until at least the woolly thing was exhausted, if not extinguished. Then she brushed her teeth and got into bed, where she slipped out of futility and into the safety and comfort of a whole other life.

## Chapter 9

Skye boarded the train from Paddington with a heavy heart, which sank further with every station they passed. She stared out of the window the whole time, yet didn't notice the changing scenery as they left the city behind and came into the country; she got quite a surprise to learn that they had arrived at Swansea, and only just managed to alight before the grumpy-faced guard came in to tell her that the train was terminating.

Skye jumped on a local bus and tried to compose herself as she completed the final leg of her journey, but coming home made everything in London seem unreal, and it was hard to feel together. She slouched off the bus at her regular stop, and the first thing she noticed was that the postbox had finally been repainted. She could hear the shouts of children coming from the park and strains of Band Aid coming out of the pub, the volume rising every time the door swung open, while the bus juddered out of the village. The air was clean and fresh, and the wintery chill stung her nostrils as she mooched down the path towards her house. She rounded the corner and paused for a minute, to stare at the familiar sight of the three bed semi-, then took a deep breath as the door flew open and her mother stepped out onto the porch.

"Louise! My love! It's so good to see..."

"Mum, I keep saying, it's Skye now. It's just what I've gotten used to."

"Skye...of course...love, what have you done to yourself?"

Skye closed her eyes for a few seconds then reopened them and locked her gaze on Chris, challenging her to comment further. "I just fancied a change, Mum. It seemed about time, my hair was so dated and I was fed up with being plain."

"Plain? Louise, Skye, love, you were beautiful the way you were. You looked so natural and sweet. But..."

"Mum, I just wanted to grow up. Ok?"

Chris opened her mouth then shut it again and blinked. "Ok, love. You do look lovely, it was just a shock, that's all. You look so...sharp. And professional. I was expecting my little girl."

Skye softened. "I am your little girl, Mum. I always will be, in a way. But I can't be a child forever. I'm a grown up now."

"I know, love." Chris reached out and stroked Skye's blazer. "I just sometimes can't help wishing I could have my little girl back." Chris's hand froze in the crook of Skye's elbow. Skye looked up and caught her mother's eyes, and in them saw something that looked like fear; they were jumpy, yet seemed frozen at the same time.

"Mum..."

"Anyway, would you like a cup of tea?"

"Um, ok. Sure. Have you got any herbal?"

Chris wrung her hands. "Oh, no. Sorry, love, just normal Tetley. But I can pop out and get some?"

"No Mum, don't be silly. Tetley's great."

"I'll go and make you a mug. Oh, and I'm afraid we haven't decorated yet, love. We were going to do it this weekend, though to be honest if it's just me and your dad I might not bother going to the trouble this year."

208

Skye felt herself tense up as she predicted the extended guilt trip that was to follow, but Chris stopped to usher Skye into the house while she went to make the tea.

Nothing much had changed at home, except that Mike and Chris had splashed out on a new kettle and toaster set which Chris found rather exciting; the kettle flashed bright blue when it boiled and the toaster cooked up to four slices of bread. The grey speckled carpets still stretched throughout the house and deep red curtains still hung from the rails in the communal areas. Pictures of Skye as a child, taken on various family holidays in Spain from the age of about three upwards, still dotted the walls, and a piece of artwork that she had undertaken as part of her GCSE coursework still hung above the disused fireplace. As always the house smelled of lavender, due to Chris's obsession with creating a relaxed and calming atmosphere, although Skye could also detect a hint of cinnamon, which showed that her mother had rooted out her festive air freshener (which got put away every January, so that it could be saved especially for the Christmas period).

"Louise! Hello! How *are* you? How was your journey?" Mike came in from the garden, stamping his feet and blowing on his hands. "Just been doing some tidying in the garden, it's bloody freezing out there! Have you got the tea on, Chris?" He called through to the kitchen and when he didn't get a reply wandered off to check the kettle, not appearing to notice anything different about Skye at all.

While she was on her own Skye took a moment to look around the room, take it all in and try and assert herself back into home life. It all looked the same, all smelled the same. But it didn't *feel* the same. She felt unsettled and uneasy in the familiar yet alien environment; it just didn't fit anymore.

"Here you go love, I brought some sherry and mince pies, too. Tuck in now, don't hold back - there's plenty more where they came from!" Skye plucked up her first mince pie of the season and lay back against the sofa, enjoying the cracking of the pastry and the tang of erupting mince.

"So, tell me about London. How's your job?"

Skye looked into Chris's eyes. Once the colour of cornflowers they were now beginning to turn a watery grey-blue. She had more lines around her mouth than Skye remembered, and her hair was looking quite white at the edges. Skye steeled herself. "It's going well, yeah. Hard work, very tiring, but I've met some nice people and it's great to be working there."

"It must be so exciting for you, love. You must be so busy what with all that hustle and bustle. No wonder you don't have time to get back and visit your old Mum and Dad! But don't you worry, we understand." Chris patted Skye's leg. "Once you've settled in I'm sure you'll have much more time for us."

Skye swapped her mug for the glass and took a sip of the sweet sherry her mother treated herself to once a year.

"So tell us about the people you've met! Have you got some good friends? And tell me more about this Dan?" Chris pinkened and Skye smiled; her mum had never found it easy to deal with that topic of conversation, despite that recent awkward conversation about the 'first time'. She must have had an aspirin that day.

"Well, yeah. There's those girls who work in the PR department, Suki and Di, who I mentioned before."

Chris nodded enthusiastically.

"They're very nice and I sometimes see them out of work. Suki lives in West Hampstead too actually, I bumped into her once and since then we've been quite friendly."

"And what about Eve?"

"Eve?"

210

"The receptionist! The one your father and I met when we came to the office! Did you ever get that plant?"

Skye felt a cloud cross her features at the mere mention of that day. "Oh yeah. She's ok. And no."

"And Dan?" Chris rather wisely changed the subject, although she flushed again and twisted her fingers uncomfortably around her schooner glass.

Skye took a deep breath. "Well, yeah. Dan." It felt odd to be talking about him to her mother, but she wanted to bring him into the conversation and feel the shape of his name on her tongue. She inhaled deeply. "He's really nice! I think you'd like him."

"And he's one of the graduates with you, right?" Chris asked, her face having returned to its normal colour.

"Yes, he's one of the graduates. He's really intelligent, and funny, and good looking. And, you know, things seem to be going pretty well!"

"Really? Oh, Lou…Skye…that's so exciting!"

"It is." Skye nodded bashfully. "But Mum, now you've got a bit used to it, what do you think…?" Skye trailed off and fingered her hair.

"It does look nice, love. It's just so different, why did you do it? If you don't mind me asking. I did love your mahogany waves. And how on earth have you managed to change the colour of your eyes? That nearly made me jump out my skin when I first saw you, I thought you'd been possessed or something!" Chris whispered the last part of her sentence.

Skye laughed. "I just needed a change Mum, you know? I've had the same hair, same look since, well, forever, then I got to the city and all the girls were so glamorous. I felt the need for a bit of a make-over. I didn't mean to be abrupt when I came in."

"That's ok, love. I understand. Why, when I was young

211

I once wanted a change, and I used all my money to go out and buy the biggest pairs of flares I could find! The first time I wore them I went flying down the stairs and your grandfather thought I'd had a fainting attack and wanted to call an ambulance! It took me ages to convince him that I'd just fallen because my flares were so big I couldn't walk in them. I'm still not sure that he really believes that was the case. Actually, do you know what, I think I've still got them upstairs! Take this, I'll go and have a look." Chris thrust her sherry into Skye's empty hand and shot off up the stairs to relive her youth.

Skye drained her glass, then on second thoughts drained her mother's, and lay down on the cushions while she waited for Chris to return.

## Chapter 10

"I just wanted to do something special for you! Is that a crime?! Jesus, Cindy!" Ryan leaped out of bed and pulled on his boxers.

"I told you, Ryan! This is just a bit of fun, I'm married for God's sake! I have a husband, I can't just go off on a spontaneous weekend with you! This," she indicated the rumpled sheets, "is all we are. I thought I made that clear!"

"Crystal." Ryan muttered, as he turned his trousers back the right way.

"Ryan," her voice had softened but he couldn't bring himself to look at her. "I'm sorry if I've misled you. But I'm happy with Tom. Well, happy enough. And I'm too old for you, you need to go and meet a girl your own age. Someone who wants the same things as you." She paused. "I think it's best that we finish this."

Ryan turned. Cindy was sat up in bed with the duvet wrapped around her waist, her breasts on show. As he eyed them he felt a wave of anger that had been latent for too long balloon inside him. His breathing deepened as the energy flooded his system, and Cindy's look of concern mutated into one of fear.

"Ryan?" She pulled the duvet up to cover herself. "Ryan. I think you should leave. Now."

He held her gaze for a while, resisting an urge to smash

up the full length mirror or punch the wall. He realised, in a brief moment of clarity, that if he stayed put he may not be able to remain in control of his actions. So he leant over, grabbed the Eurostar tickets and left without a word.

Pounding down the street Ryan was vaguely aware that his hands were clenched into fists. The acid in his stomach was bubbling like lentils spitting over the hob and his legs were tingling with heat. The humiliation he felt was out of sorts for the situation, but the floodgates were open and he was well past the point of rational thought.

As he rounded the corner onto a quiet, residential street he spotted a holly bush hanging over the pavement. It was coming closer with each stride, and his arms started to twitch as he remembered the story he had told Cindy. He thought about how good it would feel to have those spikes scrape him up and down, so the excess energy could flow freely until he felt soothed and released and somewhat back in control.

Ryan stormed up to the bush and plunged his arms into it, flailing around and groaning at the relief the pain afforded him. And then as quickly as it started it ended, and he was shocked to find himself standing in the middle of an alien street, elbow-deep in a holly bush with his arms starting to sting. The pleasure gave way to an almost unbearable pain, like a hundred wasps all going for him at once. Withdrawing his arms and glancing furtively up and down the street he pulled down his sleeves, turned, and headed for the pub he had spotted earlier.

Ryan's phone rang as he ordered his first pint but he ignored it, the vibration in his pocket and the chirpy tune getting him more fired up by the second. Just the thought of talking to the person on the other end of the line made him feel sick. Instead he ordered a pint and downed it, calling for another before he'd even returned the glass to the bar.

"Coming up. You alright there mate? It's still early, you know!"

Ryan responded to the portly barman with a glare, which he held until he had taken a first, second, third sip of his fresh pint. Then, as his feelings and awareness started to return, he pulled out a bar stool and dropped himself onto it, resting his head in his hands as he inhaled a few times and took a moment to process what had just happened. He hadn't got very far when his phone started to vibrate again. This time he reached for it, feeling both relieved but disappointed to see that the call was coming from Ash.

"Alright?"

"Mate, what are you up to? Do you fancy a few pre-gig drinks over lunch?"

"Pre-gig? Huh?"

"We've got Arena tonight, eh? Are we still on?"

"Ah yeah, sorry mate. Course. I'm in the pub now actually, having a few."

"Where are you?"

"Umm...hold on. Hey, excuse me? Where am I?"

Ryan felt his neck recoil like a turtle's under the gaze of the barman.

"King's Arms. Court Street."

"Cheers. King's Arms mate. Court Street, do you know it?"

"Yeah I do actually. I'll be there soon. Laters."

Ryan slipped his phone back into his pocket and had a look around. There were only a couple of other punters in the lounge, which seemed strange given that it was a Sunday afternoon. He glanced up and noticed the vast collection of old beer pump clips adorning the wall, next to a display of old and foreign notes. Some had signatures scrawled over them.

"Buddy, I know this isn't any of my business but are

you ok?"

Ryan just noticed that the barman had a strong Liverpudlian accent.

"You just don't look so good."

Ryan hesitated, then sighed. "Yeah. I'll live. Just, you know. Stuff."

"Ah! So is it work, women or wonga? It's always one."

Ryan took another deep breath. "Urgh. All of the above."

"Oh, you got it bad, mate. Well, here you go, on the house. It will get better, I swear. I've seen it all before and I'm damn sure I'll see it all again. It's kind of a given in this trade."

"Thanks. Good pint, by the way."

"Cheers. Want to talk about it?"

"No."

"Fair play. Well, you're in the right place now. Just sit there and have a few, and I promise you it'll all look better in the morning. Is that your mate?"

Ash was strolling towards the bar, looking all glossy and happy and pleased with himself. Ryan nodded at him and attempted a grin, but he wasn't sure it came out quite right.

"Alright, mate? You found us ok? Glad you could make it."

Ash did a double take at the barman's address.

"Er, yeah, I've been here before, it's a nice joint. You don't do food though, right?"

"Nah. We used to. Try The Admiral for a roast. Now, if you'll excuse me, I must get back to my glass polishing. Oh yeah, after I get you a drink. What are you having?"

"Pint of Pride as well, cheers. Then you ok to pop over to The Admiral, Ry? I'm starving, had a bit of a sesh last night, know what I mean?" Ash winked at Ryan, who by now was more than familiar with the code. 'A good sesh' meant a decent night out but not much to write home about, whereas if the sentence was succeeded with 'know what I mean' or punctuated with a wink it meant that there was a girl, or on occasion girls, involved. The double emphasis this afternoon did nothing to lighten his mood.

"Can I get another? Cheers."

"Jesus, Ryan, that was quick. You had that one in about two sips! You need to pace yourself or you won't last past seven! Hair of the dog is it? Oh, this is a good pint, I need this."

"Umm, yeah. Something like that," Ryan muttered. His realism was starting to fade out now that he was on his fourth pint, but he needed a few more to dislodge it completely. "Hey, shall we get a shot?"

"A shot?! It's the middle of Sunday afternoon! That's pushing it even by your standards, surely?!"

Ryan grunted. "Suit yourself. Boss, can I get a Sambuca?"

"Sambuca? Really?"

"Yes!" The venom in Ryan's voice took even himself by surprise, but it did the job. The glass had barely touched the surface before Ryan knocked back its contents, which seemed to make him gag more today than it did on a Saturday night. But the burning sensation trailing through the system was comforting in its familiarity.

"Hey man, what's up? What's happened? Is it your bird?"

Ryan looked up at Ash's face, and to his embarrassment his eyes went watery. He blinked a few times as he nodded brusquely, then shrugged his shoulders in an attempt to appear nonchalant.

"Over?"

"Uh-huh. Ditched her."

"How come?"

217

Ryan hesitated and swallowed a few times. "Too old. And desperate. Sad cow. Thought it was hot at first, you know. But then she got all needy and heavy, so I got out."

"Ah, I see. Why are you so cut up then? If you ditched her?"

"Dunno, really. Just got a lot on my mind, I guess. And I'll miss the shagging. It was the only think keeping me going!" Ryan attempted a chuckle but it came out more like the snort of injured swine.

"How's work?"

"Shite."

"What days you doing now? You gone part time, yeah?"

"Yeah. So I can write. I do three days a week but they vary, depending on when they need me. Three guaranteed though."

"That's alright, eh? How's the writing?"

"Shite. Well, going. But you know. Doing a bit with Music Mania, hence the gigs. And I'm try to get going on a novel."

"Started?"

"Yeah. Well, I've done like a thousand words or so."

"And how many words make a novel?"

"Eighty thousand. At least."

"Long way to go then. Hey, did you manage to make rent on time this month?"

"Just about. Money's pretty shite as well."

"Jesus man, you're a right walking tragedy aren't you? Forget what I said, hey! Boss! Can we get a couple more Sambucas over here?"

That was the shot that pushed Ryan to the point where he could start to see oblivion. The sight of nothingness on the horizon, coming closer with every sip, spurred him on to reach there sooner rather than later. He downed the rest of his pint and ordered another round, just as the wobbly sensation hit his knees. It simultaneously slipped in through his freshly broken skin to invade his system from all sides, creating the last clear memory he would retain from that night.

"Uuuurrrr," Ryan groaned through the pain but it didn't help. He clamped his mouth shut and turned in his bed, but the room turned with him so he rolled back round again, struggling not to retch as he did so. After a few breaths he gingerly opened his eyes, feeling almost surprised to see that everything still looked the same as it had the day before.

He shifted in bed and stretched out his limbs, and came into contact with something cold and damp. Pushing back the covers he saw an ochre-tinted tidemark stretching out across the sheet, and it was only then that he realised his boxers were wet. But before he could think any more he became overwhelmed by a huge wave of nausea, so he pushed the sheets right back and charged for the bathroom. Though he didn't quite make it in time, and his stomach rejected the poison of the night before all over the off-white lino. After a rasping breath he locked the door behind him and squatted beside the toilet bowl to finish what he had started, until his retching turned dry and the headache kicked in. Then he rummaged in the cupboard under the sink to find an old scourer and started to scrub, balling up the shower mat and shoving it straight into the bin.

Once he had freshened up the bathroom Ryan changed his boxers then stumbled down to the living room and threw himself on the sofa next to Ash, who was finishing off a bowl of Weetabix. The grey-brown mush made Ryan's stomach flip once more so he turned his head away, held his breath and counted to ten; he didn't have enough energy to run back to the toilet.

"Alright? You look a little worse for wear. Man you were in a state last night, eh?"

Ryan forced a grin as he pulled another costume down from above and slipped it over his head. "Ah yeah, mad wasn't it? Awesome night though. I'm suffering man, but I'll be ok after a coffee and some toast." At the mere mention of consumables Ryan's throat clenched up. "Did you have a good time? What did you think of the bands? I can't really remember them, will have to get on Youtube to do a review! Remember they were pretty cool though. I think. It's all a bit of a blur, to be honest."

There was a clatter as Ash dropped his spoon into his bowl and tuned to face Ryan. "Seriously, mate? We didn't see any bands. They wouldn't let us in."

"What?" Ryan creased up his forehead, suddenly realising that Ash's usual grin had been replaced by a stony, set look. He was sitting up on the edge of the settee, where he normally flopped right back into it.

"We couldn't get in because you were so drunk. You were all over the place, man! I don't even know how it happened, we drank the same amount! I mean I was on my way but you...Jesus, Ry."

Ryan thought of the extra shots he had slipped while Ash had been in the bathroom. Then he had a flashback to popping off to the cornershop for cigarettes - a sure sign that things were getting out of control - and spotting those little bottles of vodka behind the counter. He'd bet himself that he couldn't get through a whole one before he made it back to the pub, but that had been so easy he'd turned around and gone back for another, stashing it in his pocket 'just in case'.

"Shit man! What happened to your leg?"

Ryan looked down to see an angry welt in his inner

220

thigh, where the skin had opened to reveal the flesh underneath. It was almost a perfect circle, although the skin around the wound was ragged. It was flecked with black ash and Ryan knew, from experience, that the deep red would soon turn yellow and leaky before crusting over. Sometimes he picked it when it got to that point.

"Dunno man," he shrugged. "Can't remember much, to be honest."

Ash looked at him with raised eyebrows, and Ryan suddenly felt about five years old. "So you don't remember starting on the bouncers, then starting on that bloke in the queue after coming onto his girlfriend?"

Ryan let his head fall back on top of the sofa and closed his eyes.

"Or starting on me? Lamping me in the face when I tried to bring you home?"

Ryan's blood ran cold as Ash turned awkwardly to reveal a purpley-brown smudge on his cheekbone. What the fuck?

"Man you were out of control. Like, beyond a joke. Again. You need to sort it out."

Ryan couldn't even bring himself to apologise; his last few drops of energy had evaporated to leave behind just a shell and nothing more.

"Anyway, I'm going to work. Lucky you, having the day off." There was a hint of sarcasm to Ash's tone, which Ryan had never heard before.

"Ash, I'm sorry man. I don't know…I'm sorry. Shit."

Ash pulled on his coat, raised his eyebrows at Ryan again, and left. As the door slammed shut Ryan's system came to life once more, but he just managed to make it to the kitchen sink in time.

Ash was wrong. He did have work today. But there was

221

no way in hell he was going to spend the next eight hours in the office. Nor was he going to go on Youtube to research his review, nor was he going to phone in sick. He was going to fuck it all and spend the day under his duvet. Except he couldn't even do that until he had changed the sheets. He went back to the sofa and crashed out on the cushions, waiting for his next bout of sickness, which he knew would be along before too long. Maybe he could delay it if he didn't really breathe.

As he lay there Ryan noticed a white envelope on the coffee table, with 'Cindy' scrawled across it. Ash must have found it somewhere along the way and brought it back. He reached for it and opened it up, pulling out the paper print outs and fingering their edges. Then he slowly started ripping them to shreds, except for one ticket from St Pancras to Paris. That one he folded up neatly and slipped back inside.

He had planned the trip for a couple of weekends before Christmas, as he'd always liked the run up to the festive season, in contrast to the January hangover which he found almost too grim to bear. Every year he wished that people would just put Christmas away on January 1st, as there was nothing more pathetic than returning to work among wilted trees with half their decorations missing and tinsel hanging on by a thread. No, much better to know when to call it a day and move on.

So, on the penultimate Friday before Christmas, that was exactly what he would do, when he would board that train and start his new life. And today, in between bouts of vomiting and dozing and at some point washing his sheets, he would set the ball in motion by e-mailing his landlady and giving notice on the flat.

## Chapter 11

As she wandered down Bishopsgate in the icy December Monday morning Eve's thought were with fuchsia plants and Christmas. She felt a pressing need to get that plant into the hands of Skye Worthington, and had even noted down her parents' phone number from the staff database - where it had been listed as Skye's emergency contact - so that she could tell the couple when the plant had been delivered.

Her thoughts then oscillated to the upcoming holiday. Eve had plans to go back to her aunt's and couldn't wait to spend a week sat on the sofa, chatting away and overindulging. For the other 51 weeks of the year she followed a strict diet and didn't allow a single rogue calorie to cross her lips. And carbohydrates, of course, were strictly forbidden. So for that one special week she allowed herself a spot of indulgence. Not up to the same level as the majority of the population but pretty significant for her - the odd mince pie, a few slices of chocolate orange, the occasional portion of Christmas pudding and a good few lashings of Baileys; all were permitted for that week, and that week only.

As she was daydreaming about carbohydrates, cream and chocolate she realised that she had walked straight past the front door of the office. She quickly turned around and backtracked, hoping that her error hadn't been caught on camera, and entered through the automatic doors of the office, giggling quietly. Distracted, she collided with the cleaner who was on her knees, scrubbing at a mark on the floor.

"Oh my God, I'm so sorry! I didn't see you down there!" Eve scrambled to her feet, brushing the seat of her trousers. She held out a hand to the girl in the regulation blue pinafore, who was sprawled across the floor looking a bit dazed.

The cleaner reached out for Eve's hand but then looked up and quickly withdrew. Her expression mutated from stunned to one of contempt, and she assertively placed her hands on the floor and pulled herself up on her feet. She was wearing chunky heels which meant that she stood an inch or two over Eve, who had opted for Uggs that day. Eve thought they looked completely unsuitable for cleaning, but who was she to judge?

"Are you ok? I'm so sorry, that was completely my fault. I was in my own little world and I wasn't looking where I was going. I was too involved in dreams about Chocolate Orange and mince pies!"

"I'm fine," snapped the cleaner, glaring at Eve for one last time before picking up her cloth and getting back down on her hands and knees, pointedly scrubbing away at the floor once more.

Fine, suit yourself, thought Eve, as she turned and hurried over to her desk. She was late starting now and had a lot to get through today. And she was going to start by dealing with that flipping plant.

Once she had sorted herself out Eve picked up the fuchsia and headed for the lift. She knew where she was going and she knew who she was looking for, and this time she was going to concentrate so that she wouldn't crash into any more people and cause any more havoc. It was starting to become something of a habit.

*     *     *

"Hi, are you the supervisor up here? I'm looking for someone, a Skye Worthington?"

The large woman looked up from her computer and grinned. Eve recognised her from walking through the foyer. Every morning she sang out a hello, and every evening she sang out a goodbye, but that was the furthest their conversation had ever gone. She always left a trail of sickly sweet perfume in her wake, and up here the scent was almost suffocating.

She answered Eve's enquiry in a strong accent that Eve struggled to place. "Skye? Yeah, she's here. Don't know where she is right now though, off on an assignment somewhere I think. Can I take a message?"

Eve hesitated. She'd been hoping to meet Skye herself, to put a face to the name and get some idea of what was going on. But at the same time it had taken her long enough to get round to bringing the fuchsia up here, and the holiday period was looming. If she didn't get rid of the plant soon it would sit on her desk for two weeks, and no doubt be withered up and dying by the time she returned in the new year. She sighed resignedly.

"I just wanted to give her this fuchsia. Her parents stopped by a while back and dropped it in, so I said I'd pass it on to her. But do you think you could do it? Just tell her that Eve from downstairs brought it up. I'm the receptionist, that will help her place me."

"I know you're the Receptionist, you're the first person I see every morning and the last person I see every night! I know who you are!"

Eve smiled at the woman and wished she could remember her name.

"I'm Shirley," the woman offered, as if she had read Eve's mind.

225

"Thanks, Shirley. Tell Skye to pop down and say hello - it would be nice to work out who she is. I probably see her around about ten times a day but just don't know her name. Does she work up here then, with you?"

"Yes! I tell you, I'm her boss. Do you not believe me? Think I'm not enough of a dragon like that bitch downstairs?" Shirley opened her mouth and guffawed before Eve could respond. She wiped a tear from her eye then rose from her seat. "Listen, I must get on. I'll pass this on to Skye and I will see you tonight, when I leave to go back to my baby! Catch you later!" And with that she waddled away down the corridor with the fuchsia.

Back at her desk Eve dug out the telephone number for Skye's parents and carefully tapped the digits into her desk phone. A mature female voice answered on the third ring, so Eve took a breath and launched into her spiel.

"Hi, it's Eve here, calling from the Edwards, Greenwood and Benjamin office block. Is that Mrs. Worthington?"

"Yes! Yes, what's happened? Is everything ok? Has Louise hurt herself?" Chris's voice was shrill and Eve mentally kicked herself for giving the older lady such a fright.

"No, everything's fine. There's no need to worry. I just wanted to tell you that I managed to locate Skye, and I've passed on the fuchsia that you left for her."

"Oh, Eve! Thank you love, for passing it on for us. I'm glad she finally got it. And thank you for calling to tell us, that's so kind of you!" Chris's voice softened into a whisper. "She wasn't too cross, was she?"

"No. Actually I don't know. She was busy so I left it with her boss who said she'd pass it on."

"Oh, good! And does she work for that woman, the one who came down that day?"

226

"Umm, no. Not Khadijah."

"So what floor is she on then? Not the third?"

"No. She's on the eighth."

"Oh, that makes sense then! That's why that woman didn't know who she was, must be our mistake. So she's doing her PR up there is she?"

But Eve didn't have time to answer before Chris's distinct shriek came down the phone line once again.

"Oh my God, Eve, sorry love I have to go. Mike's just come in with something. I don't know what it is but it looks expensive and electronic and I don't like it. Thanks again for calling, you are a love. And have a lovely Christmas!"

The phone line went dead and Eve breathed a sigh of relief, then figured she'd better set about doing some work. It was gone ten by now and she hadn't even shuffled her papers efficiently yet, something she liked to do at sporadic moments during the day to make her look a) official and b) like she knew what she was meant to be doing.

Eve sat at her desk, tapping her acrylic talons on the blinding surface and gazing into the middle distance. Every now and then she became aware of a frown creeping across her features, and made a point of smoothing out her forehead so that she wouldn't encourage the crease marks to take up permanent residence. But a few minutes later the crinkles would be back as she tried to piece everything together. Something about the whole situation captured her imagination, and she really wanted to help Chris and Mike.

The thought of the couple made tears well up in her eyes as, for the first time since this all began, she allowed her thoughts to touch on the time when her own parents had been alive, before the crash. As the loop of images flashed through her mind, from when she had received that call, followed by the time in hospital and the ensuing funeral, she felt a tear spill over and roll its way down her cheek. She brushed it away, shut down the database, grabbed her bag and set off for Starbucks. She wasn't supposed to take a break now, but what could they do? If she wasn't there she wasn't there, and everyone would just have to wait twenty minutes while she gave herself some time. They could do with learning a bit of patience anyway, those fat cat types with all their money. It wouldn't do them any harm at all to be kept waiting for once.

Eve joined the service queue, inhaling the relaxing scent of coffee and sugar while eavesdropping on the conversations around her; one of her favourite past times. She was pondering whether or not to risk indulging in a muffin, despite her strict anti-carb rule, when she tuned into the conversation taking place between the barista and a familiar looking girl in red cashmere a couple of places before her in the queue. Both seemed completely unaware of the growing line of impatient office workers waiting for their mid-morning caffeine kick.

"Yeah, so it's pretty tough but I'm really enjoying it. And, you know, the eye candy makes it all worthwhile…!" The girl in red winked at the young girl behind the counter, before chuckling coyly.

The barista stared back with wide eyes. "I'm so jealous! I'll be going to university next year and I can't wait to get going with it all, move away from my parents, start a career, find myself a nice man." The girl blushed coyly at this point, which only served to enhance her youthful looks.

"Yeah, it's great. You'll have a ball! University days really are the best of your life. Listen to me, I sound like a right old woman! But it's fab, you'll have so much fun and meet so many people. And maybe even find a Dan of your own…!"

"Dan?" The girl's eyes widened even further. "Isn't that the blond guy who comes in every morning for his double espresso and croissant?"

"The very one." The girl nodded smugly as the barista looked on in wonderment, while Eve froze. She felt her blood start to boil and her stomach begin to churn, and lifted a hand to her forehead in an attempt to cool her overheated skin. But as she did so her handbag dropped to the floor and her phone, concealer, mascara and a few coins clattered out onto the tiles. The girl in red looked up, then flushed the colour of her jumper as she caught Eve's eye. Time seemed to stand still for just a second before she pushed past Eve - nearly knocking her down as she leant over to collect her make up - and shot out of Starbucks, leaving her coffee on the counter and the young barista staring after her in bewilderment.

"Can I get my coffee now, then?" The agitated voice of the man in front of Eve broke the stunned silence, and the barista seemed to jump back into life.

"Can I help? Hello? What can I get you?"

Eve suddenly realised that another barista had appeared and was addressing her.

"Um, no. Thanks." And Eve turned to leave, her head spinning and her insides still dancing.

The young barista stared after her in puzzlement. What was it with these young career woman types? Why were they so odd? As she turned to take the next order she wondered whether to bother with university. Perhaps she'd just stay serving coffee for the rest of her life; at least the people in this trade were sane.

Back at her desk Eve was unable to concentrate. She couldn't sit still and her mind was going a million miles an hour, attempting to work out exactly where she stood in the whole situation, as well as how angry she was 'allowed' to be. But there was no way she could get on with her work now. She shifted slightly in her seat, so that her bulging inbox was out of her line of vision, and set about carrying on with the search for Skye.

After re-logging into the staff database Eve searched for 'Skye Worthington' and double checked the information. She was definitely the daughter of Michael and Christine Worthington, who were listed as her emergency contacts, and she did indeed hold a degree from the University of Aberystwyth. But then it all went a bit odd.

"Argh!" Eve let out a grunt of frustration and ran her fingers through her hair. Nothing made any sense! And it was so frustrating to feel a part of the unfolding story when she didn't even know what the main character looked like. She resumed her tapping as she tried to come up with a plan, and before she knew it she was on her feet and heading in the direction of the lifts, where her right index finger pressed the button for the eighth floor. She was unsure of what to do and didn't know what form her plan was going to take, but figured she'd leave it to fate to decide. And, for once, fate seemed to be on her side.

The lift stopped at the first floor and a middle aged man in a dark grey suit joined Eve in the tiny room, clutching a cardboard cup of coffee, with the strap of his laptop bag hanging across his chest. He emanated a sense of self-importance almost as strong as the stench of his putrid aftershave, and smiled at Eve before winking in a way she could only assume he believed was appealing.

"You're the young lady off Reception, aren't you?" He punctuated his question with a resounding gravely cough that seemed to echo off the walls.

Eve nodded tightly.

"Bob." He extended an arm and she eyed it warily before placing her delicate hand in his sweaty paw. "Work in

JENS, up on tenth. I've just been promoted, in fact." His chest seemed to swell and Eve briefly wondered whether he was hiding a plumage of feathers under his shirt.

"Are you...shit!" Bob's self-interruption caused Eve to swing her head back to see what had caused him to curse, and the sight before her eyes nearly made her burst into giggles right in front of him. It seemed that somehow a collision had occurred between Bob's coffee and his laptop bag, with the result being that most of the coffee was now in a puddle on the marble floor while a fair few splashes and dribbles made trails down Bob's trouser leg. "What shall I do now? I need to get someone to sort that out but I have a meeting to go to!" Eve wasn't sure whether Bob's whining was rhetorical but at that moment, just as the lift pinged its arrival, her brain snapped into gear.

"I'll get someone." She expected a grateful look from Bob - maybe even a word of thanks - but instead he just snorted gruffly and carried on mopping at the stains on his trouser leg, with a questionable looking navy handkerchief. Eve rolled her eyes and exited the lift, wondering yet again why she ever bothered. Although this time it was only a means to an end.

She wandered into the cleaning department, past trolleys bearing dirty mops and used cloths, and ironically got a overwhelming desire to wash herself as she became immersed in the scent of cleaning products. She tentatively pushed open the main doors, but the desk was empty save for a giant box of half eaten Krispy Kremes and a bell perched on the corner, like the kind Eve would expect to find in an old hotel. She hesitated for a few moments, feeling creeped out by the lack of life in comparison to the hustle and bustle of the foyer, then leant over and tapped the top of the bell with her palm.

"You alright out there?" Eve jumped as a voice boomed out from a little corridor leading off behind the desk, then waited for the owner to follow. "Hellooooo? Anyone there? Can I help?"

A few more seconds confirmed that the identity of the caller was going to remain a mystery.

"Um, there's been an accident." Eve shouted out, before continuing hurriedly as the silence became expectant. "Someone spilled some coffee. In the lift. So I thought I'd pop by and see if someone could sort it out."

"That all? I thought someone had died or something, the way you started off there! I'll send one of the girls out in a sec, just let us finish our doughnuts. I'm finding out all the goss!"

"Thanks, I'll just wait here."

"Ooh now, you don't need to be doing that, you must have stuff to do. No need to wait around. Unless you want to join us for a doughnut?"

Eve smothered a giggle. "No, I'm fine thanks. I'll go back down. Thanks for your help!"

"No worries! Laters!"

Eve pursed her lips as she dawdled down the corridor, then she felt a vibration in her pocket. Genius! She pulled out her phone to read the message then started typing out a reply, as slowly as possible, so she'd look like she had a reason for hanging around the corridors.

It wasn't long before the doors swung open, causing Eve to look up from her phone, then drop her arm to her side. Because the girl coming out of them, dressed in a scarlet cashmere jumper, smart jeans and chunky heels and carrying a mop, bucket and a collection of cloths, was the very girl who, just fifteen minutes earlier, had been telling the barista in Starbucks all about how she was seeing Dan. And in a flash Eve remembered where she had seen her before. She wasn't one of the associates or trainees, as Eve had assumed, but the very same cleaner that Eve had literally bumped into just the other morning. And, if Eve had her sources right, she was also Skye Worthington, the daughter of Chris and Mike.

*     *     *

When Skye got in that night she placed the fuchsia on the table and regarded it critically. It was a pretty plant but she wasn't sure she wanted it. She knew how it had come to finally be in her possession, was aware of the journey it had made and the hands that it had passed through, and that was the problem. One of those sets of hands were tainted. Those hands of that girl, Eve, with the long black hair and impeccable white suits, who worked on reception and was always flirting with Dan. Ok, so not always, exactly. But Skye had caught them locked in conversation often enough to know that she didn't like it.

She was the one her parents had spoken to; they had sung her praises and spouted nice things, but they didn't know what she was really like. They didn't know that she was waiting in the wings to pounce, just waiting for a moment when Skye let her guard slip so that she move in on Dan and claim him as her own. Not that Dan would be interested, of course. None of this was his fault. But Skye knew that boys were easily led, and that a woman spurned was a woman crazed. There were few limits to what a crazed woman would do to wreak revenge on her bitter enemy.

As she was running those thoughts through her mind she saw that she had been fiddling with the fuchsia buds, popping them all so they were now open and vulnerable to the world, without even realising what she was doing. She watched her hands, wondering what they would do next. And right before her eyes they picked up the bud nearest to her, squeezed the stem between her thumb and forefinger then plucked it off, quickly and neatly, dropping the bud so that it fell to the floor

233

and just a bare stem remained in its place.

Skye watched as one by one her fingers picked away at the flowers, slowly but steadily snapping them off until she was left with a pile of pink and purple heads and a pot of naked stems. Now the plant was ugly. Alive, still, but ugly. No good or use to anyone, not even for putting on a shelf to brighten up a dull room or for placing outside the front door to welcome visitors into a family home.

She continued to gaze at the pot for a while longer, until her eyelids began to droop. She kicked herself into gear and rose, picking up the decapitated plant in one hand and the flower heads in the other, and wandered over to the kitchen bin. She dropped the ruined plant into it, and the dull thud the pot made as it hit the base of the receptacle provided a sense of relief. She moved off to the bedroom and climbed up on her bed, then dropped the flower heads into her cloud box where they fell to rest on the pile of photos, clippings and papers, crowned on top with the sacred silver bangle.

# The Delusion

## Chapter 1

"Passport please. Thanks, ticket? That's great. Thank you, sir."
The passport controller handed back Ryan's documents. "Hope
you have a nice break, Paris is lovely this time of year. How
long are you going for?"

Ryan shrugged, noticing an odd sense of disconnect
between his head and his body. His legs felt as if they didn't
quite reach the ground.

"Oh! Well, all the best. Merry Christmas, and all that."

Ryan smiled wryly and headed towards the train,
pulling his phone out of his pocket by force of habit, before
staring at the screen and realising that he had nothing to say to
anyone. He wandered towards a bin and dangled his phone
over its gaping mouth, then on second thoughts switched it off
before returning it to his pocket. Then he let his head hang back
and breathed in deeply, savouring his new-found sense of
freedom and the beginnings of his 'fresh start'. That sounded
much better than 'running away'.

*     *     *

"Excuse me, can you help? I'm looking for a Mr Benjamin
Sage? From Key? Could you call up to him for me, please?
Hello?"

Eve jumped and looked up to face the glamorous

middle-aged woman awaiting her service. She quickly removed her head from her hands and sat up straighter. "I'm sorry, can I help?"

"Yes, I'm looking for Benjamin Sage. From Key. Can you tell him that Angie is here to see him?"

Eve became aware that her face had puckered into a frown. She immediately smoothed out her features, then ran a hand through her hair and blinked a few times. "I'm sorry, you're looking for Angie who? Which company?"

The older woman removed her glasses and leaned over the counter. "Are you ok?"

Eve nodded dumbly, unfamiliar with being spoken to like a real person at work. "Yes, sorry. Just, you know. Don't mind me, which Angie is it?"

"I'm Angie," the woman spoke slowly. "I'm looking for Benjamin Sage. With Key."

"Benjamin! Key! Of course!" The woman moved back a few steps at Eve's sudden display of enthusiasm. "Take the lift to the fourth floor, I'll phone through and tell his PA that you've arrived."

"Thanks." The woman hesitated. "Are you sure you're ok? You look very pale. Should I get someone?"

Eve felt tears begin to prickle the backs of her eyes and she rapidly shook her head. "No, no, I'm fine. Thank you, though. Thanks."

Angie smiled at Eve before making her way over to the lifts. Eve watched her go, waving weakly when Angie turned back as she pressed the lift control button, then took a deep breath before attempting to focus once more. Her concentration didn't last long.

"Stace? It's me!"

"Hey, Eve! You alright?"

"Yeah. Well, kind of. Something's happened. But it's a

bit odd. Can you chat?"

"Yeah, for a few mins. What's happening?"

"Well, you know that Skye girl I told you about the other day?"

"Mm hmm."

Eve heard a keyboard clicking in the background.

"Sorry, just had to send an e-mail. I'm all yours now."

"Ok. Well, anyway. I've found out a bit more information, and I've double checked on the database, and she's listed as an employer of Office Imps Cleaning Company, working under Shirley Minster, on the eighth floor. Definitely not as one of the graduates training in Edwards, Greenwood and Benjamin PR Agency on the third, like her parents seem to think."

"Huh? Well, it's probably just a mistake. Or a misunderstanding or something. What's the big deal?"

"But it's not a mistake! Because it still doesn't add up - Khadijah clearly had no idea who Skye was the other day. It just doesn't make any sense!"

"But why does it involve you? I don't get why you're so het up about it!"

"I don't know... I just....it's interesting. And my work is boring."

Stacey snorted down the line. "Fair play."

"But there's something else..."

"Yeah?"

"I think she might be seeing Dan."

"What? Your Dan?"

"Yes!"

"What the fuck? What a bitch! And what a dickhead! But Eve, again, why are you getting so involved? Especially if she's shagging your boyfriend! Oh Eve, are you ok?"

"He's not really my boyfriend..."

239

"Whatever. As good as"

"He's not. And I know it sounds crazy, but after everything that happened with Lloyd I don't really blame her. It's him I'm angry with."

"Have you said anything to him?"

"Not yet."

"Are you going to?"

"I have to."

"Yeah, you do. Eve, I'm really sorry but I'm going to have to go, can we chat properly later?"

"Yeah, sure. I'm about this evening."

"Cool. But I think you should ask him today, see how he reacts and what he says. You have to know, Eve. But don't do anything rash – I know how much you like him. And I know that sometimes you can get a bit, umm, fiery."

"I won't. It's ok, I've got a plan."

"You and your bloody plans!"

"You love them as much as I do! Talk to you later."

"Bye, babe!"

Eve hung up and flicked onto 'compose message', typed out a text, sent it up to the third floor and then attempted to get on with some work. But despite Stacey's advice she couldn't stop her thoughts from escalating, and by the time she heard Dan clattering across the hall she was struggling to hold on to rationality.

Eve glanced up, noting his crisp suit topped off by a look of confusion. Her heart still flipped slightly at the sight of his wonky, chipped tooth, but she steadied it and gave herself a firm talking to; she wasn't going to let him sweet talk her.

"What's going on? What does this mean?" He hung right over the desk, breathing heavily and waving his i-phone under her nose, but Eve shrugged and feigned interest in her monitor.

240

"Just what it says." She tapped away at her keyboard, frowning at the screen.

"But why? I was looking forward to our date."

Eve sighed and turned to look at him. "It's just not what I want."

His frown deepened.

"I'm through with dating, and games and all the rest of it. I just want to start something proper, that can develop into something meaningful. I don't want any more crap."

"What crap? Where has all this come from?"

Eve sighed again and rolled her eyes. "Skye."

"What?"

"Skye."

"What?" Dan's voice rose a few tones. "Why are you talking about the sky? Did you have a heavy night last night or something? You're not making any sense."

"Not *the* sky, Skye the *person*!"

He raised his eyebrows.

"Skye the cleaner. The one you're having a thing with."

"What?! What are you talking about? I have no idea what's going on here. Who's Skye? And why do you think I'm having a *thing*," he made rabbit ears around the word, "with a cleaner? What cleaner, anyway?"

Eve peered closer at him, then suddenly leant over and pushed the vase of flowers off the counter top and onto the floor. The glass smashed and water flooded out over the tiles, slipping down between them and covering the floor in a dangerous invisible sheen.

"What the hell are you doing?" Dan jumped away from the mess and stared in surprise at the mixture of flowers, water and shattered glass. But Eve was already on the phone.

"Hi, it's Eve. I'm sorry, we've had an accident down in reception, the flowers have fallen off the desk and made a mess

241

on the floor. Can you send someone down to sort it out? Great, thanks." She replaced the receiver in the cradle while Dan looked on in confusion. Eve had no doubt in her mind that he thought she was crazy.

"Look, I don't know what's going on here but the only person I am interested in is you. Or was you. You've obviously decided you're not keen and that's fine, but I want you to realise that that's coming from you, not me. I am not seeing anyone else, and I wouldn't see anyone else while I was dating you."

As Dan was speaking there was a ping, and they both turned their heads towards the lift. The doors swung open to reveal a young girl, smartly dressed in a scarlet cashmere sweater and skinny jeans, that were partly concealed by the uniform navy blue tabard of Office Imps. In one hand she held a brush, and in the other a mop and bucket. Her make up was pristine and every hair was perfectly shaded and lying in the correct place. Her clear turquoise eyes stood out across the hall as she stared over at Dan and Eve, who felt her blood suddenly race through her heart. Eve watched as Skye's eyes clouded over with something between fear and anger, then all three of them stood frozen in a silent triangle until Eve broke the stillness by raising one eyebrow at Skye, then turning questioningly to Dan. At that point Skye fled for the second time that morning, dropping her cleaning implements with a clatter and shooting across the hallway, out of the main doors and onto the crowded pavement. Eve could see her running off in the direction of Liverpool Street station, weaving in and out of workers and tourists as she disappeared off into the distance before losing herself in the crowds of the city.

Dan turned back to Eve and shrugged. "That was weird. Wonder what her problem is. Anyway, so as I was saying if you don't want to get involved that's fine, but remember it was your choice. Not mine."

Eve frowned at Dan. "Aren't you going to admit it?"

Dan exhaled noisily. "Admit *what*? I haven't done anything!"

"But Skye…"

"I have no idea who Skye is, Eve. And I don't know what you're talking about. Look, I've got to get back, I'll see you around, yeah?"

"Hang on." Eve watched him hesitate, then turn back apprehensively. "That girl, who just ran out the door."

"Yeah? What about her?"

"She's…Skye."

Dan shook his head dismissively and shrugged yet again. "I have no idea who she is. And I have no idea who Skye is. And I have no idea what has got into you today. But I've got to get back to work." And he turned and entered the lift that Skye had just vacated, after picking up the mop and brush and leaning them against the wall, so that the doors could close and take him - yet another one - away from her once more.

\*     \*     \*

Skye ran until her legs couldn't take anymore. She had to get out of there, out of the city, and back to her world. As her thighs started to turn to stone she hailed a taxi, past caring about the cost, then once home quickly changed and washed before curling up under her thick winter duvet, where she closed her eyes and got to work, thanking God for her escape from everyday drudgery and boredom. Here, she had it all - a dream job, a perfect man, a gorgeous flat and lots of friends to share it all with. Who cared what was happening out there? It was all so much simpler in her head.

But recently her fantasy world was starting to become

243

entwined with real life, and it was easy to get confused. Just for a second here or there, before reality kicked in again. It had happened once, briefly, when she'd seen Dan up in the cleaning department. For a moment she'd thought that he had come to see her, but he was just looking for soap for the toilets. Though he had bitten off a bit more than he could chew when he had played along with Shirley's flirting. Skye had hidden behind a pile of towels, eying him up and down as he squirmed, and making sure she took in every single last detail of him. She'd noticed an unfortunate water mark down the front of his suit, spreading out from the crotch in a suspicious looking dark stain. She'd enjoyed staring at it while trying to work out how it had got there.

The world inside her head meant so much more to her now that it had started to take on such a distinct shape, and she wanted to spend more and more time there. And other people believed in it, too. They were proud of her and her achievements, and she didn't want to spoil that illusion. That time before she went to bed, or when she has just woken up, or when she was stuck on the train or managed to slip off while walking down the street, kept her going. It helped her hold onto the idea of how her life could be. How her life *would* be, one day, when everything managed to sort itself out. Those moments added a bit of sparkle to it all, and without that avenue there would be nothing; real life was just such a bloody, great big let down.

## Chapter 2

Ryan woke up in the centre of Paris, after the best night's sleep he had had in ages. He stretched then hopped out from under the covers, pulling back the curtains to look out over the city. He could see the Sacre Coeur in the distance, standing out like a wedding cake against the grey, wintery clouds, and hear the sounds of the city waking up all around him.

"Good morning, Paris. *Bonjour!*" Ryan chuckled to himself then turned away from the view, quickly showered and dressed, picked up his laptop and headed out to find a croissant.

Ryan breathed in deeply as he wandered down towards Notre Dame. A crepe stand was already up and running, scenting the air with the smell of burning oil and frying batter, while an alternative clothing store - one of the few shops that had opened up for the day - blasted punk music out into the otherwise quiet streets. But other than that many of the shopfronts were still down. It felt like New Year's Day, as if the whole city had been up late last night and was now in the midst of a national hangover.

"*Bonjour, Monsieur.* You are Eengleesh? You want to see me?"

Ryan turned to see a middle aged woman reclining in a shop front, dolled up in leather and wearing enough make up to sink a Brittany Ferry. Actually, on second thoughts, it could be a man.

He smiled. *"Non, merci."*

S/he just shrugged and went back to their cigarette, while Ryan crossed over the road to a cafe with a perfect view of the Eiffel Tower. He was sure a coffee here would be horrifically overpriced, but it was worth it for the view.

*"Cafe au lait, si'l vous plait. Et un croissant. Merci."*

Ryan basked in his new-found language skills then settled himself at a table, flipped up his computer lid and opened up a new document.

'Lone Guitar,' he typed, then screwed up his nose.

*"Voila!"*

*"Merci."* Ryan took a bite of croissant, and a sip of coffee, and then started typing.

The clicking of the keys, the print filling the screen and the flow of the movement of his fingers across the keyboard soothed and relaxed him from the inside right out, and by lunch time Ryan had already spewed out over 1000 words. It was only when his stomach rumbled that he noticed his croissant still lying on the plate beside him. He picked it up and shovelled it into his mouth, while ordering another coffee, and wondered why he hadn't done this sooner. What had London ever done for him? And why had it taken so long to realise that the best thing he could do was leave? He hadn't felt this calm in a long time, and even when that picture had fallen out of his passport that morning he had just about felt ok. Things were finally starting to make sense, and it was such a relief that he could have cried. This 'fresh start' thing was certainly the way to go.

*"Excusez-moi? Si'l vous plait?"*

Ryan blinked and tore his gaze away from the screen.

*"Excusez-moi, Je..."*

"Um, *Ingles*. Sorry, I mean *Anglais*."

"Oh thank God, my French is appalling. Can you just keep an eye on my bags while I take these two...Alfie! I'm coming, just wait a few seconds!"

Ryan turned to see a small red-haired boy hopping from foot to foot while holding onto his willie.

"I can't! It's coming out!"

"Alfie! We're going, I just need to grab Lily, wait!"

"I can't, Daddy! I need to go!"

"Alfie! Get back here, you can't go on your own!"

"Hey, I'll watch her. Go with him, we'll be fine."

The guy hesitated.

"Honestly, we'll be fine! We'll just wait right here."

"Um, ok. Ok. Ta, thanks so much. Alfie, I'm coming!"

Just then a wail ran out that seemed to reach the Eiffel Tower then ricochet right back down the Seine and straight into Ryan's ears. He looked down at Lily, whose puce face was screwed up like a piece of used kitchen roll.

"Lily? It's ok. Daddy's coming back, he's just taken Alfie to the toilet."

Lily didn't seem to give a shit.

"Um, Lily?"

The screaming escalated even more, and her distress started to fracture Ryan's insides. How could she know that her daddy would be back in a few minutes? She probably thought she was never going to see him again.

Ryan hesitated and glanced up at the toilet door. There was no sign of the father, and he couldn't bear to watch Lily cry. He tentatively reached out and touched her cheek with the back of his finger, then trailed his hand down her arm to her tiny, tiny fingers. He brushed his finger over her miniature nails, and Lily suddenly grabbed for it and squeezed it tight. He was shocked at the amount of strength in her teeny fingers.

"Ok Lily, let's get you out of there."

247

Ryan crouched down next to the carrycot and slipped his hands under Lily's shoulders, making sure his fingertips supported the base of her head. He was amazed at how naturally it came.

"Shh, shh," he whispered, as he gently picked her up and pulled her into his chest like a hot water bottle. "Daddy's coming soon, he's just with Alfie. Your big brother."

As he rocked Lily from side-to-side her wailing decreased to a snuffle, and he noticed the colour in the top of her head fade to a creamy shade once more. He slipped his thumbs under her armpits and held her out from his body, and when her eyes locked on his she fell silent, just eyeing him and sniffing occasionally.

"Hello, Lily." Ryan smiled. "My name is Ryan."

"I'm so sorry that took so long! We had a little accident along the way, and...hey, are you ok? Here, let me take her."

It was only when he felt Lily's weight being removed from his hands that Ryan realised that his cheeks were soaking. His body felt filled with a huge black hole, with just his stony heart floating in the middle.

"Mate? I'm sorry, I don't even know your name. Are you ok? Can I do anything?"

Ryan looked up and saw the Eiffel Tower in the distance, fronted by the murky waters of the Seine. A boat sailed past.

"Mate? Hello? What's your name? I'm Ryan."

The stone in Ryan's chest seemed to swell as he looked up into the other Ryan's eyes. And then he pushed back his chair and ran, leaving his computer and wallet on the table.

Ryan fell in through the doors of the hostel later that night, unsure what he had been doing with the past ten hours or so. He knew he had run along the river until he was happy that the cafe was far behind him, and then had jumped on the metro and headed up to Montmartre with only two things on his mind.

But after alighting at Pigalle and walking along the boulevard for a few minutes Ryan had realised that he wanted to be alone. He didn't even want the beer anymore. So, instead, he had wandered the streets of Paris for the rest of the day. He knew that much. But he had no idea where he had been or what he had seen. Or what he was going to do now that he had lost all his cards and cash.

"Ryan? Ryan!"

Ryan turned and retraced his footsteps back to the foyer.

"Yeah?"

The attractive Australian girl was on the desk, the same one who had been working yesterday. Normally Ryan would have a crack at her, but tonight he couldn't be bothered.

"Oh, I'm glad I caught you. Some guy came by earlier and dropped off your computer and wallet. He said he found them in a cafe? And the hotel address was in your wallet. I was quite worried about you?"

"Oh! Wow."

Ryan stared at his belongings, wishing he could thank the other Ryan for doing this.

"Are you ok?"

"Umm, yeah. I, umm...I was in a cafe and then I had to, umm...and I left my stuff behind."

"Ok." The girl frowned at him. "Well, as long as your alright."

Ryan nodded, scooped up the computer and wallet and headed off in the direction of the lifts.

## Chapter 3

"Hi Shirley, it's Eve. Is there any news from Skye?"

"Nope. And I tell you what, I think it's better for her that I ain't got none. She's got no job here now, you know. I'm not having my staff doing a runner in the middle of a shift. I don't expect to see her again, and I'd give up hope too if I were you. It's been a week now, you must have more important things to do down there in that shiny white palace than worrying about Skye, you've been calling at least once a day since this happened! I'd forget about it if I were you! Why are you so bothered anyway?"

"Oh, no reason." Eve paused. "I just...I don't know. I feel sorry for her, I guess. I met her parents and they are so sweet, and I think something's going on. I think she's having something of a hard time. That's all."

"Hard time? I'll show you a hard time! You come up here and try and run this department when your imps don't bother showing up for work, or don't know their dusters from their dishcloths! I don't know…"

"Well, thanks Shirley. I'll let you get back," to your doughnuts, Eve added in her head.

"Oh, anytime love, you take care of yourself. Come up for a doughnut and a cuppa soon, eh?"

"Will do." Eve hung up and took a few deep breaths, before settling into her usual course of action whenever a crisis arose: brewing up a nice big mug of fruit tea.

Eve pondered what to do as she inhaled the sweet, strawberry scented vapours. It was just like her, to get embroiled in some other family's problems. But the world could just be such a vile place, and she wanted to help people. In the end came up with two options: phone Skye's parents, or get Skye's home address off the database and go and find her for herself.

That evening Eve found herself standing outside a miserable looking fried chicken shop in the heart of Cricklewood, in North West London. The shop had already opened up for the evening but the only person inside was a large, dirty looking middle-aged man slouching behind the counter who, as Eve had been watching, had stuck a finger up his nose, had a good poke around and then gone straight back to flipping burgers. The smell of frying grease and cooking chicken crept into her nostrils, tinged with the fresh, warm scent of detergent from a nearby launderette and the sweet edge of the shisha cafe a few doors down.

Eve pulled out the slip of paper bearing Skye's details, stamping her feet against the cold, and re-read the address. She was definitely in the right place but needed to get to flat B, which was presumably above the fast food outlet. She looked around the shop and spotted a worn wooden door, with black paint peeling off in strips, flanked on one side by an intercom system. Eve wandered over, routed out the button for flat B and held her finger down firmly on the buzzer.

She waited a minute or so. She tried buzzing again, then stepped back on the pavement and eyed the building. The Victorian brickwork of the flats did have potential, but it was covered in a layer of dirt. Wooden window frames, desperately in need of a coat of paint, were rotting and chipping away, and the windows were lined with dirty, off-white nets, apart from one that was covered with cardboard and newspaper. And it was at that point that she saw one of the curtains on the first floor twitch. As she looked in the direction of the movement she saw a flash of blonde disappearing behind the net, so with renewed determination Eve went back to the flat and pressed her finger down on the buzzer three times, then held it down extra long for good measure.

"What?"

The abrupt voice coming out through the speaker took Eve by surprise.

"Oh, hi. It's Eve here. From the office. Is that Skye?"

There was no response.

"Um, ok, um, I just wanted to see if you were alright. You disappeared so quickly from work the other day and no-one has heard anything from you since. I'm worried about you."

"I'm fine." Skye spoke curtly and Eve rested her head against the wall, sure that she wasn't going to get very far, but relaxing into the sense of relief flooding through her body at just having found Skye.

"Can I come up?"

A pause. She was beginning to wonder whether Skye had gone, but then she spoke again.

"No. Listen, I'm fine. Everything's good. Thanks for being concerned, though. Take care, and have a great Christmas." A click echoed out into the freezing night air.

Eve sighed and turned to leave. At least she knew Skye was ok, for the time being. But she knew she needed to do more. She'd probably have to phone Mike and Christine. Unless...

A new idea formed in her mind as she hurried back down towards Kilburn tube station, turning for one last glance

253

of the flat as she strode down the road. She stumbled as she spotted Skye leaning out of the window, her usually perfect hair looking as if she had fallen asleep with it wet, her eyes sallow and her cheeks thin. A cigarette hung out of the corner of her mouth and as Eve watched Skye exhaled a puff of blue smoke into the clear black sky. It merged with the orange glow of the streetlights. Eve caught Skye's eye and her heart started to thump as she froze, worried that if she so much as moved a muscle Skye would rear and buck. Skye held her gaze for a second, before taking another drag on her cigarette, retracting her body into the window and slamming the glass shut behind her.

"I'm not sure about this, Eve." Dan eyed Eve dubiously over the top of his pint glass.

"Please, Dan. Come on, we need to do something."

Dan wrinkled up his nose as he took another sip of lager. "I don't know. It just seems a bit," he hesitated. "Far-fetched. And weird." He put down his pint and leaned back in his chair, folding his arms over his chest in a way that made his biceps bulge and Eve's mouth salivate. "Can't we just stay here? It's nice and warm. And we managed to get a booth, you know how hard that is. I want to celebrate our reunion! I thought you were never going to speak to me again." He touched her hand gently and leaned forward in his seat.

Eve chuckled and glanced over at the log fire burning at the far end of the room. She could feel the heat tickling her calves, and the air was warm with the scent of mulled cider. She snuggled back into the corner of the darkened booth and for a second felt tempted by Dan's suggestion. But then the image of Skye dangling out the window flashed into her mind and her eyes snapped open.

"No. We have to do something, Dan."

"But I don't think it would work anyway!"

Eve sighed. "Well, maybe not. But I think it's the least we can do. Seriously, something's not right. She honestly told that girl in Starbucks that she was going out with you and that she worked in PR. Both of which are obviously blatant lies."

Dan nodded.

"And now she's disappeared from work, and she's hiding out in some horrible flat in a horrible area. And she looked awful, Dan. All tired and haggard. I just want to get in there, see if she's ok."

"But it's nothing to do with us." Dan squirmed. "I've never even spoken to the girl, I barely even know what she looks like. What does it matter to us if she's a compulsive liar? Have you ever spoken to her?"

"Not really. But I'm worried. I just want to make sure she's ok. I feel involved, I've met her parents and…" she trailed off, not quite ready to tell Dan about losing her own parents and the connection she felt to Mike and Chris because of it.

Eve looked up and fluttered her fake lashes, assuming a doe-eyed expression. She laid her hand on top of his and as her leg brushed against his thigh she felt him shudder.

"Ok! Ok." He drained his glass. "I'll do it. Just tell me where you want me to go and want you want me to do, and I'll go there and do it. But you owe me."

Eve smiled back at Dan, holding his gaze as she took a sip of her spritzer, and felt a glow of warmth oozing through her body. It felt like happiness, though she couldn't be sure. It was such a long time since its last visit.

"After you." Dan mock-bowed as Eve boarded the Jubilee line train, and she bee-lined for the last available seat as he propped himself up against a pole. "Where are we going anyway?"

255

"Cricklewood. It's just up from Kilburn."

"Ok." Dan reached for one of the free papers that lay strewn around the carriage. "Want to do the crossword while we travel? One across, 'baby eel'."

"Elver!"

"Wow, that was quick!" He penned in the answer. "Two down, Spanish queen. Five letters, begins in R. How am I supposed to know any flipping Spanish queens?!"

"Reina."

Eve winked as Dan looked down at her.

"Reina. It's Spanish for queen."

"Aha! Very good! Three across..."

And they spent the next fifteen minutes arguing over answers, apart from a brief recess at Swiss Cottage where the train stopped rather abruptly and Dan careered into a bunch of youths, complete with hoods and earphones. Much to his embarrassment, and much to Eve's amusement.

The duo alighted at Kilburn and set off up Shoot-Up Hill, walking for about twenty minutes before they reached Skye's flat. As before the chicken shop was deserted except for the obese owner, who today appeared to be biting his nails while mixing salad. The air was still heavy with the smell of frying oil and washing powder, and the flat still dreary.

Eve led Dan up to the worn black door and was about to press down on the buzzer, when she noticed that the door was open. She glanced at Dan, but without waiting to see his reaction pushed open the door, then crept into the darkened hallway.

Eve nearly tripped on the threadbare carpet, that appeared to be draped over the stairs rather than tacked down at the edges. When she arrived outside the door she saw that it, too, was hanging open, so she tentatively pushed it further and peered inside. She recoiled as the stink of damp and rotting fruit hit her nostrils, but forced herself to go into the living room. A faded, burnt-orange sofa faced an ancient-looking coffee table, scratched and peppered with cigarette burns and ash. A single hard backed chair rested by the window, which looked out onto a paved yard covered in rubbish from the chicken shop. The carpet was a dated ochre colour, although there were a fair number of brown stains which gave it something of a speckled effect.

"Skye? Are you there?" Eve's voice echoed around the bare apartment as she picked her way through the discarded lager cans, enroute to a doorway branching off from the main living space.

She gently pushed open the door and peered into the chamber. The room stank of cigarette smoke, and again the number of possessions was pitiful. An unmade bed rested in one corner of the room, the duvet and cushions deprived of covers and cases. The floor was covered with an ill-fitting brown carpet, and an old net curtain - stained yellow from years of tobacco abuse - barely covered the tiny window pane which was speckled with watermarks and bird shit.

"Eve?" She jumped a mile as Dan came behind her and placed a hand on her shoulder. "Eve, I don't like this. It's a shit hole, it's creepy, it stinks and there's no-one here. Let's go."

Eve couldn't speak. How could Skye be living in such a place? This picture didn't correlate with Skye's image, nor with the parents who had spoken so proudly of their daughter. They had seemed so, well, *normal.* And this most certainly wasn't. Nothing about the situation was.

"Eve, let's go. Come on." Eve allowed herself to be led back through the filthy living room, down the treacherous staircase and out onto the street. She was glad of the freezing cold air that slapped at her cheeks as she exited the building - it reminded her that she was still awake and not drowning in a nightmare. Not that that wouldn't have been preferable.

They walked silently down Cricklewood Broadway, towards the tube station. Eve's head was tangled with thoughts of Skye and that flat, and she couldn't stop wondering about how things had ended up this way. She was about to voice her thoughts to Dan when she looked up and caught a familiar face. Skye was scurrying along, her shoulders hunched up against the cold, wearing joggers and a scruffy jacket with a bottle of milk tucked under her arm.

Once she had passed Eve halted and grabbed Dan's arm, making him jump and cry out in surprise.

"She's here!" Eve hissed, turning around to watch Skye fading into the darkness.

"Where? What are you doing?!" Dan sounded perturbed, and verging on fed-up, as Eve grabbed his hand and started to drag him down the street.

"We're going back. She must be on her way home so we're going back to her house to do what we came here to do."

"But...ok! Fine!"

Once they were back outside the flat Eve paused, appearing to think for a moment, before turning to Dan.

"Go on, in you go."

"What? Why me?" His eyes seemed to pierce into her soul and Eve suddenly felt an involuntary shudder run down her spine.

"You promised! She won't talk to me but I think she will to you, you have to go in!" Her voice was indignant, although distracted somewhat as she tried to avoid being thrown off course by the forces soaring through her bloodstream. It was as if someone had just spiked her with adrenalin.

"But...I don't know..."

Eve suddenly reached up and grabbed Dan's face in her

258

hands, pulling him towards her and placing a big kiss on his lips while pushing her hips up against him. His lips were slightly parted in surprise and she briefly slipped her tongue between them. He tasted of coke, from the can he had been sipping, and as she pulled away from him his breath felt warm on her tingling lips.

"Will you go in?" She spoke softly and seductively, licking her lips as she eyeballed him and challenged him to refuse.

"On it." He stuttered as he stumbled towards the door, all objections firmly silenced.

*      *      *

Skye poured milk onto a bowl of stale cornflakes as she thought forward excitedly to the evening ahead. Tonight she was going to be praised for her contract with that client, and Dan and her were going to step up their relationship by having 'the talk'. She'd felt it coming for a long time, and now that she felt confident enough to discuss those hidden demons with him she was keen to get started on it.

As she became more eager to slip into her special space she abandoned her cornflakes and, almost on autopilot, glided into her room and sank down on her bed. She closed her eyes and slipped out of reality, feeling a wide smile spreading over her face, and then she was gone.

Skye jumped when the buzzer went. It took her a second to work out where she was and what that noise meant, but as the buzz resounded around the flat for a second time she jumped up and went to the intercom system. She hesitated before picking up the phone, then lifted it to her ear and waited for the other person to talk.

"Hello?"

259

It was a well-spoken male voice.

"Skye?"

Skye jumped a mile. How did he know her?

"Skye? Are you there? It's Dan." A pause. "From the office. From Edwards."

Every muscle in Skye's body froze. She felt that even if she had wanted to move her fingers, or stretch her toes, it would have been impossible. She couldn't even blink. But she must have made some kind of noise, because Dan seemed to become aware of her presence.

"Skye? You're there." It wasn't a question. "Can I come up and talk to you?"

"Huh?" Skye's throat cracked.

"We're worried about what's happened to you. I just want to talk to you and make sure you're ok, so I can go back and tell the others."

"I'm fine." As Skye came more fully back to consciousness her voice became spiky and sharp.

"I just want to talk. Two minutes? Please?"

"No." And she hung up the receiver before he could respond, ignoring the buzzer which continued to echo around the flat a few more times before it fell silent.

*    *    *

Eve was reluctant to admit defeat, but had to concur that if Skye didn't want to talk she couldn't force her, so eventually they gave up and headed back to the station once again.

Like last time Eve turned before she lost sight of the flat, and jumped when she saw Skye peering out of the window. A sense of deja vu caused her breath to catch. She paused and the girls stared at each other for a second, until Eve tentatively raised her hand. Skye reacted by shooting back

260

behind the grimy net curtain, leaving it waving in the breeze as if it was telling Eve to go home. Eve cursed herself for having scared Skye off, and as she turned and walked alongside Dan she held the picture of Skye's thin, exhausted face in her mind. It was the huge, terrified eyes that made Eve shiver, the way Skye had been peering out of the window like a child left alone, desperately hoping that her mum would be back soon. The eyes held a mixture of anger, sadness and wistfulness, but something more, as well. Eve shuddered, knowing that look would haunt her when she tried to get to sleep that night, and felt a stab of desperation penetrate her heart. She wondered when that feeling would realise its futility.

Eve reached out and slipped her hand in Dan's. She didn't even think about the action as it seemed so natural, and it was only once she had wrapped her fingers around his that she wondered whether she had overstepped the mark. Holding her breath she turned to look up at him, but he was smiling down at her. He held her gaze for a second before leaning over and kissing her ever so gently on the lips, then they continued along the road to the tube.

*     *     *

Skye extinguished her cigarette and wandered back into her bedroom, where she lay back heavily on her bed and closed her eyes.

"Sorry about that babe, it was no-one. Just an unwelcome interruption. Now, where were we?" And as she placed her hand on her breast, tweaking her nipple so that it stood to attention, it became Dan's fingers doing the work. "I love you, Dan," she whispered, before he closed his mouth over hers and trailed his fingers further southwards.

"I love you too, Skye," he murmured into her mouth,

his breath warm and tasting of red wine. "I really, really do."

Skye smiled as he started to kiss her, and thought once again about how lucky she was that the love of her life could never, ever leave her.

## Chapter 4

"I'm going to call her parents."

"Eve, don't you think you should bow out now? You've done what you can. It really doesn't have anything to do with you."

"I know, Dan." Eve tapped her nails on the receiver of the office phone, which was as white and shiny as everything else in the entrance hall. At least on the outside. The buttons on the inside were engrained with foundation and blusher way too deep to ever come off. "I know, and I know Skye is going to hate me even more, and her parents are going to be so worried and hurt, but...but that poor girl. She needs help, Dan. If this got worse and I hadn't done anything, I just couldn't live with myself. I just couldn't..."

"Ok, Eve. Listen, you do what you feel you need to do, ok? I know well enough that you're going to go ahead with this anyway. So just give me a shout and let me know if you need me, ok?"

"Thanks, Dan, Are you still coming down for lunch?"

"Yep, see you at three. Sorry it has to be so late. Anyway, I've got to go now."

"Ok, see you later. I'll tell you how it goes."

It was Chris who answered the phone, sounding so relaxed and trouble-free that Eve almost hung up without saying anything. But she forced herself to stay on the line, knowing that she was the only one who could help Skye and that she couldn't risk leaving it until it was too late.

"Mrs Worthington? Hi, it's Eve here. The Receptionist from the office where your daughter works. We met recently and I passed on the fuchsia plant for you…"

"Oh yes, hello dear! How nice to hear from you again. How can I help? Is Louise so busy now that she has employed you as an assistant to organise her busy social life and make calls back to the oldies?" Chris laughed uproariously at her own joke and Eve felt her eyes sting with the onset of tears.

"Mrs Worthington…"

"Chris, please."

"Ok, Chris," Eve took a deep breath. "I think there's something you should know. About Skye."

"What?" Chris's voice became sharp.

"Is your husband home?"

"What's going on?"

"Is Mike home? Would he be able to come on another phone? I'd like to speak to both of you together."

"What the hell is going on? Is she alive? Is she in hospital?"

"Mrs Worthington…Chris…Skye is alive and she's not in hospital. Please get your husband on the line so I can talk to you both." Silence ensued and Eve wondered for a second whether Chris had deserted the call. Then she heard scrabbling down the line and a male voice spoke, gruff and worried.

"Mike speaking, what's going on?"

"Are you both there? Ok, look. I don't know how to break this to you in any easy way, so I'm just going to say it. Skye's been lying to you. She doesn't work for Edwards PR but as a cleaner in this building. She…"

"What are you talking about? Of course she works for Edwards, she's one of the graduates there. Is this some kind of joke?"

"Please, listen to me." Eve implored, though she didn't blame Mike for his abrupt reaction. "I have some stuff to tell you, and I know how it will sound. Believe me, I've run through it in my head enough times, trying to make sense of it all. But I'm telling the truth."

There was a pause before Mike's voice came back down the line. "Look, I don't know what you're talking about, and I don't know what your game is, but I've got things to do. You need to find a better way to spend your time." Then there was a click on the line, and Mike was gone.

"Hello? Chris?" An exhalation of breath confirmed that Chris was still there. "Chris, please listen to me. I'm telling you the truth. I'm really worried about your daughter, I think she needs help."

"Are you on medication?" Eve could hear the hope in Chris's voice, and would have found the question laughable if it hadn't been such a serious situation.

"No!" She slammed a fist down on the counter top and watched a biro roll across the surface, dropping onto the floor with a delicate tinkle. "No, I'm not. Please, just hear me out. Please. It's important."

There was a silence, followed by a sigh, which Eve took as a sign to continue.

"Look, after you left the other day I looked Skye up on the database, so that I could take the plant up to her. She was listed as working for Office Imps Cleaning Company on the eighth floor. I know, I thought it was just an error in the system too. But I remembered that Khadijah didn't seem to know who Skye was, so I went up and investigated on the eighth floor. And I met the manager of the cleaning team, Shirley."

A sharp intake of breath on the other end of the line made Eve pause.

265

"Skye said her boss was called Shirley," Chris practically whispered.

Eve closed her eyes. Skye must have slipped up somewhere down the line.

"Well, Shirley knew exactly who Skye was. She took the plant for her."

Chris didn't respond.

"And then I met Skye. She was mopping the floor, all dressed up in the cleaning uniform. But then when I was in Starbucks I overheard her telling the waitress about how she was working for Edwards and was seeing this guy."

"Dan."

Eve's heart thumped.

"Yes. But I know Dan, and he doesn't actually know who Skye is. And Skye saw me when she was saying all that stuff, and now she knows that I know something's going on she's stopped coming into work. I've been to her flat, so I know she's ok, but she's disappeared from the workplace. And I'm worried about her."

"Are you jealous?"

"What?" Eve's head jerked up out of her hand. "Jealous?"

"Yes. Our daughter is a very successful PR career girl and has a great new boyfriend. And you're just the receptionist, and you want this Dan for yourself. So you're going out of your way to destroy our daughter's life. Is that it?"

"Chris, please! I wouldn't. There's something else as well."

"What?"

"Well, I went up to her flat in Cricklewood the other day…"

"Cricklewood? She lives in West Hampstead. She has a lovely flat there, with a garden and a balcony and a nice flat mate called Anna. We've seen the pictures..." Chris trailed off, suddenly sounding a lot less certain.

"Chris..." Eve crossed her fingers, hoping against hope that Chris would believe her. "She doesn't. She lives by herself above a chicken shop in an area called Cricklewood. And the flat is, well, horrible."

"No, it can't...I don't understand..."

"Nor do I, but I'm worried about Skye. She seems to be living some kind of double life. I think you'd better come and see if you can get to the bottom of it all. Can you come up?"

"Oh my God. Eve, is it happening again?" Chris's voice caught.

"What, Chris? Is what happening again?"

"Well, there was this time at university. In Aberystwyth. She...I'm sorry, I can't..."

"Chris, it's fine. Just tell me when you can be here."

Chris sniffed. "Tonight. We'll leave right now."

"Right, take my number." Eve rattled off her personal mobile number. "And call me when you get here."

"Well, we'll go straight to Skye's place. We've got her address right here."

"What is it?"

Chris started reeling off an address, then stopped. "That's not right, is it?"

Eve shook her head, momentarily forgetting that Chris couldn't see her.

"Eve? Is that where Skye lives?"

"No. Phone me as soon as you get here and we'll talk. I don't think we should just go barrelling into her flat, she's in a very precarious position and we need to think before we act."

"What's her real address?"

"Just call me when you get here, ok?" And Eve hung up the phone, feeling guilty for cutting Chris off but wanting to make sure that she and Mike couldn't go to Skye's without talking to her first. And, most importantly, just wanting Skye's mother to get off the phone and get up to London.

## Chapter 5

"Mike, Chris, hi. Good to see you."

"Where is she? You said you'd tell us when we got here and here we are. Where is she?"

"Chris! Wait!"

"No, Mike! She's my baby and I want to see her!"

Eve took a deep breath and clenched her jaw. "Chris, listen, let's get a coffee and have a chat. Then we can go up to her flat."

"Coffee?! You think I can drink a coffee right now?"

"Chris! Calm down. I think that's a very good idea, Eve. Let's go in here and decide how to manage this."

"I..."

"Chris," Eve saw Mike squeeze her arm. "Coffee first."

Chris opened her mouth but just exhaled, appearing to cave in on herself as she slouched against her husband. But she allowed herself to be dragged into the little cafe outside Kilburn tube station, and sat quietly while Mike wandered off to order. Though she wouldn't even look at Eve, let alone talk to her.

"Here, Eve. No sugar, right?"

"No, that's great. Thanks Mike."

"That's ok. Listen, I'm sorry I was rude on the phone earlier. I..."

"No, Mike. It's fine. Honestly."

269

"It's not, Eve. I should have listened to you. I shouldn't...."

"Mike, seriously. It's ok." Eve wrapped her hands around the boiling mug. "Let's just focus. We need to act fast, but we need to be careful. I'm worried about Skye's fragility, so I really think we need to proceed with caution. That's why I wanted to talk with you first."

Mike nodded.

"I just don't want her to do another runner and vanish altogether."

Eve glanced down at the table as she noticed Mike's eyes glazing over. He coughed, and she gave him a moment to compose himself before continuing.

"Look, before we head up there I was just wondering if, I mean, on the phone you mentioned something about Aberystwyth? Has this happened before?"

Eve watched as Mike and Chris, who had so far remained mute and still, made eye contact. A single tear trickled down Chris's cheek. Eve felt the connection between them, the story that still bound them together, and sensed that she had gone too far.

"I'm sorry, you don't even know me. Shall we go?" Eve went to pick up her handbag but Mike put his hand on her arm and gently encouraged her to sit back down.

"Yes, this has happened before. When Louise was at university. We had no idea that anything was amiss - Lou would phone and tell us all these wonderful stories about her life at university, and we thought she was happy. Then she stopped calling so much and when she did she seemed so distant and angry, though she'd still talk about all the same things. And then one day we got a call from her friend, Amy, saying that she was concerned about Louise and didn't know what to do. Amy said that Louise was rarely coming out of her room and had made up some lie about having a relationship with a young man who claimed to not even know her name. Apparently Louise had stopped going to lectures and didn't go out socialising, yet when Amy spoke to her she talked as if she was living the high life. The call from Amy was similar to the one we got off you, but, you know…we never really got to the bottom of things…" Mike broke off, hanging his head guiltily, and Eve became aware of Chris trembling next to her. "We took her to a doctor and he prescribed a few things, and she tried counselling, but didn't stick with it. And we didn't make her." Mike looked up and met Eve's gaze with desperate eyes, as if begging for forgiveness. "She seemed better, Eve. We thought it had gone away and that we could forget about it and move on. It just seemed like a phase, so we figured it was a reaction to leaving home and everything, but that she'd got better and that was it. We didn't want to think, or maybe admit, that…"

Eve placed her hand over Mike's and squeezed, his skin feeling surprisingly soft despite its outward wrinkles. "Mike, you don't need to explain to me. I just want to help you now. Shall we go?"

Mike blinked a few times and sniffed loudly before nodding. "Yep, let's go. He rose from his seat and put out his hand to support Chris. "Oh Eve," he exhaled heavily and rubbed his forehead with his free hand. "How could we have got it so wrong? How could we have let this happen again? I just wanted her to be better, I just wanted it to go away. And I really thought it had."

"Shh, let's not dwell on that now." Eve patted Mike's arm before wrapping her coat more tightly around her tiny waist. She suddenly felt as if she was mothering a small boy, and wanted to give him a hug. "Let's just go and deal with the situation and take it from there, ok?" Eve made towards the exit

271

of the cafe, turning to ensure that Mike and Chris were following, and led the party out onto the street. It was only once they were outside that Eve noticed they didn't have jackets to protect themselves against the elements of the December evening.

She led the way up Shoot-Up Hill towards Cricklewood, along the route that was becoming increasingly familiar to her, while puzzling over what the pair had revealed. It all seemed a bit extreme - so Skye had struggled to settle into university and had told a few lies to add a bit of gloss to her life. Didn't everyone do that from time to time? Eve knew that she had one persona for the office, that differed from the one she presented to her flatmates, and yet another which she employed when she visited her aunt. They were all slight variations on the truth, with certain things emphasised and others remaining unvocalised, depending on who she was with. But that didn't make her unstable, or ill. And most people did the same thing. But then again most people seemed to know where the boundaries lay, and it didn't seem as if Skye fell into that camp.

As they arrived outside the chicken shop Eve halted, and one look at both Mike's and Chris's faces told her that they had genuinely had no idea that Skye was residing in such a place. Mike's face was as white as a sheet and Chris held one hand over her mouth, looking as if she was about to vomit. And that was before she had been inside.

"Wait here," Eve instructed, and made for the buzzer. "I think it's best if I try and get in first. She's getting used to my visits, but she might freak out if she knows you guys are here. I'll go and see what reaction I get, ok?"

Chris and Mike nodded mutely and Eve strode off towards the door, appearing much more confident than she actually felt. She didn't have a game plan and had no idea how this whole thing was going to go, but she knew that someone had to take the lead.

She held her finger over the buzzer, but no voice came over the intercom. After trying three times and getting no response she tentatively pushed the door, and it fell open. Turning to look at Skye's parents she indicated that they should stay where they were, then she went in and crept up the same staircase that she had wandered up just twenty four hours earlier. Once again the door to Skye's flat was hanging open, and Eve frowned. Didn't the girl have any sense of security?

Not much had changed in the flat since the previous day - it still smelled unclean and stale, the rubbish hadn't been taken out and lager cans and cigarette packets still littered the surfaces. The unmade bed was still visible through the open bedroom door, and the flat still lacked any kind of personal touch. Eve walked across the dirty carpet towards the bedroom, glancing around for any kind of clue as to what the hell was going on. And there, lying on the desk, was a notebook, lying open at a page covered with scrawled writing and doodles. Without thinking about it Eve grabbed the notebook, stashed it in her handbag and scurried back down the way she had come.

"She's not in." Eve announced, as she exited the building. "But I've found something that might help." She dug into her bag for the notebook, but as she looked up she noticed that Chris and Mike had slipped past her vigilant guard and were already making their way up the stairs.

"Hey! Wait!" She ran back towards the door. "Come back a minute, I've got something, just…just…" but she knew it was futile. She watched them disappear in through the open flat door and cringed, unable to imagine what would be going through their minds when they saw the dump that had become their daughter's home. But the notebook stole her focus and she scuttled over to the nearest lamppost, where she used the

273

orangey illumination to aid her in reading the childish scrawl that covered the page.

*I know it's not the best way to live, but I just can't help it. Reality is a big let down where nothing goes as intended. I had so many dreams and hopes and ideals, but they've all been dashed; I've failed and I don't know how to succeed. But when I close my eyes I have a life. I have a successful career, an amazing flat, great friends and the perfect boyfriend.*

*I'm not mad. I choose to dream; it's not like I can't help it. And I know what's real and what's not, but I also know that I don't like Louise's world. I like Skye's. And with each day that passes I spend more time there.*

*Sometimes I do it all day - just shut my eyes and slip away. I meet people and build relationships, develop my career and plan for the future. Every time I return I pick up where I left off. I'd rather be there than anywhere else, and I don't want it to end. Then nothing would have any meaning. I could cut back, but it's hard to change a habit. And it doesn't hurt anyone. Does it really matter, anyway, if I'd rather be in there than out here? Being there makes me happy and happiness, at the end of the day, is all I've ever wanted.*

Eve finished reading Skye's poignant words and became aware of the tears trickling down her cheeks, leaving cold trails as they hit the freezing air. What on earth had happened to Skye? How could she have become so disillusioned with life that she would rather fantasise than be around real people? And why had nobody helped her?

Eve realised that there was more so she turned over and scanned the following page, and if she thought the first admission was a shock the next bit nearly gave her heart attack. She felt her insides turn to jelly as she read the final paragraph.

274

*No-one knows how things really are there. Not mum, not dad, not even Amy. And they'll never know, because this is our little secret. But this is right. This way we're both a part of something and I know we can always be together, just the way it was meant to be. And now you can never leave me. And I promise that I will never leave you, either. We both know things are better this way.*

Eve jumped as a banshee wail echoed out round the still winter's night. She spun around to try and identify the source of the noise, her brain flailing around as it tried to grab hold of a way to make the sound stop, then she realised it was coming out of Skye's apartment.

The door to the flat swung open and Chris and Mike came stumbling out. Chris's wailing subsided as she came out onto the pavement but tears continued to flow down her cheeks, and Mike's eyes were rimmed with red. Eve brushed her own tears away and, on impulse, ripped that last page out of Skye's journal and stuffed it in her pocket. She held the book discreetly by her side and hurried over to them.

"I'm sorry..." she started, then stopped. What good was that going to do? "Mike, can I help? Here, let me take her other arm."

Chris only seemed able to support herself through leaning on Mike, who had his arm around her shoulder and his cheek resting on the crown of her head. Eve tried to take her other arm and slip it around her waist but Chris resisted, just turning to glare at Eve. But after a few seconds she turned back to Mike then slowly collapsed onto the pavement, coiling up into herself and once again emitting a low wail that sent shivers down Eve's spine.

"Come on love, that's not going to help." Mike

275

crouched down next to Chris, wrapping his arms around her and talking into her hair. But in response Chris's wailing intensified until words became audible.

"Why is she doing this? Why is she lying to us?" Chris's sobs took over her speech once again as she buried her face in Mike's shirt sleeves. "How could I let this happen? After everything…my baby…why couldn't I keep her safe?" And then her words gave way to wail after wail as Chris worked herself up into a state resembling hysteria. Ordinarily Eve would have felt uncomfortable witnessing such a scene, but her recent discovery was taking over her mind and she didn't have space to feel awkward.

"Mike, I've found something out." She indicated the notebook, but Mike didn't react.

"I've got to get her inside, we need to go somewhere. Help me!"

Eve slipped the book back into her handbag and took Chris's right arm, as Mike pulled her up by the left. This time Chris didn't resist, but she was like a dead weight and did nothing to help them support her.

"Come on Chris, we'll get you to a hotel. It'll be ok." Eve didn't have to meet Mike's eye to know that his optimism was all a front. "Come on love, there you go."

Eve struggled under Chris's weight; she was a short woman but rather round, and she leaned heavily on Eve's shoulders. As Eve battled to keep herself on her feet she inhaled the scent of lavender from Chris's blouse collar, and thought with a jolt about how, that morning, Chris and Mike would have just got ready for the day as usual, with absolutely no idea of what was to come.

As she noticed a taxi approach Eve waved her free arm manically, and once Mike and Eve had bundled Chris into the back Eve opened the passenger door and jumped in next to the driver.

"To the nearest hotel. A Holiday Inn or something." The driver nodded and pulled away from the kerb, and away from the hovel that Skye called home.

It only took about ten minutes to arrive at the nearest Marriott. Eve left Mike and Chris in the car while she went and negotiated a room, and once she had a key card went back out to pay the taxi and get the couple inside.

Chris had stopped bawling, but silent tears still ran down her cheeks. She even got out of the taxi by herself and walked into the foyer without any help, although she moved like a robot with her eyes staring soullessly into the middle distance.

Eve led them to the room, and as soon as she opened the door Chris made for the impeccably white covered bed, pulled back the sheets and crawled under the duvet without even pausing to take off her shoes. Mike followed and slipped her loafers off her feet, murmuring consolingly the whole time, then placed her shoes gently on the floor. He pulled the covers up to her chin and tucked them in around her as if she was a helpless child, before moving back over to Eve, while Chris lay facing the wall. Her eyes were unblinking and her face expressionless. Eve gave Mike a sympathetic look, but bit her tongue as she thought about the latest bit of news she had to break.

"We need to talk." She muttered, and Mike nodded. "Out there - I saw a coffee machine and there were a couple of chairs, we can talk but keep an eye on Chris at the same time." Eve led the Mike out of the room towards the seating area while wondering, yet again, how she had managed to become so embroiled in all of this.

## Chapter 6

Rather than trying to explain what she had found out Eve handed Mike the notebook, open at the relevant page. She held her breath as she watched his frown deepen the more he read, then sat back as he finished but flicked back to the beginning to read it again. A flash of guilt flickered through her belly as she thought of the other sheet of paper that was hiding in her pocket, but she felt that Mike was dealing with enough for the time being.

Finally Mike placed the notebook on the wooden coffee table and picked up the plastic cup of coffee that Eve had bought for him, taking a sip before turning to her with a frown on his face.

"God, I never knew it was this bad. Shit! Sorry." He briefly rubbed a palm over his mouth. "We were so wrong. We thought..." Mike trailed off and Eve let him have some time. She tried to warm her fingers by wrapping them around the polystyrene cup of murky brown water, but they were still practically frozen rigid and the coffee's effort was futile.

"What can we do?" Mike's frown deepened. "It seems as if...I mean...we thought..." he took another sip of the lukewarm, weak excuse for coffee while Eve took a deep breath.

"Well, she seems to be living in a fantasy world." She paused, but he didn't speak. "It sounds like she just daydreams, all the time. I think she must have dreamed up a whole new life for herself, and she pretends she lives that life instead of living in the real world."

"Is she mad?" Mike questioned, but Eve shook her head, drawing on her Psychology 'A' Level for support.

"I don't think so. If you read what she's written it suggests that she knows what she's doing, and that she knows what's real and what's not." At least at the moment, she added to herself.

"So what is it then?" Mike sounded agitated.

"I don't know. It sounds like a massive disillusionment with life. There may be depression in there, or something else, but I think she's just decided that she would rather spend time daydreaming than, well, living."

"So you're telling me that Louise, or Skye, has been lying all this time about her job, and that instead of being on this graduate scheme she's been working as a cleaner."

"Well, I don't think it's as straightforward as just lying. But essentially, yes." Eve nodded.

"And her friends and her boyfriend don't exist? Well, not in the way that she talks about them."

Eve nodded again.

"And that she's lied about where she lives, and that instead of getting on with her life and sorting herself out she would rather lie on her bed daydreaming about the ideal life, and experience that in her head."

Eve continued nodding.

"It all seems a bit far fetched to me." Mike ended, and Eve turned to meet his eye. But he swung his head around to gaze at a crack in the wall.

"Well, given the evidence - what I've told you, what you've seen for yourself and especially what's written here," Eve picked up the notebook and slapped it against the edge of the wooden table, "can you think of a better explanation?'"

It was a while before Mike responded. "So what now? I can't...I mean I thought...before..."

"What did happen before, Mike?" Eve spoke gently but she suddenly felt as if she has downed three espressos rather than half a cup of brown water.

Mike rubbed a hand down his face and breathed in deeply. He looked up into Eve's eyes, and for the first time she realised how sad his copper-tinted gaze looked. The whites of his eyes seemed to have ever so slightly yellowed.

"No. She hasn't done this. I mean, she's always been a dreamer, has our Louise. But this is something else. Anyway Eve, what can we do?"

"I don't know. I really don't know. We can go back up to her flat, but as I've said I'm concerned about scaring her. I don't know how she'll react to you being here." Eve paused. "You could write to her?"

Mike shook his head. "No, I am going to go back up there. I need to see her and talk some sense into her. Bring her back to Swansea with us, get her sorted out."

"Mike, I'm not sure it'll be that simple. She's in a state, and I think we need to tread carefully."

"Well what the fuck else can I do?!"

Mike's outburst made Eve jump, and he seemed to scare himself too. He let his head drop into his hand, then Eve noticed a tear slip out of the corner of his right eye.

"I'm sorry." He sniffed. "I'm sorry. I think I need to go to bed. I'm going to go and check on Chris and try and get some sleep. Will you come back tomorrow?"

Eve nodded.

"Promise? We need you." Eve took Mike's hand.

"I'll be here at nine, I promise." In her head she was already calling in sick with the flu; it was about time she had a

281

break anyway.

*     *     *

Skye came home and kicked off her shoes, tossing a few coins onto the countertop and flicking a warm lager out of her four pack as she made for her room.

The last rays of winter sun tickled the underside of the old net curtains as she curled up on her bed, pulled the naked duvet right up to her chin and slipped into her perfect world, though she struggled to stay awake. It didn't matter though - it wasn't going anywhere. She pecked Dan on the lips, wrapped her arm around him and rested her head on his chest, then fell into a deep, dreamless sleep.

But when she awoke something felt different. Something was missing. She didn't have many possessions; she had binned most of her stuff when Anna had asked her to move out of the flat in West Hampstead. Apparently, they 'didn't gel'. So when something had gone astray it became quite obvious. Glancing over at her desk she realised that her precious notebook, where she recorded all her thoughts and feelings and documented both her real and fantastical worlds, had gone. She jumped up in a panic and rummaged around her room, pulling her bed and the cupboard out from the wall and yanking the bare drawers off their rollers. She was relieved to see that her cloud box was still hidden on top of her cupboard, pushed right to the back so that it was out of view, but the notebook was nowhere to be found. As she gave up and flopped onto her bed she felt hot and cold shivers running up and down her spine, and a sense of nausea developed in her stomach as she mentally kicked herself for being so slack on security. Someone must have taken it, so someone had been here and, worst of all, someone else knew. And she bet she knew who. With that final thought she turned and punched the wall, but the force had no effect on the solid barrier between herself and the outside world. And that just made her feel even more pathetic. Skye reached for her duvet and wrapped herself up in it, then pulled it up over her head and wept.

*    *    *

"Phone her." Eve had spent all night tossing and turning and wondering what to do for the best, then had finally come up with a plan in the early hours of the morning. Since then she had lain awake weighing up the pros and cons, then had got up and had a rushed breakfast, pulled on any old clothes and headed back up northwest. She'd been in the hotel foyer at nine o'clock sharp where Mike had been waiting for her, looking as if he hadn't slept a wink. He was wearing the same clothes as yesterday, which were creased and scruffy and smelled musty.

They were sat in the hotel dining room with a cup of coffee each, although Mike's was untouched. Chris was still in bed - indeed had barely moved since she had deposited herself there last night - so it was up to Eve and Mike to lay some plans.

"And say what? Tell her that I know everything?"

"No!" Eve's eyes widened. "No you mustn't, we can't risk scaring her off. Just chat to her."

"Chat to her?" Mike's face was disbelieving. "What, like nothing has happened?"

"Exactly. Talk to her like you normally would, then tell her you're coming to London to visit and you'd like to see her. Say you're coming up today, for a last minute Christmas surprise for Chris, and that you want to meet her for lunch. Try and set a time and a place, and we'll take it from there. Use my mobile, I'll set it to withhold the number," Eve paused and

283

fiddled with her keypad. "There you go."

Mike took the phone cautiously, as if it was a bomb about to go off in his hand. "I don't know if I can do this," he said dubiously, but Eve fixed him with a hard stare.

"You have to." She instructed. "I'm going to pop to the bathroom."

Mike nodded dumbly and started tapping in Skye's number, and Eve didn't return to the breakfast table until he had laid down the phone and had a few minutes to think. Then she went over and resumed her seat opposite him, eying him expectantly.

"What happened?"

Mike sighed. "She sounded so normal. Said she was at work, had a meeting to go to, was going out for lunch with the other graduates. She said that Khadijah was working them all to the bone as the holiday period is looming. She said everything was going well with her flat in West Hampstead, but that she couldn't meet us tonight as she'd arranged to have dinner with Dan and his family. She sounded so normal."

Mike repeated his opening sentence and looked at Eve, who saw his eyes silently pleading with her to tell him what to do next.

"I don't know what to do." His voice broke at the end of that sentence. "Is it all lies, Eve? Is she really just lying to me, so blatantly and outright?"

"As I said before, I don't think it's as straight forward as that." Eve paused. "Does Skye have any siblings?"

Mike looked up. "No. Why?"

"Oh, I just had a thought. You know, sometimes siblings have ways of getting through to each other. I thought that if there was a brother or sister we could call on, it might help." She bit her lip and waited for Mike's response.

"No, she's all we have." He spoke heavily. "We wanted

more, you know. But we just couldn't…and…well this isn't the time or the place. She's always been an only child." He paused. "So what do we do now?"

"I guess," Eve hesitated. "I guess we're just going to have to confront her. I can't think of any other way. I thought we'd get to meet her for lunch, as Skye, and then we could take it from there. But I didn't really think beyond that…"

"Shall we go now?" Mike's chair wobbled on its two back legs as he stood up suddenly, but it managed to resettle itself gently on the floor.

"Sure," Eve drained her cup. "What about Chris?"

"I'd rather leave her here. I can't see her going anywhere if we go out, so let's just go and get this over with. Let's get a cab, I don't think I can drive. Anyway, I can't remember where I left the car last night, and I don't want to waste time looking for it."

"Ok." Eve stood up to join Mike and together they set off for the main road, where she flagged down a taxi and gave the driver Skye's address.

\*     \*     \*

Skye was in the middle of one of her favourite fantasies, out at work drinks with Dan, Suki, Di and the rest of the crew in a snazzy bar in Hoxton Square. They were sipping cocktails and chatting and jibing when Dan caught her eye and smiled at her.

"Follow me," he mouthed, setting down his glass and getting up out of his seat. She raised her eyebrows but he just brushed a finger over his lips and winked at her. Skye jumped to her feet and followed him into a dark corner of the bar, where he turned and grabbed her around the waist, pulling her into him so sharply that she gasped for breath. Before she had time to think he bent down and placed his lips on hers, kissing her roughly and passionately. She could feel his stubble tickling her lips and was aware of his strong muscles as she ran her hands over his back, and revelled in the now familiar scent of his aftershave mingling with his natural scent. He tasted sweet and fruity from the cocktails and she devoured him greedily, feeling him grow and swell as he pushed himself against her. Finally he pulled back half an inch and stood eyeing her, his blue eyes glazing over with a mixture of yearning and desire.

"I want you so much. I need you. I love…" but just before he finished those three little words the buzzer echoed around Skye's flat and her whole body jerked. She lay still, afraid to move for fear of giving herself away, and thanking God that she had tightened up on security since the disappearance of her notebook. Then the buzzer went again, and again.

She slithered off the mattress and crept across to the window that overlooked the main street. Very carefully she moved the net curtain a fraction of an inch to the side, and then jumped back in shock, tripping over a six pack of lager and crashing to the floor with a bang. She lay there, frozen in shock, too afraid to move. What the hell was her dad doing out there? And how on earth had he found her?

She felt her cheeks flush with anger as the rage coursed through her bloodstream. That interfering bitch, Eve. That was how. She'd already been up twice, and now she'd got onto Skye's parents, had told them where she was hiding out and had sent them down to find her. There was no other explanation. Well, she wasn't answering that door. Her parents couldn't hang around forever, but until she was confident that they were safely back in South Wales she would ensconce herself in this building and make sure that they couldn't get in. She wasn't having them - or anyone else, for that matter -

spoiling her magic.

Skye closed her eyes to block out the world, and drifted back into perfection while lying right there on the dirty, threadbare carpet. Her left leg was still twisted over the six pack of lager that had caused her to fall, but she didn't even try and straighten it.

*     *     *

"No answer." Mike sighed and rubbed his hands over her eyes. They had been waiting outside Skye's flat for twenty minutes. "Come on, this is hopeless. Let's go check on Chris."

Eve felt her heart ache as she followed Mike down Shoot-Up Hill, his previous straight back curved over into a 'c' and his hands pushed deep into his trouser pockets. They didn't speak again as they traversed Kilburn, negotiating Christmas shoppers and unpredictable traffic. Eve could hear the shouts of children in a local school out at play, and smell rotisserie chickens roasting on a spit.

The pavements became emptier once they came out the other end of the High Road, and as they passed the cosy cafes and food places Eve couldn't help gazing in wistfully and thinking about how nice it would be to be sat inside with a coffee and a mate, just chatting about Christmas and daft New Year's resolutions. But as they approached the Marriott she pulled her attention back, and laid a hand on Mike's arm as the lift took them back up to Chris. She hoped he found it somewhat reassuring.

"Chris? Chris, can you hear me?" Chris was still lying on her side in the bed, in the same position as when they had left her. Her eyes were awake and glassy, staring ahead but focusing on nothing, and her skin was completely drained of its colour. She hadn't reacted as Mike and Eve had come into the

287

room, and had shown no sign of consciousness when Mike tried to talk to her. He was now gently tapping her arm, but getting no response, when Eve slowly became aware of a sour smell diffusing through the room. Sniffing inquisitively she leant over the bed, where the smell became more obvious.

"Mike?" Eve leant over and touched his elbow. "Mike? I think Chris has soiled herself. Chris? Can you hear me? Chris?"

Mike gently pulled back the covers to reveal a large dark stain spreading out from beneath Chris's hips. He looked up at Eve, and together they managed to haul Chris to her feet and direct her over to the bathroom. But although she responded to their instruction she did so in a kind of trance.

"We're going to clean you up, Chris. I'm going to nip out and get some bits and pieces while Mike helps you into the bath. Can you get up, Chris? Here, let me help you. The warm water should help you relax. I'm going to go now, but I'll leave you with Mike and I'll be back in a bit. Ok?"

Eve dashed up to the Primark they had passed on the way down to the hotel. She grabbed a few supplies then hurried back, entering the room to see Chris sitting up in a chair wearing one of the hotel's bathrobes, while Mike perched on the end of the bed. His face was red and his eyes swollen.

Eve knocked on the door, although she was already inside, then crept towards Mike. "Hey, I'm back. I managed to grab a pair of trousers and a jumper, and I got some underwear as well." She spoke softly and placed the items on the bed.

Mike looked up and smile wanly, then sniffed and reached for a tissue from the box on the bedside. "Eve, I'm sorry. You shouldn't be dealing with this." He blew his nose. "I'm not even sure why you are, anyway. Wouldn't you rather be out with your friends? Celebrating Christmas or something? You don't want to get involved in this, Eve. It's so...so..." he

288

dropped his head into his hands and took a breath, then straightened up again. "So messed up. And it just keeps getting worse. I thought it would go away, if we ignored it enough. But..."

Eve placed a hand on his shoulder, feeling the cheap acrylic wriggle its way into the natural lines of her palm. "Has this happened before? With Chris, I mean?"

Mike nodded. "Yes. Oh Eve, the last time was horrific. It's like she barrels through like a steamroller, so strong and together and ironing out any lumps and bumps lying in her way. And then occasionally something happens to trigger this."

Eve followed his gaze and eyed Chris's huddled form under the covers.

"It's as if all the sadness and grief spills over in one massive gush. I never know what to do for the best. Then, just when I'm about to give up myself, she bounces out of it and things go back to normal. And I just pray that that's the last time it'll happen. She's been through so much, you know. More than she should have had to deal with."

There was a heavy pause until Mike seemed to snap into action mode, slapping his hands on his thighs and jumping to his feet so that Eve's hand flew off his shoulder. She wrapped her arm around herself.

"Eve, I need to get her home, this is no good to anyone."

"But what about Skye? What are you going to do?"

Mike sighed and wiped a hand over his face, holding his breath for a second before replying. "I honestly don't know. I haven't a clue what to do for the best, but I do know that I need to get Chris out of here."

Eve nodded. "Yep, ok. Listen, I'll keep an eye on Skye for you, while we try and come up with a plan for getting her home too."

289

"Would you do that?" The gratitude in Mike's face almost reduced Eve to tears. "You're so, so kind." Mike touched her arm gratefully and Eve blinked rapidly as she tried to retain her composure. "I don't where we'd be without you."

Eve shrugged and breathed deeply before she opened her mouth. "I lost my parents. In a car crash, not that long ago. I miss them, and you and Chris reminded me of them, that day in reception." Eve felt her eyes brim over and the next thing she knew she was in Mike's arms, the tears she had been suppressing cascading down her cheeks and soaking into his old sweater. She buried her head in the starchy acrylic, his universal late middle-aged man's smell reminding her of her own father, as he stroked her hair and shushed her. She closed her eyes tightly and she was almost back in her own father's arms, being comforted after scraping her leg or falling off her bike. But she soon pulled away, sniffing and wiping her eyes, though smiling through her tears. "Thanks," she whispered, but Mike just shook his head.

"Anytime," he smiled back at her and for the first time in a long while Eve felt an inkling of that special support and security that only a parent can bring, and that she hadn't felt since that awful night. She briefly allowed herself to re-experience the feeling that everything would be ok because Daddy was there, before she forced herself to focus.

"Come on then, let's get you guys home." Eve moved to help Mike get Chris up on her feet, and together they supported her back to the station and up and down a few side streets until they found the car. While Eve waved them off she felt wistful yet strong, and she knew that she would do everything in her power to restore the family and give Mike back the home life he deserved.

\*    \*    \*

Skye woke up with a jump, taking a minute to work out why she was sprawled across the living room with her legs going numb and her head resting on an old cigarette packet. But then it came back to her. Her dad had been outside; her parents knew. They had broken through her stories and come up to Cricklewood to find her. With that interfering cow, Eve, from reception. What did she have to do with anything anyway?

Hauling herself to her feet, and staggering slightly as she attempted to kick life back into her left leg, Skye wandered the floor of the tiny flat as she tried to work out what to do. She felt a pang in her heart as she thought of home, of her own bed and the security it offered, but she knew she couldn't go back. She'd moved on now, and to return would be to regress. Ok, so things weren't ideal, but she was coping. And this set up was only temporary, while she got herself together. She needed to sort things out for herself, and if she let her parents in now they'd never let her do that. She owed this, at least, to both of them. After everything she had put them through. Because if it hadn't been for her...but she couldn't allow herself to finish that thought. She couldn't handle that pain in her heart, the numbing of her face or the contractions in her stomach that came with it, not to mention the nausea and shame that washed over her in tsunami-like waves. They reminded her repeatedly that it was all her fault, and that deep down she was a bad person who had caused bad things to happen. Things that had spoiled everything for everyone.

Without realising what she had been doing Skye found herself standing in the middle of her bedroom, clutching her sacred cloud box which she had taken down from the top of the cupboard. It was about the only thing she had left of her former life. She gently placed the box on the bed and removed the lid. Inside the fuchsia petals had darkened and withered, but the silver bangle continued to glimmer and shine. She reached down into the pile of newspaper clippings, photos and leaves of paper covered in her ineligible scribblings, and thumbed through the records and evidence. She sighed deeply as her mind wandered, and although she didn't want to she knew what she had to do. Indeed if she wanted to carry on with this life there was only one thing for it.

Carefully replacing everything in the shoebox she placed the entire contents in her metal wastepaper bin and lit a match, then watched as her collection tanned and withered before disappearing into nothingness. It had taken years of snooping and searching to collate that stash, but it disappeared in seconds. The photographs made the smoke smell slightly plasticy, but the papers had well and truly dried out and caught the flames easily.

The silver bangle was the only thing that didn't burn, although it remained charred and blackened by the smoke. Once the fire display had ended and it had had time to cool Skye fished out the bracelet and threw it under her bed. She couldn't see it, but she would know that it would always be there. Just in case.

And then she breathed a deep sigh of relief. Now everything was gone, and no-one would ever know. Now Louise was completely free to be Skye.

## Chapter 7

Ryan finished re-reading the first part of 'Lone Guitar' and laid his head on his desk. It was shit. The biggest load of bollocks he had ever read.

He slapped his right hand down on the table then hauled himself up, slouched over to the drawers and pulled out his British phone. He unscrewed a bottle of red as he switched it on and waited for his messages to come through.

There was a text off Ash asking for last month's rent, and a text from Maura, just checking in. Just those two, plus about a hundred junk e-mails as well as one from Lara, telling him that he couldn't write his column from Paris and therefore they would have to let him go, and one from his parents, wishing him a happy Christmas and asking him to phone if he had a minute.

Ryan flipped back to the main screen and checked the date. December 25th? Really? How had that happened?

"So this is Christmas," he said, he voice sounding strangely loud in the bare room. "And what have you done? Another year over..."

He walked over to the window and opened it wide, the cold air slapping his face and reminding him that there was a whole world out there. And then he drew back his arm and, with all of his might, threw his phone at the wall on the other side of the courtyard.

Ryan bundled himself up, grabbed his keys and scurried out of the room. Down in the foyer he popped online to send an e-mail to Maura, then he went out to wander alone, yet again, along the river, ducking into a corner shop along the way to stock up on beer, wine and, on second thoughts, brandy. That should all go nicely with the packets of paracetamol he had back in his room.

Walking along the Seine with his plastic bag and his plan Ryan started to feel at peace. It had all been brewing at the back of his mind for some time now, even before all of that stuff with Zoe. But then, when he had found her, he had started to feel like life was worth living and that he could get through it. As long as she was beside him. But then it had all just become too hard. And now, at last, things made sense, and that feeling brought with it a sense of calm that had evaded him for far too long.

Ryan stopped on the Pont Marie and gazed into the water, watching the choppy waves lap at the side of the river. The wind had numbed his face, but he felt as frozen inside as out. It was confusing - he should be feeling sad, or angry, or scared, or something. But there was nothing. Just the sense of a big, gaping hole where his body should be.

Ryan put his bag down on the floor and pulled his wallet out of his pocket, rummaging around in his receipts to find the photo he had slipped in there the other day. He felt the need to carry it around now, and to make sure that it was always near him.

He gazed at the fuzzy image, and in his mind's eye could see Zoe smiling at him, just the way she had when it had been taken. He smiled back at her and then leaned over and dangled the image over the river. He was about to let go when he suddenly changed his mind, snatched his arm back and

294

slipped the paper into his back pocket. He just couldn't do it. Instead, he opened up the Cognac and took a long, warming gulp.

Ryan polished off half the bottle in one go, before resting it on the top of the bridge and taking a breather. Then he noticed a discarded safety pin lying down his feet. He bent down and snatched it up, rubbed it between his fingers to clean off the dust, then rolled up his sleeve and trailed it down his forearm, feeling that sense of calm prevail once more. Then he chucked it into the Seine, picked up his bag and hurried back to the hotel room.

A few hours later Ryan had finished off the brandy and most of a bottle of red. He was slumped against his bed in the hotel room, and struggling to summon the energy to even blink. It felt as if someone had stuffed him like a teddy bear, so that all his nerves were insulated and all his senses muted.

Taking a deep breath he picked up the plastic container next to him and shook it, listening to the pills rattling around. He flicked open the lid and tipped a few into his hand, and suddenly all his feelings came back to life. The fear started flooding through his veins, causing him to throw the tablets across the room, and the sadness started to engulf him from the inside. But then the physical side took over and his stomach started convulsing. He jumped to his feet and ran to the bathroom, then vomited all over the floor.

Once he had finished he grabbed a spare toilet roll and started to mop up, between fresh bouts of retching and waves of the shakes. His brain seemed to have turned itself back on as he began to make sense of where he was, how he had got there, and what a mess he had managed to land in, and he felt more and more scared by the second. But there was one key thought that eclipsed all the others to hammer repeatedly at his brain, right behind his forehead: 'I can't go on like this,' it said. But the futility of it all still made him angry, and as the fear in his veins turned into aggression he hauled himself up by the sink and eyed himself in the mirror.

"December 25th." He said to himself. "Happy fucking Christmas." And then the glass shattered.

"Maura?"

"Ryan? Oh my God! Where the hell are you? You're on an international number?"

"Maura..." Ryan broke off as he tried to fight the tears.

"Ry? What's going on? Ryan?"

"Maura, I can't do it anymore."

"What? What have you done? Where are you? You better not have done anything stupid. Where the hell are you?"

"Maura, calm down. I haven't done anything stupid. Well, I nearly did. But then I stopped."

"Ry..."

"I'm in Paris, Maura. I thought it would be a fresh start, but it's all gone wrong. I just..." Ryan sniffed as the tears spilled over. "I just...I just can't stop thinking about the baby."

"What? What baby, Ryan? What the hell is going on?"

"My baby. Mine and Zoe's baby." Ryan couldn't hold back the sobs any longer. It was just such a relief to say it; it had been weighing down his body for all that time and now, finally, it had been released.

"Oh my God, Ryan." Maura's voice was softer this time. "I had no idea. Zoe's pregnant? But she's with someone else."

"Zoe was pregnant. For 13 weeks. And then, suddenly, she wasn't." Ryan looked down at the scan picture that he had been carrying around with him for the past year. He was surprised he hadn't worn it out, the amount of time he had spent gazing at it. He'd promised Zoe that he had got rid of the

296

photo; she'd said that would help them both move on. But he couldn't bring himself to do it. He ran his finger over the fuzzy image of the baby and wondered, yet again, whether it had been a boy or a girl. If it had been a boy they were going to call him Tommy. If it had been a girl they were going to call her Lily.

"What happened?" Maura whispered.

"It just went away." Ryan heard his voice wobbling. "One day it was there, and we were about to start telling people. And then it was gone. And that was that. And…" Ryan sniffed. "And I wasn't even there. I was away on a stag do. A fucking stag do, Maura! Pissing about in some dive in Brighton while Zoe went through all that. I lost my phone, she was trying to call…how could I have left her?"

"Oh, Ryan…"

"I was so scared when I found out, Maura. I didn't feel ready. But Zoe had always wanted to be a mother, so we talked about it and decided to keep the baby. And then it became so great, Maura. I finally felt that I had a purpose in life, and I couldn't wait to be a family! But then, overnight, it all went away. I haven't been able to do anything since, Maura. Except screw up. And get drunk. And…"

"And what?"

"Nothing. Just that." Ryan ran his finger up the scratch on his arm. "Maura, I need you." And then he burst into tears.

"Where are you, Ryan?"

"Paris."

"Right. I'm on my way. Text me through your address, I'll be there as soon as I can."

The following morning Ryan woke up to the sound of someone hammering on the door. It took a few moments to wake up properly and work out where he was, then he stumbled out of

297

bed, opened the door, and fell into the arms of Maura.

"Ryan..." She held him tight for a couple of minutes, then gently pushed him into the room, closing the door behind them. "I got the first train out this morning. Ryan, what the hell are you doing?"

Ryan looked around the room at the empty bottles, the discarded paracetamol tablets, and the pathetic half a baguette. "I don't know, Maura. I thought...I mean...I felt...I don't know. I had to get away, but it didn't make anything better." He sat down heavily on the bed.

"Why didn't you come to me?" Maura sat down gently next to him.

"I...it was hard." Ryan shrugged. "I didn't know what to do and it all felt like too much." He slipped his fingers under the pillow and extracted the scan picture. He wordlessly handed it over to Maura.

"Oh, Ryan," she took the picture. "I had no idea, I just assumed the relationship had run its course."

Ryan inhaled deeply, and felt his lower jaw start to tremble. "It was so difficult, Maura. And afterwards…" a pain in his chest made Ryan pause.

"What happened afterwards, Ry?"

Ryan closed his eyes and steadied his jaw. "I know it doesn't make any sense, Maura, but after the miscarriage I couldn't cope with how much I loved Zoe." He opened his eyes and saw Maura's frown. "I know. I know how it sounds. But I got so scared that she would leave me, too. Or that someone would take her away from me." Ryan felt that familiar, deep sadness swelling up inside of him and this time, for once, he didn't try and squash it back down. "I became so paranoid about it, and that just destroyed everything. I couldn't be with her, but I couldn't be away from her. So in the end I just kind of shut down, and ended it all." He felt his body begin to shake uncontrollably. "And it was the worst mistake I ever made." The sadness suddenly became all consuming and he flopped back onto the bed, rolling over to bury his face in the pillows. "I just..." a tear trickled onto the cotton cases. "I just want Zoe back."

"Ryan..."

He felt Maura's hand give his leg a gentle squeeze.

"I know. I know it's too late." He turn his head around to look at his friend, wiped his eyes and let his gaze drift around the room. He felt a kick of disgust in his gut at the sight of it. "Maura?" Ryan placed his hand on hers.

"Yes?" She turned her hand round to slip her fingers between his.

"Will you take me home?"

# The Defeat

## Chapter 1

"Ok, love. Bye, Eve. And thank you."

Mike felt that concrete balloon sink back down onto his diaphragm yet again, as Chris hung up the phone, burst into tears and collapsed onto the sofa next to him. It felt like too much effort to lift his arm and wrap it around her, but after all this time he knew his place. He heaved up the leaden limb and draped it across Chris's shoulder, but she didn't acknowledge its presence.

"No change?"

She shook her head, then turned her gaze on him. It still made him jump to see how grey she had become in the past few months.

"I'm going to phone her."

"Chris! No! We've been over this, you have to stop calling!" Mike reclaimed his arm and ran a hand down his face. His skin seemed to have dried out so much recently. Or perhaps it had started to resemble newspaper much earlier, but he had just never noticed before.

"We can't risk Louise disappearing, or doing some kind of damage to herself. We just need to sit it out while we work out what to do. If you keep hassling her..."

"We've been sitting it out for months! Just like we sat it out before! I can't keep 'sitting it out' and doing nothing, Mike! It's not helping. Plus it's never got us very far in the past, has it?"

"And whose fault is that?! I never wanted to go along with it; you know I wanted to talk about it! I needed to talk about it, for me and for the family! You weren't the only one hurting, you know." His last sentence dropped a few decibels; as much as it was bursting to come out he knew that this was neither the time nor the place. He was sure Chris had heard, but she didn't react.

"Is it our fault? Have we really been that bad as parents? I just wanted to protect her. I didn't want her to grow up with the burden, and the sadness. It's still inside me, you know, like a hollow pit that just can't be filled. I didn't want her to live like that, all empty and regretful, always living in a different world." Chris paused as the irony of her words seemed to hit her, and the tears started to fall anew.

Mike hesitated, before putting his arms around her once more and pulling her into him. He felt her collapse into the softness that his once muscley chest had mutated into, and was aware of her sniffing the nape of his neck. Once upon a time he had treated it to cheap deodorant spray, then designer aftershave, then a bit of Old Spice, before relaxing into his natural musky smell when building a family took priority over his appearance. But now he knew that his skin smelled of tobacco, from the cigarettes he had taken up. He'd expected Chris to be angry that he'd started smoking again, but she'd confessed to finding the faint scent of toxicity that lingered in his shirt collar comforting. She'd said that use of her senses reminded her that she continued to exist - despite how she felt on the inside - and also took her back to her earlier years, when life had made sense. He wished they could go back there for real, and not get it so wrong this time.

Chris sighed. "You were - are - right, Mike. We should have talked about it, and been more open. She had a right to know and we messed up, and now we've ruined her. I'm so sorry Mike, so sorry. It's all my fault." Her voice trailed off as the tears took over, and she sobbed into his yellowing collar. He was surprised that there were any more left, given the amount she had shed over the past few months, but it seemed they'd finally rebelled against more than two decades of suppression. Once the first ones had been freed the others followed in droves, sometimes fast and desperate, sometimes slow and steady, but always, always present.

"Shhh." Mike kissed the top of the head, in the middle of her parting. It was a lot wider and thinner now than on that day when he had first kissed her there, and he always liked to think that the strands had worn away because of his kisses over the years.

"I'm going to call her again." Chris stirred and pushed herself up out of Mike's grasp, that had strengthened in protest to her statement of intent.

"Chris, don't." She turned to look at him, her washed out blue eyes tired and sad, the lines around her mouth finally admitting that time was defeating her. Her lips had been full and rosy but were now pale and drawn, and her once groomed eyebrows were sprouting hairs in all directions.

She raised her eyes to break their connection and gazed off into the kitchen that led off from the lounge. They used to spend hours gazing into each others' eyes, never reaching that awkward point where one would have to break away, but these days Mike had noticed that she seemed more comfortable regarding objects than people. Every time it happened it was like being spiked in the heart with a pin. It may not sound like much, but if you poked the same bit of skin with a pin hour after hour, day after day, week and week, it would soon turn septic and scar.

He followed her gaze and regarded the sparkling

305

counter tops and the spotless lino on the floor. Until a week ago the surfaces had been stained and dull, strewn with dried up food while the bin overflowed with microwavable cartons. The lino floor had sported a layer of crumbs and dust balls and the hob had remained caked with burnt sauces, which had overflowed from pans that Chris had set boiling and then forgotten about. Dirty dishes had piled up in the sink, and the whole room had been fragranced with the pungent stink of rotting waste tinged with the acrid scent of burnt food. Mike had tried to tidy up but it had made Chris angry, so he eventually gave up, tired of feeling the sharp end of her tongue.

But then, once Christmas had passed and the new year had commenced, Chris had flipped to the complete opposite end of the spectrum, and the kitchen had once again become her haven. Or her cell, which was more how Mike saw it. Now it was pristine once more; the hob glistening and the countertops scrubbed until you could eat your dinner right off them. No crumb was allowed to reside on the floor for longer than three seconds, and indeed if Chris saw just one lying about she would be straight in there with the brush and the mop, and the whole surface would get another going over with antibacterial spray.

Though the kitchen was rarely used for cooking now. Chris didn't really eat anymore, just a bowl of softened cereal every now and then and, of course, the bowl was washed, dried and polished the second she finished her last mouthful, and carefully placed back in the cupboard where it belonged. Mike still ate, but his cooking skills were somewhat limited and he was the one who had been responsible for the build up of paper cartons in the bin - lined with traces of lasagnes, fish pies, curries and pasta bakes - that Chris hadn't liked him to remove. He rarely cooked in the kitchen these days, though, as he couldn't cope with Chris's obsession with cleanliness and order, and had taken the microwave out to his shed so that he could make as much mess as he wanted in peace. He knew that Chris didn't like it, but he also knew that she didn't have the energy to challenge it so, rather like a triumphant child who had got their own way, Mike slowly moved his life out of his house and into his garden retreat.

Chris sighed and turned once again to dial the landline number, which Eve had somehow managed to obtain and pass on to them.

"Don't." Mike snapped, his tone making her jump so that she dropped the receiver. It clattered onto the laminate floor and lay still as Chris turned back to her husband. "Don't." He repeated. "It won't help. It's more likely to make things worse and push her away even more."

Without commenting Chris bent down, picked up the receiver and recommenced pressing buttons. But a few moments later she had to accept defeat, and replaced the receiver in its holder. She silently left the room and Mike could hear her padding up the stairs.

A few seconds of silence followed before the phone rang, its shrill tone clashing with the fading tension in the air. Mike reached out for the receiver, and picked it up at the same time as Chris picked up the extension in their bedroom.

"Hello? Mike Worthington speaking."

"Oh my God, Skye? Louise? Please, talk to me!"

There was a pause before a familiar voice came down the line.

"Chris? Mike? Hello? What's going on?"

"Louise?"

"No, Chris. It's Amy."

"Amy? Oh, Amy…"

For a split second Mike felt reassured by the normality of the call, but then he tuned back into Chris's sobs. "Where

307

are you, Amy? Are you back?"

"Yeah, I cut my trip a bit short. I was ready to come back and get on with my life, meet a woman, settle down, you know."

It still sounded unusual to Mike, to hear Amy speak like that. Not that he'd ever had a problem with her sexuality, but it was just a different world out there now. He fully supported it - indeed had been involved in a bit of anti-homophobia campaigning back in the day - but he couldn't help but experience a little jolt of surprise when she spoke about her girlfriends so openly. What an improvement, though, compared to all that negativity Caroline had been battling just a few years ago. Mike suddenly dropped a pen he didn't know he had been holding, and realised that Amy was still talking.

"I'm in London again, now. I've been back a week and have been trying to get hold of Louise, but I can't get through on her phone and she won't reply to my e-mails. I wondered if she'd changed her number but then I thought…it's not good news, is it?"

Chris sobbed once more. "Love, something's happened. She's lying again. But it's more, it's much worse. I don't know…I can't…Eve is helping, but I think you'd be best. Thank God you're back. Please help us, Amy! She might listen to you." Silence ensued. "Amy? Are you still there?"

Mike heard Amy inhale deeply. "Chris, I was so worried about this. Shit! I never should have gone away and left her, I knew she wouldn't cope!"

"What? What do you mean?"

"Ok, Mike. It's like this. When Louise was at Aberystwyth she wasn't very honest about her life."

"I know, she told tales but she was young, and she was lost. She was just silly. This is different."

"Chris, it's not. I can imagine what's happened. She's

living in a fantasy world, isn't she?"

Mike was taken aback by Amy's matter-of-factness. "How do you know this? Have you spoken to her?"

"No, but it's what happened in Aber. The same thing has happened again, I almost saw it coming."

"No it's not! In Aberwystwyth it was just a few lies, this is a whole world Amy! She's not even living in reality!"

"Chris! It's the same! She had a world in Aber, she lived in fantasy there. She used to spend all her time daydreaming, she told me about it when she was better. She told me that she knew what she was doing but it got out of hand, and fantasising became all she wanted to do. But she never believed the dreams when she was in the real world, she did know the difference. Which in a way seemed even stranger. Then suddenly, one day, it started to get better. She seemed to move on and stopped spending all her time in her room, and started living properly with the rest of us. I don't even know what happened, and I was just so glad to have her back that we never really talked about it. But she didn't tell you the truth because she didn't want to worry you. So she told you that she'd just got a bit carried away and unsure of herself, but that she was sorted out. But Chris, it was so much more than that. It was really, really scary. And I just hoped it wouldn't come back."

"She's changed her name. She's calling herself Skye. Did she do that in Aber? She's changed her looks, she's dyed her hair and changed her eyes and become a whole other person. I could barely recognise her when she came to stay, Amy! It was so much worse than that time after she finished at university."

Mike bit his lip as he waited for a response.

Amy hesitated. "No. No, Chris. she never did that. Oh, God. Did you mention someone called Eve? Who's that?"

309

Mike explained about Eve and the part she played in the whole situation, finding it a relief to have an outlet for it all; he'd had to be so strong for Chris in recent months.

"Ok, I'm going to go and see this Eve. I'm back at my parents at the moment so I'm not far from London, I'll go up there tomorrow and find her. And we'll have a talk. Then I'll call you."

"Oh, Amy." Chris's tone had dropped in both pitch and volume. "Thank you. Thank you so much. We'll talk to you tomorrow."

Mike was ready to put the phone back but Amy's voice came out of the speaker again, a lot sharper and livelier.

"Hang on, something's bothering me. What did you say about graduation?"

"Oh, you know Amy, when Louise finished at Aber she wasn't well at all. She wouldn't get out of bed, she barely spoke to us and wouldn't see her friends. I guess she was living in her fantasy then, too. Right here, Amy! In her own home! And we didn't help her..." Mike's voice wobbled. "I just thought it would pass...but it's getting worse, Amy. She seems to be slipping further away from us, and I'm not sure she even knows who we are anymore. Sometimes Chris does manage to get through to her, but she speaks to her own mother like she's a stranger. It's got a different quality this time, Amy. I don't know what we're dealing with anymore, and no matter how much I try I can't even start to understand it."

"Hold on." Amy's abrasiveness was incongruent with Mike's softer tones. "After university? I thought she went travelling? Went to Australia, then spent time in Asia doing voluntary work or something? That's what she told me when she was staying with me. I mean, that was why we hadn't seen her for so long, and why she couldn't come to graduation? But we did e-mail. She met someone there and stayed longer than intended, but then she had visa problems and they broke up and then…"

Amy stopped abruptly but the shock realisation ricocheted through Mike as well.

"Fuck. Oops, sorry Chris, Mike. But, I mean, fuck."

Mike heard Chris hang up. "Amy, listen, I've got to go. Please, go and see Louise, and see what you can do. Please." And Mike put down the receiver before she could reply.

## Chapter 2

"Oh, shit. Urgh. Gross."

Eve stared down at the cold, purple tea that she had just spat out, and was dripping through the paper and onto her desk. She glanced at the clock and was surprised to see that it was over an hour since she had made the cup. She was re-reading, for the hundredth time, the slip of paper she had torn out of Skye's notebook, and trying to find some kind of meaning and sense in it all.

A deliberate cough made her jump, and she glanced up to see that a line of people were waiting for her attention.

"Oh my gosh, I'm so sorry! I was so distracted!" She pushed the paper aside and smoothed down her hair, feeling her skin flush as she smiled her sweetest smile. But the man continued to glare at her from stony eyes behind thick glasses.

"Lancaster."

Eve tried her smile once more, but again he was unresponsive. "Ok, you have an appointment?"

The man nodded once.

"Can I take you name, please?"

He just exhaled rudely and Eve felt her skin start to tingle in agitation.

"Fine, fifth floor." She knew she was breaking all sorts of regulations by letting him through security without complying with protocol, but rather than stress about that she resorted to glaring at the man and challenging him to respond. He seemed momentarily surprised then headed over to the lift, turning back to look at the desk on his way, as if he could feel Eve's eyes boring into his spine.

"Excuse me?" A timid, polite voice asked for Eve's attention, and she turned to see a young woman standing on the other side of the counter, who looked like a carbon copy of herself with her blonde hair, curvaceous figure, tanned skin and black trouser suit. "Are you Eve?"

Eve nodded. "Can I help?"

The girl sighed and smiled wanly. "Yes. I'm Amy, Louise - sorry Skye's - best friend. I want to know what's going on."

"Oh my God, Amy! I'm so glad you're here. Chris and Mike said you were coming. I need to talk to you. Hang on a sec. Can I help?" Eve turned to the woman tapping her heel impatiently behind Amy.

"Yes, I have an appointment at Chestertons at two, my name is...."

"Yes, yes go on up, eleventh floor. Lift is over there." Eve waved her hand vaguely in the direction of the steel doors across the entrance hall and turned back to Amy. "I have something I need to show you. Let's go, it's practically my lunch break anyway and someone will come to cover soon." Eve shrugged herself into her white jacket and slid out from behind the counter, puzzled by the angry and demanding look coming from the woman who was looking for Chestertons. It was the eleventh floor, the lift was right there, and if she had claustrophobia the stairs were right next to it. Jeez, how helpless could someone be?

Eve recounted her story to Amy, finding that relaying it in one go - without interruption - helped make some vague sense of it. Amy didn't speak but listened with a pale face and

314

damp eyes, from time to time running her hand across her forehead or through her hair, and occasionally shaking her head as if to check that she wasn't dreaming.

"But there's something else, too." Eve twisted her face into a grimace, even as she felt the weight lift off her chest as she prepared to share her secret.

Amy widened her eyes in encouragement for her to continue, and in response Eve pulled the scrap of paper, that she had grabbed from her desk as they were leaving the office, out of her handbag. She handed it over to Amy, who read wordlessly while Eve put her head back and closed her eyes. She felt like a balloon that had finally been allowed to deflate.

"Shit."

Eve sat up straight and nodded.

"I can't believe this! Where did you get it?"

"From her flat."

Eve saw that Amy was about to question her further, but seemed to decide against it.

"My God. I can't...I don't...Jesus, Eve!!"

Eve waited while Amy took a few deep breaths, rubbed her hand over her forehead and flopped back in her chair, biting her lip.

"But actually, now, things are starting to make a bit more sense. The whole thing, from the beginning. Shit! I can't believe it. Can I keep this?!"

Eve hesitated then nodded, deciding that she was happy to let Amy relieve her of that sheet of scrawl. "What are you going to do with it?"

"I'm going to talk to Chris and Mike about it."

Eve nodded. "I should have done that. I was going to send it to them this week. I just...I don't know. They have so much to deal with and I hoped it would get better and we could all move on. But it hasn't, and now I don't know what I'm

315

doing." Eve felt a couple of tears of relief roll down her cheeks.

"It's ok, Eve. We'll sort this. You've been amazing, by all accounts. You've done way more than most people would have even considered. You don't even know Louise!" Eve felt Amy's soft palm rest on her hand, seeming to emit the warmth of those far-flung places which Amy had just returned from. She looked up and smiled at Amy, and the girls shared a moment of peace before Eve voiced her latest concern.

"Amy, you know how you said that Skye, or Louise, always knew the difference in uni, between reality and fantasy?"

Amy nodded.

"Well, I don't think she does anymore."

"Me neither." Amy raised her eyebrows. "I think she's lost in it and I don't think she knows who she is. I've never seen anything like this before. She certainly never got this bad in Aber."

*     *     *

Skye hesitated as the landline burst into life once more. She considered leaving it but then decided to answer, just in case it was Dan. After all, she'd only installed the landline for him, really, in case he couldn't get her on her mobile for some reason; it would be silly to go to all that trouble and then not answer his calls.

"Louise?" The person at the other end spoke in a whisper, as if predicting the reaction they were about to evoke.

"Louise doesn't live here!" Skye's voice came out shrill and stressed, tired yet flying. "I keep telling you, now stop calling! If I hear from you again I'll call the police, you hear? Leave me in peace!" Skye slammed down the phone and glared at the receiver, frustration pounding at her temples and her palms sweaty with irritation.

As she eyed the phone it started to ring again, but she left the machine to get it. Taking a deep breath she got up and wandered into the kitchen, where she grabbed a chilled lager out of the fridge, finding a sense of peace in flicking back the ring pull and inhaling the bittersweet scent as the effervescing liquid sprayed over her naked arm. She held the can to her lips and relished the first slug as the machine kicked in, and that all too familiar voice resounded out into the silent living room.

"Louise, please. I just want to talk to you. Just pick up the phone for five minutes then I'll leave you alone. I promise. Don't do this to me Louise, please. Five minutes, that's all I ask."

Skye exhaled, then slammed her can down on the kitchen counter before storming into the living room and grabbing the receiver.

"Louise. Doesn't. Live. Here. Stop. Calling. Me." Then she reached down to the cracked and worn skirting board and yanked the cable out of the wall. She dropped it onto the stained carpet where it snaked back to the phone, sad and dejected as it became deprived of its utility and necessity in life.

Why couldn't she get the message? Louise had moved on from this flat, and as far as Skye knew she no longer existed. She'd tried disconnecting the phone but eventually always had to plug it back in, had tried changing her number but somehow that stalker always got hold of the new one. She was obsessive and couldn't let it lie. What was her problem? Why couldn't she just accept things and move on? The flat was Skye's home now, and that was the way it was going to stay. That woman needed to get a grip.

*Something was niggling at the back of Skye's mind, but she*

317

*suppressed it and wouldn't let it come to the forefront. She knew what it was, really, but she preferred to think that that wasn't the case. It was just so much better for everyone that way.*

Just as Skye felt her body relax her mobile burst into life. She eyed it warily before looking at the screen, and yep - it was that number, *again*. Skye sharply hit the end call key, shoved a few things in her bag and prepared to go out. Just before she was ready to go she plugged the landline back in, hoping that would avoid more calls to her mobile, and even as she was locking up the flat she heard the monotonous ring of the telephone echoing around the halls. She rolled her eyes, shook her head and pursed her lips before running down the stairs and out into the unusually quiet street, the sound of the old fashioned bell still ringing in her head. She inhaled a breath of the chilly late-spring night air, nearly retching on the smell of rotting rubbish that lay outside the silent chicken shop, snuggled into her oversized duffle coat and set off to meet her friends.

She used to walk this road cautiously, careful to avoid tripping on uneven paving or twisting her ankle in a pothole. But now she knew the path like the back of her hand and scurried along, executing the familiar dance that ensured she wouldn't fall. A couple of red double-deckers roared past, followed by an old banger that should have been scrapped at least a decade ago. It remained oblivious to the billowing fumes blowing back into Skye's face and momentarily poisoning her. She coughed as the vapours caught the back of her throat and her eyes started to water, then she put down her head and tottered along to the station.

Meanwhile a voice was emanating through Skye's empty flat, sounding slightly electronic through the distortion of the phone line.

"Louise, love, please don't do this. We're so worried about you. Please just talk to us. Louise, we know who you really are, you don't have to pretend. We're not angry or disappointed, but we just want you back with us so we can make you better. We'll get you the best private treatment and have the real Louise back in no time." At that point the voice broke, and the woman on the other end sighed as she tried to compose herself. "Louise, you're not well. Skye doesn't exist, and we should have made that clear a long time ago. Your job doesn't exist, your penthouse doesn't exist and Dan, as you know him, doesn't exist. Please realise this, so we can help you. Please let Skye go and come back to the real world. Come home to your mum. I want you back."

When Skye got in early that morning she saw the red light flashing on her answer phone, but hit delete without even listening to the message.

She retrieved a dirty glass from the clutter on the sideboard and filled it with water, sipping thoughtfully. The cool water - tinted with dregs of lager - refreshed her somewhat, although she was still dreadfully tired. It had been a long night, out partying with the rest of the Edwards crew. Well ok, wandering around Carnaby Street and Soho while watching everyone else having a good time, and picturing the others in her mind. But that was almost better than actually being involved, because that way she remained in control. Nothing got too scary or overwhelming, and everything went exactly as she wanted it to.

Skye took her glass through to the bedroom, put it down on the side and closed her eyes for a quick power nap. Dan would be over soon, and she wanted to make sure she looked fresh for him.

He came around about an hour later and the two of them

set off to wander the streets of Hampstead. They peered into the windows of all the little trinket shops and fashion boutiques before stopping off for lunch in a quaint little cafe, that served the best fair trade coffee and home made *pain au chocolat.*

Then, once they felt refreshed, they stood up to leave and as Dan reached over to brush a stray piece of flaky pastry from Skye's cheek, he whispered something in her ear that made her body tingle and her heart jump.

"How about we go back and check out the rings in the jewellery shop?" She turned to look at him questioningly, aware of what was about to happen but at the same time unable to comprehend it. Before her eyes Dan got down on one knee, took both her hands in his and gazed earnestly into her eyes. He only got the first two words of his question out before Skye hauled him to his feet and flung her arms around him, crying into his shoulder and shouting 'yes, yes' at the top of her voice, over and over, unable to stop. He started to laugh and she joined in, then they were kissing, passionately and desperately, to the backdrop of the sound of people exclaiming and clapping.

As they pulled apart a waitress arrived, carrying a bucket of ice containing a bottle of Cava and a pair of crystal glasses. Dan popped the cork and Skye watched the frothy, sparkling liquid tumbling into the champagne flute. When she drank the fizz bit her tongue, but tasted like liquid diamonds.

Skye smiled to herself and rearranged her pillow. For a brief second she came back to the real world, but there was nothing there for her. She re-entered her world greedily, eager to retain the perfection and satisfaction she found in her mind, as she knew it was far greater than anything she could ever hope to reach in real life.

320

## Chapter 3

"Ok, girls, I must dash. Seriously! But it's been great catching up, and thanks for your cards and bits. It means a lot. It really does." Skye smiled around at the Edwards girls, excited to see that their eyes sparkled almost as much as the diamonds on her finger. "Oh ladies, I'm so lucky to have you! What would I have done if I hadn't met you? If I'd gone to work for Linburn's instead? Ooh, it doesn't bear thinking about!"

"Come on, don't be silly! We did find each other, and that's what counts. Go on, get back to lover boy. See you in the morning. And give us one last hug before you go!"

"Ooh, big squeeze Di! Suki, you too. See you bitches tomorrow, I've got to get home and titivate. Lover boy is actually away tonight, but I have to look hot as hell for him tomorrow!" Skye pouted and stuck out her chest as Di leant over and slapped her on the arse.

"Go on then, bugger off so the rest of us can cry into our cocktails without being accused of putting a dampner on your big night. See you in the morning. Mwah!"

Skye grinned then turned and strutted out of the bar, pausing at the exit to flash her left hand at the girls one last time, before stepping out into the bright lights of Soho and making for Leicester Square station.

A short while later Skye swept into her flat feeling as if she was cocooned in a soft, pink mist, which would protect her from all the bad in the world forevermore. She almost bypassed the letter lying in the hall, half covered up by the mat; it was only that her heel caught in the brush that she happened to glance down and see the ivory envelope peeking out. She kicked off her heels then slipped her fingers under the seal, pulled out a hand written sheet and started to read.

Skye suddenly realised that it had grown dark. It had been a struggle to read the last couple of paragraphs. What was this letter all about? It seemed to be from her mother, and was telling her that she, Skye, didn't exist. What the hell? Why would anyone write such a thing? Let alone her own mother? She was too confused to feel scared or worried; it was just the most bizarre thing. She wiggled her fingers and watched them move. She breathed in the crisp, cool air that was filtering in from the open window, filling her lungs before she expelled it back into the atmosphere. They were certainly still working.

*Something fluttered at the back of her mind. She was aware of what it was, but she wasn't going to let it out.*

Skye dropped the paper back onto the table and stood up to flick on the light. The yellow haze shone garishly out from the naked bulb, the glare too big for the tiny, bare room. When did the light become so stark? She was more accustomed to soft lighting these days, preferring the relaxed, sensual atmosphere of the dimmers in her cream painted living room. She ran a hand through her hair, and yelped as it caught in a tangle which pulled at her scalp.

As she turned back to face the table she noticed something lying on the floor. It was a photograph, with two sentences on the back, written in different hands. The first was a careless teenage scribble, as if written by someone who had something more interesting to do. 'The Gower,' it read, '29 July 2002'. And below was something in more careful, even print. 'Remember her? We miss her. We want her back. We love you.' Skye frowned and turned the picture over. It showed a young woman with long, dark curls paddling in the sea, laughing and shouting at someone off camera. The sky was cloudy and overcast and the girl was fully clothed and wearing a cardigan, despite the fact that it had been taken in the middle of summer. Her jeans were rolled up to her knees and were spattered with sea water, and she was trailing her fingertips over the surface of the ocean. As Skye studied the photo she suddenly became aware of the scent of salt on the air. Then her fingertips felt wet and cold, and her jeans heavy, as if they were waterlogged. She could hear the squawk of seagulls in the distance, mingling with the cries and shouts of children on holiday.

And then, as quickly as the sensation arrived it vanished, and she once again found herself standing in the middle of the kitchen, staring at a random picture of a strange girl. She peered closer. The girl had copper coloured eyes with long dark lashes, and her skin was highlighted with a hint of gold. She was smiling and her eyes were shining.

Mum! She must call her mother, she wasn't well. And when had she last spoken to her? It must have been Christmas, when she had called from Dan's. But that was, shit! It was spring now, she'd noticed the buds on the trees for the first time today. And she saw a daffodil last week. Why hadn't her parents tried to call her in that time? What if they were both ill? What if they had died? Oh, but then mum couldn't have written the letter. Of course.

Skye wandered into her room to get her mobile, then realised she had no idea where it was. She hadn't used it in ages, and couldn't remember the last time she'd even seen it.

She stood in the middle of the room for a minute, then slouched back into the kitchen and picked up the photo again.

The eyes looked familiar. Actually, the whole face looked familiar, as if Skye had met her once, a long time ago. She tried to search back through her memory but just came up against a blank wall. Sighing, she slipped the letter and photograph back inside the envelope and turned it over to examine the postmark, but there wasn't one. In the corner where the stamp should be was a phone number, with the name 'Amy' written underneath it. Amy? That name had been written in the letter. Was Amy her real friend, or one of her invented ones? It was just so hard to know these days. She could call the number and find out, but she didn't seem to have a mobile anymore and the landline only took incoming calls. She shook her head vigorously and shoved the letter into the kitchen drawer. Maybe one day she'd study it again, to see if she could find any clues and return it to where it had come from.

Skye checked her watch. It was late and she needed to get some sleep; she'd had a busy time in the office lately and this was the first evening off she'd allowed herself in some time. Dan was away for the weekend, and while she missed having him around she was secretly glad of a night to herself now, as something was unsettling her. It was niggling at her stomach enough to make her feel nauseous, and her head was starting to hurt. She started to massage the muscles in the back of her head, and decided to skip her usually strict routine of cleansing, toning and moisturising. She threw on her joggers and an old t-shirt, pulled back the duvet, climbed into bed and closed her eyes.

But she struggled to drop off and tossed and turned, getting tangled in the sheets and more restless as the night wore on. Though she must have fallen asleep eventually, because suddenly she was wide awake and the pale light of morning was sneaking in from behind the curtains. Her head throbbed and her eyes were wet, and when she brushed her hand over her pillow she was shocked to feel how damp it was. As she came to she felt the tears build again and tried to fight them, but she couldn't, and they ran down her cheeks at an alarming rate. She cried silently, all her energy taken up with the tears so that there was no more left for wailing or sobbing.

After a few minutes she hauled herself up off the mattress and blindly negotiated her way back to the kitchen. She opened her 'things' drawer and pulled out the envelope, pausing before she extracted the contents. She looked around and took in the dire state of the bedsit, the clarity with which she viewed her hovel shocking her like she had just been slapped in the face. The dirty kitchen was layered in yellowing paper that was peeling round the edges, and sporting dusty cobwebs. The stained orange, cracked linoleum was sticky underfoot. The appliances were at least twenty years old and caked with greasy gunk and congealed remnants of past meals. The area around the fridge stank of rotting bananas, and the rest of the kitchen reeked of cheap cigarettes. An ashtray of butts was gathering dust on the white, plastic kitchen table and a collection of lighters and discarded cigarette packets lay scattered around the room. A half drunk Red Stripe perched on the sideboard and a collection of empty cans was accumulating beside a bin that was overflowing with waste. No memorabilia dotted the shelves, no photos were stuck up to trigger happy memories and no personalised mugs or special breakfast bowls adorned the counter tops. What had happened to her minimalist lounge with fresh, cream walls and soft, relaxing lighting? Oh, yeah. That's right. That was in her other world. But when did it all start getting so muddled?

As Skye observed the tragic space she found herself

fiddling with her hair, absent-mindedly pulling out a lock and running it between her fingers. But then it caught her eye and she refocused her gaze on the strands she held. Hidden beneath the platinum blonde, chemically straightened mane was a single, dark curl, that stood out in stark contrast to the silver-white background. Skye pulled the curl further out into the room and studied it before reaching for the cracked cabinet mirror, which had long ago fallen off its hinges. Dropping the curl she held the mirror up to her eyes and looked deep in through the windows to her soul, and her heart started racing. They were light brown, but usually they were a striking turquoise - people were always commenting on their exotic colour. Her palms started to grow sweaty but she stared herself out, daring the girl in the mirror to look away first. Then, as she peered deeper into them, she felt a shiver shoot up from her feet to the tip of her head, leaving her scalp tingling in its wake. Those eyes belonged to that girl in the photograph.

An image flashed through her mind, sharply and suddenly like a bolt of lightning. It was of the girl in the photo, and she seemed so close that Skye could smell undertones of dewberry and feel a few strands of the girl's hair tickle her cheek as they waved in an absent breeze. She smiled at Skye, who lashed out to push her away, causing the mirror to fall to the floor and shatter with a crash. A piercing scream filled the flat and Skye jumped, slapping her hands over her ears to shut out the noise. But then she realised that the sound was coming from herself, and it scared her so much that she screamed even louder. Her temples started to throb and she closed her eyes to the outside world, but a picture of the girl, running across a shoreline and laughing, shot into her mind. Skye stepped backwards onto the broken shards of glass, which embedded themselves in her foot, but she was barely aware of the pain and the subsequent warm trickle of liquid that flowed out of the gashes and onto the lino. But she did notice a sudden silence, although it didn't last long before a whimpering sound replaced it. This time she knew it was herself, but she couldn't make it stop. It sounded like an animal that had been caught in a trap and given up hope of ever being rescued, and it intensified as she curled herself up into a ball before collapsing onto the broken diamonds.

Another image emerged, of a little girl eating an ice-cream in a park on a sunny day. Skye turned her head sharply to the right and heard the crush of broken glass against solid bone, but when the shards pierced her skin it felt more soothing than painful. She turned back the other way and felt the warmth spread through her other cheek. Picture after picture continued to flash through her mind, like a relentless slide show set on a loop, as Skye continued to writhe and whimper. There were family Christmases, beach holidays, picnics in the woods and school days. Then teenagers, dressed to the nines and going to parties, watching videos and munching pizza. There were celebratory parties and emotional goodbyes, and then a young, blonde woman at a heaving university campus, her face a picture of hope and ambition. And at the centre of every image stood the girl in the photo, her dark curls shaping her pale face, her haunting eyes staring piercingly and accusingly into Skye's own azure irises.

And then there was more. An older woman, again familiar, and a man. Skye recognised the way the man stood slightly behind the woman, his hand resting on her upper back, a few tan coloured age spots peering out from beneath the fraying cuffs of his jumper. The woman was short with curly dark hair, highlighted with grey and sticking out at odd angles. She held her hands together and had a composed aura, although the wild hair hinted towards a more scatty side of her personality. She had a kindly smile but sad eyes, that reached out to Skye in an imploring manner that Skye couldn't quite grasp.

Then everything stopped and Skye froze, her muscles locking and her eyes staring into blankness. The eerie silence scared her more than the sound of her own pain, and she felt her stomach churn until she thought that her bowels were about to give way. She knew something was coming but she didn't know how to prepare for it, how to face it or how to escape from it. The terror of the anticipation caused her breath to shorten and her heart to race, and then again it all stopped, and a sense of calm prevailed. Skye breathed in deeply, feeling the oxygen flood her body, reaching right down to her fingertips, through her core and into her legs. Her muscles softened and her eyelids felt as if someone had attached lead weights to the ends of her lashes, but she fought to keep them open as a white light shone out across the room. Her head momentarily filled with white noise, distracting her from the beam, but then it stopped almost as soon as it started.

Skye followed the trail of light, and felt her mouth drop when she saw a baby levitating just out of reach. She was only a few weeks old, sleeping peacefully under a fluffy, pink cover, yet snuffling like it was tough work. A small tangle of pale hairs lay flattened on her crown and her tiny fingers were just visible, poking through the mesh holes of the blanket. She smelled of baby lotion and milk.

Skye watched the baby's chest rise and fall, feeling her eyes well up with tears again. She sniffed loudly then paused, but the baby slept right through. She reached out to touch the baby's head, to stroke her downy hair and to run her fingers down her soft, rosy cheeks. But the infant was too far away. She sat up and stretched further, but still couldn't reach, and she felt a pulse of desperation shake up her brain like it had been plugged into an electric motor. All she could think about was how she had to touch the child, but no matter how much she stretched the baby stayed just out of reach.

Skye felt an urgent need to protect the baby and keep her safe from harm, no matter the cost to herself. It wasn't right; why was the baby on her own? Why was no-one looking out for her? The baby exhaled deeply and a bubble of spittle formed in the open crater of her mouth. In the silence that followed Skye heard it softly pop, so that saliva dribbled down her chin, leaving a silvery trail in its wake before it pooled out in a damp stain on the creamy cotton sheet lining the mattress. Why was no-one there to wipe it up? Again Skye reached out, to clean the baby's chin, but she still couldn't reach. She stretched until it felt like her arm would fall out of its socket, then let it flop to the ground with a massive grunt of frustration. The baby snuffled again and Skye froze, watching her mumble and rearrange her arms. She threw them back over her head so that they lay out on her pillow at right angles to her body, the delicate skin on her underarms exposed to the elements of the dingy kitchen.

Skye felt the baby sense her presence as she inclined her dainty head towards her. The older girl tried to call out and wake the infant, but her voice wouldn't work. And then the child seemed to blur around the edges, the definition of her body becoming fuzzy and her pinkened skin becoming paler, as a gentle hum resounded in Skye's ears. It was similar to the white noise, but not as loud or distorted. Though its volume increased as the image of the baby faded.

Skye felt the panic rise in her chest once again as she watched the baby fade into the sheet - she couldn't let the baby leave; the connection was almost tangible, and for the first time in her life she felt complete. She climbed to her feet to try and get closer but the child rose with her, continuing to float at eye level and just beyond arm's reach. Then a rush of goose pimples ran over her entire body as Skye finally realised where she had seen that baby before. She was in her cloud box, which Skye had burned when she wanted to make everything vanish. She was part of that stash of evidence she had built up as she had discovered more about her past; that baby had been in the photo that had taken pride of place.

Soon, the sheet was visible through the translucent skin of the child. Skye felt as if someone was ripping out her heart as she became overwhelmed with a sadness that seemed to saturate every cell, and make her limbs feel heavier as the child faded further. But just before she disappeared completely she opened her lids and turned to face Skye, who made contact with eyes similar to those of the girl in the photo. Similar, but not the same; they were paler, but their look - and expression - were familiar. Skye felt a warm golden haze sweep over her body and, once again, the panic subsided and was replaced with a sense of calm and stillness. And then Lucie spoke. She was just a baby yet she opened her mouth and talked, her voice as gentle as a butterfly on the breeze.

"Let me go. Live your life. I'm gone, but you're not. Make the most of it, I love you." And with that the baby reached out her right arm towards Skye, and finally Skye was able to touch her. For just a second their finger tips joined before the sizzling crackle of electricity jumped between them, jolting Skye so that she stumbled backwards, striking her head on the countertop as she fell and landed once again in the pile of jagged splinters of glass.

When Skye came to she felt the warm river of blood running down from the temple. Her limbs stung and burned as if she was being eaten alive by a swarm of red ants. She tried to move but her legs refused her mind's instructions, so instead she stretched a bloodied arm out over the lino and grabbed her

330

mobile, which was lying in the middle of the glass. Hadn't she been looking for that last night? She tapped in the eleven digit number, her fingers dancing a routine her mind could barely remember.

The phone was answered on the third ring, and it was at that point that she burst into tears. Once the initial outburst had subsided she spoke, and her voice sounded different. It was hoarse and strained, but there was a hint of a lilt to it, of a sing-song Celtic accent.

"Mummy," she whispered. "Mummy, it's Louise."

"Louise, thank God..." Louise could hear crying, although she wasn't sure which sobs were hers and which were her mother's. There was a scuffling sound and then her father's voice came down the line.

"Louise? It's your dad. Stay there, we're on our way and we'll be with you in a few hours. We love you, we're coming." Louise clicked the end call button and at that point there was a knock on the door. She struggled to her feet and went to answer it, and was met with a glamorous blonde mane and sun-kissed skin. Amy looked tired and bedraggled, yet was smiling. She held out her arms and Louise fell into them, allowing her tears to flow afresh.

"Amy," she muttered, unable to voice much more. She felt Amy massage her back and stroke her head, and it made Louise feel like a new born. She clung onto Amy until a flash of dark hair caught her eye in the corner of the landing. Raising her head she made eye contact with Eve, who hesitantly stepped out of the shadows. "Eve..." Louise reached out an arm towards her, and as Eve stepped forward Louise pulled her into the embrace.

"Thank you." She whispered. "How did you know? How are you here?"

Amy stroked Louise's hair. "I've been here every night,

just waiting. I knew you'd need me, so I just waited." Louise felt a fresh wave of emotion pulse through her body.

"Eve? I'm sorry, I..."

"Sshhhh, it's ok."

Louise pulled back to meet Eve's smile before collapsing once more into the embrace. She felt every muscle in her body relax as she finally let go, and released Lucie into the atmosphere around her. She could have sworn she saw a pale blue haze drift out of the window and into the sky, and with that she felt her knees give way as she slipped into blissful darkness. But this time, even as she lost consciousness, she knew she was going to come out the other side, and that it was all going to be ok.

.

# Postscript

*Dear Skye,*

*As you won't talk to me it leaves me with little choice but to try a letter. I don't know where your mind is right now and I can't imagine how you must be feeling. But I'm trying, Skye. You have no idea how much. Amy showed us a diary entry that you wrote and I've pieced everything together, and it's finally starting to make some sort of sense.*

*There's something you need to know, Skye, and there's no easy way to say this. You don't exist. You died as a baby. I know this because I found you. You were just six weeks old, but your lungs had stopped working. It was so sudden and no-one really knows why it happened. They call it SIDS, Sudden Infant Death Syndrome. Other people know it as cot death. I put you down to sleep and I thought I'd followed all the rules, but I must have done something wrong. I curse myself for it every day. I came in to check on you and you had just stopped breathing. Simple as that. You looked so peaceful. I called an ambulance but when they arrived they said it was too late. I held you in my arms until they prised you away, saying that you had to go for the post-mortem.*

*Then there was the funeral. It was the worst day of my life, cremating you, Lucie. That was when we started calling you Skye. It reminded me that you were free, released into the atmosphere, flying high in the sky. In some tiny way it lifted the pain. A tiny, tiny, way. At least I knew you were around, that*

335

*your spirit was there. I could imagine you watching me.*

*You left behind your twin sister, Louise. She's still here, living in London now. But we're worried about her. She's created you, as you may have been, but she's lost herself. She's stepped into your shoes but she doesn't seem to realise that she can't be you, because you're dead. She needs help, but we can't reach her.*

*It's all my fault. I never let her talk about you, never let her bring up the subject. It was just too painful for me. I see now how much those actions have damaged her, but I thought I was doing the right thing. I didn't think she'd remember you, you were both just six weeks old - how can such a little mite realise what's happening? How could she have understood that she had a sister who had just disappeared? I thought she'd just assume she was an only child. I did mean to talk to her about it when she was older, but somehow the right moment never seemed to arise. I know how wrong it was of me, but I just couldn't face it. The pain was, is, all-consuming and never-ending, and the only way I could cope with it was to push it down, right down where it would be too deeply embedded to surface again. I thought it was only me I was hurting and that didn't matter; I was already so saturated with pain, what more was a little extra? I just wanted to protect Louise. I'd bear the pain for both of us, and she'd grow up thinking she was an only child, until we were both ready to cope with the truth. It seemed the best way.*

*But I didn't account for sibling connections, or for early memories which could be re-found through searching and hunting for more information. I'd heard about those bonds that form between twins, but I didn't believe in it. I think now that Louise always knew that she wasn't whole. I guess she asked questions, searched for missing photos, went through old newspapers and records. All the information is there - it just*

336

*needs to be found by someone who's looking. She put the pieces of the puzzle together, and now something has happened. Lucie, Louise thinks she's you. She's forgotten herself. And I don't know what to do. I should have acted sooner but it was too painful, and now it's gone too far. Lucie, Skye, please help. Whatever you can do, please help her understand. I've already lost one darling daughter, and I want Louise back. I love you, Skye, and I always will, but you're gone. Louise is still here, and I want her just how she was. My darling Louise, my daughter, your sister. Skye, if there is anything you can do please do it. I'll be praying and hoping and ready to support her.*

*All my love, forever,*
*Your loving Mother.*

# Acknowledgements

First of all, massive thanks to Mum and Dad – and all those who came before – as without your support I would never have been able to follow my dreams.

Thanks to my friends and family who have believed in me, supported me and shared in my excitement throughout this journey.

Thanks to Jenn Ashworth, whose tips and pointers enabled me to convert my story into something resembling a novel, to Tanya Back for my wonderful cover, Abby for the early read throughs and thoughts, Fiona for launching with me and to Jennifer Loiske, whose support, encouragement, Lulu teaching and virtual shoulder has kept me going through the tough times, and helped me reach the point where I am actually able to do this. Thanks a million!

And, most of all, thank you to you, for picking up my book and reading it through to the end. I hope you enjoyed reading it as much as I enjoyed writing it.